# UTTERLY DARK

## AND THE
## TIDES OF TIME

*Utterly Dark and the Tides of Time* is something very special. It's a book that takes characters we love, in a world where we've already enjoyed wonderful adventures, and continues their stories seamlessly — but takes things in completely new, unexpected directions too. As ever, Philip Reeve surprises and delights us with his unique imagination and powerful writing. And then, to cap it all, he hits us with one of the most satisfying and special endings I've read for a long time. It's a book to remember — I hope you love reading it!

Liz Cross, Publishing Director

| | |
|---|---|
| FICTION | Territorial Rights: World |
| 320 pp | |
| ISBN 978-1-78845-288-5 | David Fickling Books |
| Publication Date: 7th September 2023 | 31 Beaumont Street |
| Price: £7.99 | Oxford OX1 2NP |
| Format: Paperback | www.davidficklingbooks.com |

For PR requests, please contact Fraser Hutchinson pr@davidficklingbooks.com @DFB_storyhouse
For rights requests, please contact Bronwen Bennie bron@davidficklingbooks.com

Also by Philip Reeve

Utterly Dark and the Face of the Deep
Utterly Dark and the Heart of the Wild

**Mortal Engines Quartet**
Mortal Engines
Predator's Gold
Infernal Devices
A Darkling Plain

**Railhead Trilogy**
Railhead
Black Light Express
Station Zero

**Fever Crumb Trilogy**
Fever Crumb
A Web of Air
Scrivener's Moon

**Mortal Engines 'Expanded Universe'**
Night Flights
The Illustrated World of Mortal Engines

**Goblins Series**
Goblins
Goblins vs Dwarves
Goblin Quest

**Larklight Series**
Larklight
Starcross
Mothstorm

**Other Novels**
No Such Thing As Dragons
Here Lies Arthur

**With Sarah McIntyre**
Oliver and the Seawigs
Cakes in Space
Pugs of the Frozen North
Jinks and O'Hare Funfair Repair
The Legend of Kevin
Kevin's Great Escape
Kevin and the Biscuit Bandit
Kevin vs the Unicorns
Adventuremice: Otter Chaos
Adventuremice: Mermouse Mystery

# PHILIP REEVE
# UTTERLY DARK

## AND THE
## TIDES OF TIME

David Fickling Books

31 Beaumont Street
Oxford OXI 2NP, UK

UTTERLY DARK AND THE TIDES OF TIME
is a
DAVID FICKLING BOOK

First published in Great Britain in 2023 by
David Fickling Books,
31 Beaumont Street,
Oxford, OX1 2NP

www.davidficklingbooks.com

Text © Philip Reeve, 2023

Cover and inside art by Paddy Donnelly.

978-1-78845-288-5

1 3 5 7 9 10 8 6 4 2

Papers used by David Fickling Books are from well-
managed forests and other responsible sources.

MIX
Paper from
responsible sources
FSC® C018072

DAVID FICKLING BOOKS Reg. No. 8340307

A CIP catalogue record for this book is available from the British Library.

Typeset in 12/16pt Goudy by Falcon Oast Graphic Art Ltd
Printed and bound in Great Britain by Clays Ltd, Elcograf S.p.A

For my father, Michael Reeve, who took
me to Wildsea in the 1970s.
(Or at least, to lots of places very like it.)

# 1

# A SHIP FROM THE DEPTHS OF THE SEA

Utterly Dark lay awake, and the old house on St Chyan's Head sang to her its symphony of night-time noises. Mice scritched and scratched inside the walls, oak beams and floorboards creaked like old men's knees, and the windows shifted gently in their frames as the night wind leaned against the glass. Out in the hallway, the grandfather clock tick-tocked, tick-tocked, and softly chimed the quarter-hours. And down in the cove, the small waves whispered on the shingle, reminding Utterly that it would soon be time for her to leave this place and all its dear, familiar sounds behind.

She got out of bed in the long-after-midnight dark. She went to the window and folded back the shutters.

The sky was piebald, with patches of bright moonlight showing among drifts of cloud. Out on the horizon, a line of cold light gleamed like the edge of a blade. And black against the glimmer of that light, Utterly could see the outlines of the Hidden Lands.

The house at Sundown Watch had been built there on the clifftop as a lookout, where the Watchers on Wildsea could keep their vigil for those strange islands. The Hidden Lands belonged to the Gorm, that immensely old and powerful being who ruled the sea, or maybe *was* the sea. They came and went as they pleased out there where sea met sky, visible to mortal eyes only when the Gorm desired it.

Tonight, a tiny point of golden light was shining on the shore of the nearest, largest island.

Utterly waited. She knew something was going to happen, but she did not yet know what it would be. Would the Gorm herself appear, as she had sometimes before, taking the form of a white lady, or a kelp-woven giant, or a gang of shambling Men o' Weed? But no: there was only the sea, and the moonlight, and that far fire glowing. Utterly's hot breath fogged the window pane. She wiped the glass with the cuff of her nightdress.

Far to the west, so far that even Utterly's sharp eyes could barely see it, the sharp reflection of the moonlight shifted, slithering off a long, low wave that rose there suddenly and came sweeping towards Wildsea. It was just a hummock in the sea at first, but as it drew nearer to the land it rose and darkened, gathering weed from the great forests of kelp which swayed below it as it passed. It gathered up other things as well; the shards of ship-wrecks: masts and spars and age-blackened hulks. The timbers tossed inside the wave as it rushed on. It stirred them and shuffled them and slammed them together and fitted one broken plank against another until it carried a whole ship on its foaming crest; a ship black as bog-oak, with pennants of weed trailing from her ragged rigging.

The wave roared. Veins of foam marbled its dark face, streamers of spindrift trailed from its crest, and the black ship rode upon it. It was entering shallower waters now, racing up the long, granite roots of the island of Wildsea. It grew taller, taller, until it was as high as the cliffs and the black ship was on a level with Sundown Watch. Its summit curled and crumpled into creamy foam, ready to crash down and drown the cliffs, the coast, and all the little homes that slept behind the dunes.

And there, on the very brink of breaking, the wave stopped. It stood still, a wall of water with the black ship balanced on its brow.

'Utterly,' it whispered.

And Utterly knew the time had come for her to leave.

2

# THE PROMISE

Utterly had been preparing herself for this moment all winter.

'When spring comes again, I will go to you,' she had told the Gorm the last time they had met. And now spring *was* here again, with blizzards of blackthorn blossom and bleating, bouncing crowds of lambs, and Utterly knew the Gorm would be expecting her to keep her promise. For although she had lived all her thirteen years at Sundown Watch, Utterly was the Gorm's own daughter.

But, now that the time of her departure had arrived, she realized she must have been secretly hoping all winter that she would not really have to say goodbye to Sundown Watch, and Wildsea, and her friends. Why, Uncle Will, and Aish, and Egg, and Mr and Mrs Skraeveling were far more like family to her than the terrible old Gorm, who had let her wash ashore here in a mermaid's purse when she was just a baby.

But it was because she cared so deeply for Uncle Will, and Aish, and Egg, and Mr and Mrs Skraeveling, that Utterly knew she had to go. Because the Gorm was a fickle and tempestuous sort of person; quite literally tempestuous at times. Utterly, leaning closer to the window and peering to north and south along Wildsea's rugged coast, saw the wave waiting there, and knew that if she broke her promise, the Gorm might let the wave break too. The Gorm cared nothing for the land, or for the small lives of those who lived there. The Gorm would think nothing of drowning the farms and cottages of Marazea, and washing away the new vicarage which had only lately been built to replace the one she had destroyed on a previous visit. So Utterly knew she had to leave her friends, for their sake.

She washed her face, then quickly dressed, and packed the little bag she had hidden under her bed. She did not think she would need very many things among the Hidden Lands, because the last time she visited, the Gorm had made her all sorts of fine clothes out of magic. But she packed her comb and hairbrush, because she thought the Gorm might not know about such things and would expect her to brush her hair with a sea-urchin or something, which would be a disagreeable experience both for Utterly and the urchin. And she took the pocketknife that Uncle Will had given her for Christmas, and a length of string her friend Egg had given her because he said you should always have a good piece of string about you. And she took a slice of Mrs Skraeveling's fruit cake, wrapped in a muslin handkerchief, which she had borrowed from the pantry. (However magical the Gorm was, Utterly doubted she could conjure up a fruit cake half as good as one of Mrs Skraeveling's.) Then, putting on her cloak and tying her bonnet ribbons very firmly under her chin, she went out of her bedroom for the last time.

Uncle Will was spending the night at Aish's house on the Dizzard, as he often did now that he trusted Utterly to keep the Watch for him, so she did not need to worry that he would hear her creeping about. Mr and Mrs Skraeveling were snoring softly in their room a little further along the hallway. Utterly wished she could wake them and say goodbye. She wished she could say goodbye to all her loved ones, but she knew she could not, for they would only tell her not to go, and she *had* to go. So she crept past Mr and Mrs Skraeveling's door as quietly as a mouse. But when she reached the foot of the stairs she darted half-way up to plant a farewell kiss on the nose of the little wooden tortoise on the landing newel post, the one friend whom she knew would make no fuss. Then she went down again, and the stairs let out the softest creak beneath her small weight.

Egg, asleep beside the kitchen range with Tab the cat curled up on top of him, opened his eyes at the sound. 'What's this?' he wondered, rising up all tousle-headed. Tab slid off him with a complaining little *miaow*. 'Hush, puss,' Egg whispered. 'There's shenanigans afoot . . .'

From the far end of the house came another sound; the snick of the back-door latch as someone quietly closed it. Egg narrowed his eyes. 'Utterly,' he said.

Egg had sensed that something was troubling his friend since back before Christmas, maybe ever since they had come home from Summertide. He did not have any very clear recollections of the events that had unfolded there, for they had been events of a magical sort, and magic has a way of fading from human minds like the dew from summer lawns. But Egg was pretty sure Utterly had met the Gorm upon the downs of Summertide, unlikely as that sounded, so far from the sea. And it seemed to him the old Gorm had laid some heavy burden on her, and that this burden had been growing heavier and heavier as the months went by.

Egg would have liked to help her carry it, but whenever he asked what was amiss, Utterly had told him it was nothing. But Egg had kept his ears and eyes open all the same. He had heard her sigh, and seen her run her fingers over the chair backs and stair rails, and gaze sadly at Will Dark and Aish, and even at his own self when she thought he was not looking at her. It was as if she had been privately bidding them all farewell and trying to fix them in her memory.

'And now she's sneaking off,' he told the cat. 'Sneaking off to go a-swimming with that old Gorm, and not even a goodbye! Well, it won't do, Utterly Dark! It won't do at all!'

A late frost lay thickly on the lawn, which sloped down to a hedge and a gate. Beyond the gate, where the land ended and the path led down the cliff to Blanchmane's Cove, the great wave stood frozen like a painting, and the black ship waited, balanced on its crest. The ship had swung side-on to the house, presenting its rows of rotted gun-ports for Utterly's inspection. She had no name that Utterly could see, and no crew.

Utterly went down the lawn and through the gate. She gathered up her courage and stepped from the cliff's edge on to the slimy wooden slope of the ship's flank. She climbed cautiously up the row of steps let into the timbers. Soon she stood on the deck, between two shapeless lumps of rust and barnacles, which she suspected had once been cannons. The ship was full of small low-tide sounds; drippings and tricklings and the tiny creakings and crackings of wet things drying out.

The rigging made thin, inky shapes against the sky, criss-crossing lines and triangles all blotted with clumps of weed, like geometry exercises drawn with a spattery pen. Utterly went carefully up the wet stairs to the quarter-deck, half expecting to find the Gorm herself there, but it was empty.

'Utterly!' shouted a voice, but it was only Egg, dashing across the frosty lawn. He hurdled the gate and came to stand at the cliff's edge, staring up at her. 'I *thought* you was up to something, Utterly Dark,' he panted. 'The way you've been sighing and sorrowing about, like you was off on some journey and thought you might never come home . . .'

'I *am* off on a journey,' said Utterly. 'I *won't* ever come home. Oh, Egg, the Gorm is calling to me and I have to go!'

'No you don't!' Egg stretched out his hand to her. 'That aquatic old article can't follow you on to dry land. She can weave up her Men o' Weed and her storms and hurricanes if she wants, but we'll keep you safe from her, Utterly.'

'You don't understand, Egg,' said Utterly. 'I *promised*.'

And then, knowing that her mother was not the most patient person, and fearing what might happen if her patience wore thin, she turned away. The wave seemed to know of her decision, and subsided. It did not break, but simply sank back down into the sea, carrying the black ship with it. The ship turned too, the wheel spinning as if at the touch of an invisible helmsman. Then, although the wind was set against it, it began to move swiftly away from Wildsea, out across the Western Deeps towards the Hidden Lands.

'Utterly!' shouted Egg, descending the steep cliff path to Blanchmane's Cove on his bottom, in an avalanche of dislodged stones. The ship was black against the moonlit levels of the sea. 'Utterly!' he shouted, clattering down the shingle, pounding across the sand, splashing into the shallows. He could see Utterly standing on the ship's high stern, but she did not turn at his call. The waves, which had been small till then, suddenly grew huge. They shouted 'Utterly' too as they crashed down all around Egg. One knocked him flat, a second came down on him as he surfaced, a third turned him upside down and threw him back upon the beach.

He lay on the sand, soaked through and shivering, listening to the triumphant laughter of the surf. He felt unstrung; almost too weak to pull himself together and stand up. When he finally did, the cove was empty, except for the big waves heaving and plunging in the moonlight. Way out upon the western sea the Hidden Lands showed dark, like silhouettes of islands cut from black cardboard, and the sails of the Gorm's strange ship glowed faintly as it sailed towards them. The little windows of its stern reflected the moon, and Egg thought he saw a lighter-coloured smudge above them, which he fancied was Utterly's face, gazing back towards the land and loved ones she had left behind.

# 3

# GOOD NEWS AND BAD

Will Dark, the Watcher on Wildsea, had an unusual marriage. Rather than moving into Sundown Watch with him when they were wed, his wife, Aish, kept up her own house on the north end of the island, for she loved the woods and crags there, and would not leave them for all the world. She would often come to Sundown Watch to stay a week or two, but always she would feel her own hills calling, and go home to them. Then Will would go to stay with her at Dizzard Tor. He had long since accepted that Utterly was quite as capable as him of keeping the Watch, and anyway, Aish had her own lookout place, on the summit of the tor, which offered almost as good a view of the Western Deeps.

There Will and Aish had sat together the previous evening, watching the sun go down over the sea. Once the last light had died and there had been no sign of the Hidden Lands on the horizon, Aish had taken Will's hand in hers and said, 'I have good news, Will Dark. At least, I hope that you shall think it good. I did not want to tell you until I was quite sure, and now I am, so you shall hear it.'

And she took his hand and pressed it to her tummy.

Will, waking next morning in her curtained bed, took a moment to remember what it was that had filled his dreams, and now his waking, with such a curious admixture of happiness and worry. Then he remembered. Aish was going to have a baby.

'Two babies,' she had said, in the soft twilight up there on the tor. 'They are twins. I can feel them in there, dreaming their small dreams. I declare, I do not know how it happened. I mean, I *do* know, of course, but it has never happened before. I am sure I should remember having children.'

When she told him, Will had felt only happiness. Now, with the light of the new day peeking in between the bed curtains, he felt other things. Still happiness, of course, and fatherly pride, but also doubt. What sort of father would he be? His own father had been a stern and distant man, and Will had no desire to be like that, but perhaps fatherhood would make him *become* stern and distant?

And far worse than his doubts about his own character was the great fear he felt for Aish. So many women died in childbirth, and he could not bear the thought of losing her. He reminded himself that although she looked no older than he did, Aish had lived on Wildsea since the woods were young. She was . . . Will hardly liked to use the word, it sounded so outlandish, but it was true, wasn't it? Aish was an immortal goddess. Granted, she was only a goddess in a small way, the local deity of Wildsea and its woods. But surely even small, local goddesses must be immune to the perils that attended mortal childbirth?

So Will did his best to put away his fears, and snuggled against Aish as she slept, and thought what a strange journey he had made. For when he lived in London as a young man he had loathed the very memory of his Wildsea childhood and hated the thought of ever coming back to live here, and yet here he was, so very happy, and so very deep in love, and now soon to have children of his own. How pleasant it would be to have more children at Sundown Watch, bringing happiness and laughter to the old house which he had once thought so gloomy. He hoped they would turn out as well as Utterly and Egg, who were growing into such agreeable, polite, considerate young people –

'Ahoy, Will Dark!' shouted Egg at that moment, whisking the bed curtains aside and letting in the dazzling morning sun. 'Aish! Wake up, you two slug-a-beds! While you've been a-snoring here, Utterly's sailed off in some wormy, haunted-looking great ship. She's gone! Gone off sea-bathing with the Gorm among them Hidden Lands! And what are we to do?'

They went pell-mell out of the house and up on to the tor's high summit, Will in his nightshirt, Aish wrapped in a dressing gown. They stood in the blustering wind that had risen with the sun and looked west, and there, just as Egg had said they would, they saw the Hidden Lands. But the ship that had taken Utterly away had long since dwindled from sight, and as they watched they saw the Hidden Lands begin to dwindle too, growing vague and gauzy until you would have said they were only patches of low mist drifting there above the Western Deeps, and then even those were gone.

'I was afraid of this,' said Aish. She took Will's hand, and put her other arm around Egg's shoulders, pulling him against her side. 'The old Gorm has called Utterly home.'

'But *this* is her home,' declared Will. 'What does the Gorm want with Utterly anyway?'

Aish sighed sorrowfully. She had guessed this day would come, and she knew that there was nothing to be done. She loved Utterly like her own daughter, and had often wished that Utterly *was* her own daughter.

She felt certain she would have made a better mother to the girl than that cold old Gorm. Why, the Gorm had let little Utterly wash ashore on Wildsea in a mermaid's purse when she was a baby, and left it to her father, Will's late brother, to raise her . . . But Aish was a fair-minded and forgiving sort of person, so she wiped her tears away and said, 'The Gorm loves Utterly dearly. She will let no harm befall her out in the sea's deeps. She has taken her home to the Hidden Lands, to keep her company there, and to learn her Gormish ways.'

'What ways?' demanded Egg. 'You mean like how to drown folks, or turn herself into a great huge seaweed giant? Utterly wouldn't want to do that.' He sounded doubtful though. Now that he thought about, turning into a great huge seaweed giant *did* sound diverting. 'But why would she just up and leave us like this?' he asked. 'Without even saying goodbye?'

Will sat down on the edge of the tor and put his head in his hands. 'Utterly is a good, brave girl,' he said. 'She feared the Gorm, and she wished to spare us another disaster. She must have decided it would be best for everyone if she were to keep her departure secret. I honour her for it, though I regret it exceedingly. If only she had told us what she was planning! She has been out of sorts lately; I am sure we have all noted it.'

'Oh, if only I had tried harder to find out what was troubling her,' said Egg, growing angry at himself.

'She still would not have told you, Egg,' said Aish.

'There is nothing else for it,' decided Will. 'As soon as it is light I shall ride over to Merriport and charter a boat to go after her. I fetched Utterly home from the Gorm's lands once before. I shall do it again.'

'But the Gorm's lands have hidden themselves,' said Aish, 'and I doubt there is a captain in all the Autumn Isles foolish enough to risk his ship upon such haunted seas. And do you really think the Gorm will let you defy her for a second time, Will Dark? If she sees you coming to take Utterly from her she will drag you down and drown you, and you are needed here. You are needed more now than ever. You have responsibilities. You cannot go gallivanting off across the dreadful deeps with no thought for those you leave behind.'

Will looked up at her, and thought how happy he had been a few short hours ago, and how sad he was now. 'But I must do *something*,' he said.

'I'll go if Will Dark won't,' vowed Egg.

Aish wrapped her strong arms round the both of them, as if to anchor them to her island. 'We must wait and see,' she said. 'That is all we can do. We know the old Gorm will not harm our Utterly, for she loves her every bit as much as we do, in her own damp, salty, Gormish way. So we can only wait, and see what happens next.'

She and Will went back down to the house to dress and breakfast, but Egg wanted to be alone. He squatted on the tor's top and watched the sea. Pale wandering pathways of calm water wound through the darker, choppier parts, but they led nowhere, and no Hidden Lands showed themselves out there in the west. The ship that carried Utterly away was growing harder to remember, as if it had been nothing but a dream. Magic was tricksy like that: more vivid than real life when it was happening to you, but harder to keep hold of than a snowflake or a soap bubble. Would Utterly fade from Egg's recollections too? Would he wake one day and find he had forgotten her face, as he had forgotten the face of the river girl whom he dimly recalled meeting on Summertide?

'I won't forget,' he said firmly, glaring at the empty horizon. 'We'll wait and see for a bit, like Aish says. But if that old Gorm don't let you come home soon, I'm coming after you, Utterly Dark, and that's a promise.'

4

# SWIM WITH ME

The Gorm was waiting for Utterly on the shore of the nearest of the Hidden Lands. She stood on a black rock with the surf breaking around it, and held up a brand of driftwood, which blazed with butter-yellow flames. Her white dress glowed in the gathering daylight, and her black hair swirled above her head as if she were deep underwater.

Once, looking up through sunlit tropical seas, the Gorm had seen a young woman glance down laughing over the side of a boat. The young woman had been so pretty, and the moment so affecting, that the Gorm had tipped up the boat, and drowned her, and copied her face and body for her own. That was the form she used nowadays when she wished to move among human beings and have them worship her. It was the form she had used when she walked on the beaches of Wildsea and first met Andrewe Dark beachcombing there. And it was the form she wore now, to welcome her land-loving daughter back into the deeps.

'Utterly,' she said, as the wave drove the old ship hard aground on the sand beside her rock. She tossed her driftwood torch aside and stepped from the rock on to the quarterdeck, smiling down at her daughter while her swirling hair alternately hid and revealed her face, and her eyes turned from grey to blue, then to twinkling silver like a summer sea.

'Mother,' said Utterly, making her best curtsey. 'I have come as I promised.'

Any ordinary mother, indeed, any human being at all, could have told that Utterly's heart was breaking as she said those words. But the Gorm had little understanding of such things, for she had no heart of her own. She did not even know a name for the feeling that came to her as she took Utterly's hand and led her towards the ship's prow. She only knew that Utterly was hers, that she had been too long upon the dry land, and that it was good to have her home at last.

The ship, its voyage done, collapsed back into fragments. The prow, with Utterly and the Gorm upon it, tilted forward until they were able to step easily off on to the shore, and then the waves gathered up the pieces and drew them back into the deep, leaving not one barnacled spar or rusty nail to mar the pale perfection of the sand.

Offshore, on shelves of rock, basked the long-necked dragons who had followed the Gorm here from the seas of long ago: overhead the pale gulls cried their cries. The shadows of the birds' wings swept across the cliffs, and Utterly followed them with her eyes, up and up, until she saw the house that stood on the clifftop.

It was not the sea-cave palace she remembered from her first visit to the Hidden Lands, but a house of a far more modern and convenient sort, with glazed windows shining in the morning light. There was even a sort of tower or turret at one end. Its proportions were rather peculiar, and its roofs seemed covered with mother-of-pearl rather than ordinary slate, but it had clearly been intended as a copy of Sundown Watch, and as she followed the Gorm up the sandy path to its front door, Utterly felt grateful that her mother would take such trouble to help her feel at home here.

Inside the house the walls and ceilings were all pink. It was like stepping into a colossal seashell, and, like any self-respecting seashell, it echoed softly with the sound of the sea.

A table stood nearby. The Gorm steered Utterly gently towards it. 'Now,' said the Gorm. 'What shall you have for breakfast, daughter?'

'What do you usually eat, Mama?' asked Utterly.

'I?' asked the Gorm, as if such a question had never occurred to her. 'Why, I become a whale and drink down whole nations of plankton. Or I become a shark and feast on seals and drowning sailors. Or I become a white worm and sup on the delicious steams that spew from drowned volcanoes in the deepest hollows of the sea.'

'Perhaps I do not feel hungry, after all,' said Utterly, who somehow did not fancy any of those delicacies. 'I had a tolerably large supper at Sundown Watch, only a few hours ago, and I ate a piece of Mrs Skraeveling's fruit cake on the voyage.'

'But that was in another world,' said the Gorm kindly. 'This is my world, and it is a new day, and new days begin with breakfast, don't they?' She was trying so hard to be a mother that Utterly felt quite sorry for her. 'I shall show you how to be a shark,' the Gorm decided. 'No – a great killer whale; nothing but piebald muscle, and hunger, and joy in your own sleek strength. Oh, you cannot imagine how wonderful it feels to be a killer whale.'

'But I do not wish to be a killer whale,' Utterly objected. 'Nor a shark, nor a worm, nor any other creature.'

The Gorm watched her with shifting, sea-coloured eyes, and sighed. 'How sad,' she said. 'How small. You have been too long a-land, Utterly. There is too much of your father in you. You will come to understand. I have so much to show you. But first . . .'

She clapped her hands, and two Men o' Weed entered the room. They looked just like the slimy, slopping creatures who had terrified Utterly when they first appeared on Wildsea, but she was more used to them now, and these two seemed very meek and biddable monsters. They carried in trays of silver tableware, a rack of toast, and bowls of fruit. They set it down, then fetched chairs, and placed them at opposite ends of the table, so that Utterly and her mother could face each other as they ate. One picked up a silver teapot and poured liquid from it into a porcelain cup. The liquid was clear like water, but filled with floating green-brown specks, like the torn-up seaweed that sometimes stained the waves in Blanchmane's Cove.

'What is it?' asked Utterly, picking up the cup and sniffing it. It had a brackish smell.

'What would you like it to be?' asked the Gorm.

'I generally take a cup of tea with breakfast,' said Utterly, and, looking down again into the cup, saw that the liquid had turned brown like milky tea. It smelled like tea, too. She took a sip. It was as good as the tea from Mrs Skraeveling's pot. She drank the rest, then turned her attention to the buttered toast, the marmalade, the fruits whose names she didn't even know, whose sweet juices trickled down her chin when she bit into them. And although she was fairly certain that all those things might just be slabs of weed or slimy sea cucumbers if you looked at them in one way, here in the Gorm's home they were as delicious as her imagination could make them.

When she had eaten, she went with the Gorm out through an arched door into a sort of garden, where the hedges had been clipped into the shapes of dolphins, whales and octopodes. Statues of gods and nymphs stood among the hedges, and between them stretched green lawns speckled with clumps of primroses. Here and there Utterly saw a broken pillar, or a section of tumbled wall, as if many other houses had stood here in the past, and the Gorm had let each of them fall into ruin in its turn.

A path of white gravel led up a low hill behind the house. At the top, Utterly stood beside her mother and looked out towards the west, where countless other islands showed upon the morning sea; far, far more Hidden Lands than any Watcher on Wildsea had ever suspected. She glanced back over her shoulder, past the gardens and the Gorm's white house, hoping for a glimpse of home. But there was a haze upon the eastern sea, and she could not make out the familiar hills of Wildsea at all.

'Forget that place, Utterly,' said the Gorm, guessing at once what she was looking for. 'You live in my realm, now. Here all things can be as you wish them. Come.'

She took Utterly's hand and began to run down the long western slope of the island, and what was Utterly to do but run beside her? They ran so fast that Utterly's bonnet blew off and her hair came undone and streamed out behind her like a black flag. The long grass flicked at her feet and her bare legs. Ahead of them the land ended, and she could hear the surf booming against the cliff's foot, far below.

Utterly tried to slow herself, but the Gorm ran faster, pulling her along. And just as they reached the brink of the cliff and Utterly braced herself for the fearful drop into the sea, she realized that they were already underneath it; the air that rushed around them was cool water, the birds they startled from the grass were fish, and the grass itself was fields of seaweed, giving way to silvery sand as they went further and further from the shore. The sun, shining down through the waves overhead, filled the water with moving pillars of light, and the Gorm let go of Utterly's hand and went gliding between the pillars in the form of a great golden fish.

Utterly looked down, and found that the sandy sea-floor was falling away below her. She could see the line of her own footprints, stopping short a few yards beyond the place where her mother's footprints ended. The Gorm-fish turned with a flick of her powerful tail and came gliding back between the sunbeams to join her.

'Swim with me, Utterly,' she said. 'I have so much to show you.'

# 5

# INTO THE SEA OF TIME

Utterly swam. Borne on the sea's strong currents as if upon underwater rivers, she swam with the seals and the death-white whales beneath their glittering ceilings of ice, and among schools of gaudy fish in shallow oceans as warm as bath water. She dived down into the endless night of the great deeps, where the angler fish dangled their cold lamps and unknowable shapes moved dimly in the everlasting dark. The weight of all the miles of sea above would have crushed any other swimmer as flat as a flower pressed between the pages of a Bible, but it never troubled Utterly. Any other swimmer would have grown quickly tired, and numb with cold, but Utterly could swim tirelessly, and did not mind the deep-sea chill at all. Even the whales had to rise to the surface now and then and fill their mighty lungs with air, but Utterly breathed water so contentedly that it very soon stopped seeming strange to her at all.

Often, when she saw a particularly dear little comical fish or sea horse, or a particularly grand and Romantic underwater vista, she would wish that Egg or Uncle Will were there to share it with her. But now that she could swim so easily, she reasoned it would be a simple matter to swim back to Wildsea and tell them of all the exciting things she had seen. She would go tomorrow, or perhaps the day after. And in the meanwhile, she did not miss her friends too badly, because there were so very many things to divert her.

And always at her side, or close at hand, her mother swam. Sometimes the Gorm took on her human form, but more often she was a dolphin, or a whale, or a gigantic squid, or just a rippling silvery movement in the water. 'Become a fish,' she urged Utterly. 'Become a wave. There are so many better ways to swim than flapping and kicking with those landling limbs. You are of the sea, Utterly. Be one with it. You can turn back to your human shape in an instant if you wish it.'

But Utterly did not wish to become a fish. It seemed to her that her small body, in which she had lived so happily and thoughtlessly for thirteen years, was an essential part of her Utterly-ness, and that if she were change it on a whim into something with fins or tentacles instead of legs, or dissolve herself into a wave or a deep-sea current, as her mother sometimes did, then she would become someone different. And perhaps that different someone, being no longer so human, would laugh as lightly as the Gorm laughed when they passed a place where ships lay wrecked, and sailors' bones were whitening among the sea's wild gardens.

Although she was old and cold and fickle, and almost entirely lacking in patience, the Gorm seemed to understand. When Utterly explained that she did not wish to change her shape, she merely sighed, as if she knew Utterly would come around to the idea one day, and it was simply a matter of waiting. Then, perhaps sensing that Utterly still missed the land, she led her up out of the deeps to those higher portions of the sea where the sunlight shone, and on to shores where people had raised up temples to the Gorm, and lit fires upon the beach by night to honour her.

The Gorm was flattered by such gestures. She basked in mortals' fear and adoration the way a cat basks in a beam of sunlight. Utterly followed her ashore, and watched the people bow down to her, and offer her plates of fruit, gold necklaces, the roasted flesh of bulls they slaughtered for her on the shore. Sometimes she might accept a necklace or a ring, and laugh at how brightly it glittered. Utterly felt rather proud to have a mother who was so respected. But when they were back in the sea and the Gorm turned once more into a whale or a wave, the gold would fall from her and be forgotten, which Utterly thought a dreadful waste.

Not all the Gorm's worshippers had gold to offer her, nor bulls and goats to sacrifice. On one of the shores she visited with Utterly, the people had nothing to give the Gorm but people. A boy and girl no older than Utterly had been pegged out on the beach for the rising tide to drown. Their skinny arms and legs were lashed to stakes driven deep into the sand.

The Gorm walked out of the waves with Utterly behind her and stood between the two spreadeagled, trembling bodies. She knelt, and gently brushed away the sandflies, which speckled their frightened faces. Further up the beach, above the tideline, a knot of villagers stood watching. Some looked grim, some sobbed and wailed, but all fell to their knees when the gaze of the Gorm swept over them. Smoke rose from the roof-holes of their huts a little way inland. A wave came rushing up the sand, swirling over Utterly's feet and foaming around the offerings. The boy sobbed with fear; the girl clenched her teeth to stop herself from crying out.

Utterly felt that she must do something. 'Mother,' she said, 'please do not drown them.'

The Gorm just murmured, 'Hush, child,' and did not raise her eyes from the two shivering sacrifices on the sand.

Utterly grew angry, and stamped her foot. Since she was standing upon wet sand the stamp was almost silent, but the movement drew the Gorm's attention.

'Why must you be so cruel?' demanded Utterly.

'I am not cruel,' the Gorm said, quite astonished to be scolded in this way. 'They all die anyway. It is far better to die young and beautiful, and in the sea, than to grow old and ugly and go down as dry bones into the dry ground. Besides, the people of this place have left them here as a gift to me. It would be rude not to accept it.'

'They only did it because they are afraid of you.'

'As they should be, Utterly. I shall take these two, and hang them in the deep, and the ones who are left will remember to fear me.'

The scared eyes of the boy and girl moved from Utterly to her mother as they spoke, as if they were watching a shuttlecock being batted to and fro.

'If they are a gift, then you may do with them as you please,' said Utterly. 'You do not have to drown them. You could choose to show them mercy.'

'Mercy is a human invention, Utterly. It has no place in my ocean.'

'But I *know* you can be merciful,' insisted Utterly. 'For you did not drown Egg or my Uncle Will when they came looking for me in the Hidden Lands.'

'I spared them for your sake, Utterly.'

'Then you must spare this poor boy and girl for my

sake, too,' declared Utterly, 'or, or, or I shall never speak to you again!'

The Gorm's eyes turned a dangerous shade of white. No one had ever dared to speak to her in such a way and escaped un-drowned. But then she smiled, and her eyes became blue again. This was her child, her Utterly, and she longed to please her.

'Very well,' said the Gorm. 'We shall be merciful.'

Another wave came rolling in. It was a wave so big that Utterly had to strain to see its foaming summit as it curled above her. But as it broke it split in two, passing on either side of Utterly and the Gorm. The boy and girl strained at the ropes that held them, but the two halves of the wave roared past them and they were only damped a little by the spray.

The onlookers at the top of the beach stood astonished at the spectacle. The wings of the wave rushed up the shingle and curled towards them like two herds of white horses moving at a gallop. The onlookers broke and scattered, running towards their huts, but the white horses of the wave ran faster. The thunder of its breaking blotted out their screams. The sea gathered them up. It gathered up the fragments of their flimsy huts too, and their thin brown dogs and scrawny cattle, their hen coops and blankets and baskets and shoes and fishing poles, and even the driftwood temple they had raised to honour the Gorm. Then it dragged the whole lot shrieking and howling and bellowing and clucking and clattering and gargling back down the long slope of the shore into the deeps.

'There,' said the Gorm, contentedly. She stooped to snap the wet ropes that had tethered the boy and girl to their stakes. They scrambled up and cowered trembling on the sand.

Utterly took the Gorm's cold hand and went with her back into the sea. She did not ask her to be merciful again.

On more civilized shores, instead of staking out their children for the Gorm, people had raised statues in her honour. Utterly noticed that the Gorm was always pleased by these, even when they were no more than a driftwood log with seaweed hair and two cowrie shells hammered in for eyes. And sometimes, beside the statue of the Gorm, there was another, smaller figure.

'They are learning that the sea has a daughter,' said the Gorm.

'How?' asked Utterly, looking at a marble carving that was clearly meant to be herself.

A white city lay beside the evening sea, and this statue of the Gorm and her daughter stood upon its shore. They had stood there for so long with each high tide washing around their lower parts that their marble legs were armoured with barnacles.

'These statues have been here for ages,' said Utterly. 'But it is only a day since I came to find you in the sea . . . or is it two days? Or is it three?'

Now that she came to think about it, she had no idea how long she had been swimming with the Gorm.

Her mother laughed. 'Oh, Utterly! They have made this image of you because their ancestors saw you come from the sea with me long, long ago. Don't you recognize this place? It is the same beach where we showed such mercy to that boy and girl. They remembered us, and now their descendants have raised these images in thanks.'

Utterly looked around. It was late evening and no one was about, but lamps burned in the windows of some of the buildings. She could not imagine how many years must have passed since the huts that had stood here once were washed away.

'I don't understand,' she said.

'Then I shall show you,' said the Gorm.

She put her arm around Utterly, and led her back into the sea. They dived beneath the breaking waves, and down, and down, and when they rose once more to the surface Utterly saw that volcanoes were ablaze on the horizon. Warm rain was beating down so hard it seemed the sky was trying to put out the fires, and failing. The air smelled of sulphur. The moon hung so huge and low that Utterly did not realize it was the moon at first: its face was not white but black, and veined with glowing traceries of fire.

'This is the dawn of all things,' the Gorm said, lifting her face to the ashen rain. Black rivulets trickled down her pale cheeks. 'Mortals and little beings like that creature Aish think time flows like a river,' she said. 'They are born in the river and borne *on* it; it carries them along, from the past, through the present, into the future, and they can never hope to go any faster than it flows, nor ever turn back and swim against its current. Even the Oldest Ones, who dwell in the fires at the heart of the Earth and sang those fiery mountains into being, must obey its pull. But for me, time is not a river. Time is a sea. It has its shallows and its deeps. Its myriad currents lead to every part of it, and I may swim as I like within it, through all the many ages of the world.'

6

# A SAIL IN THE OFFING

For the mortals Utterly had left behind, time was indeed a river, and a whole month had flowed past since she had left them.

Reverend Dearlove and his wife were visiting Sundown Watch. The news that Aish was to have twins was all around the island by that time – indeed, it could hardly have been kept secret, because Aish had already grown remarkably round in the waist. Mrs Dearlove had always been a little shy of Aish before, because Aish seemed to know so much more than she did about everything, but she had borne three healthy children of her own (Lucy, Horatio and little Emily) so at last, there was a subject she felt she could talk to Aish about without boring her or seeming foolish. Talk they did, while the shadows lengthened in the garden, and Mrs Skraeveling brought more tea, more cake, and eventually joined them at the table to share her own accounts of motherhood.

Will and Reverend Dearlove, much alarmed by all this female business, had retreated first into the house, then down into Blanchmane's Cove. It was there, in the warm spring sunlight, with the waves crisping against the shingle, that the vicar raised the other matter of which all Wildsea had been talking; the one that was too sad to mention over tea and cake.

'Will,' he said. 'It is an entire month now since Utterly disappeared. Do you not think it time to hold a memorial service and erect a little stone for her beside your family tomb in the churchyard?'

'Why should we do that?' asked Will. 'Utterly is not dead!'

'I know you wish to believe that she is not, and, to be sure, hope springs eternal. But it has been a month, Will. It might be best that you stop hoping to meet with Utterly again in this life, and console yourself with the certain knowledge she is with God, and that you will be reunited with her in Heaven. I know Egg said he saw a ship sail away with her to the Hidden Lands, but is it not possible that Egg dreamed the ship, or just imagined it? It seems more likely that Utterly came walking by the sea that morning and slipped in and drowned, just like your poor brother before her.'

Will, who had been turning over the last high tide's delivery of sea-wrack with his foot, stopped and stood looking out to sea. 'That *is* more likely,' he admitted. 'Or, at least, it would be, if we were anywhere but Wildsea, and if the missing girl were anyone but Utterly. But we *are* on Wildsea, and those seas out there are the Gorm's own realm, and Utterly is the Gorm's own daughter. Utterly is not with God; she is with the Gorm. Don't tell me you do not believe in the Gorm, Simon. You must recall how she trampled your house flat, obliging us to build you a new one?'

Reverend Dearlove looked sadly puzzled. The truth was, he did *not* recall it. He recalled fragmentary glimpses of a massive figure looming over Wildsea, but he had convinced himself they had been a nightmare, and that the destruction of his old vicarage had been the work of an ordinary tempest or an honest hurricane. Memories of magic did not linger long, Will knew. Even he, who had visited both the Hidden Lands and the mysterious Underwoods, had only the most confused recollections of the things he had seen and done there. If he had not had Aish to help him remember them, he might well have forgotten them entirely.

'You must trust me, then,' he told Reverend Dearlove. 'Utterly is with her mother, who will let no harm come to her. And, being Utterly, she will be sure to persuade the Gorm to let her come home again, if only for a visit.'

'But it has been a whole month,' said Reverend Dearlove again.

'Time may move differently among the Hidden Lands,' said Will. 'Utterly will return. All we can do is wait.'

'"All we can do is wait"?' said Egg disgustedly. He was lying among the grass and the dancing pink pom-poms of thrift at the very edge of the cliff, looking down at the two men on the beach below. The sea breeze carried their voices quite clearly to him up the cliff face, and he had listened to everything Will said. 'All we can do is wait? You are supposed to be her guardian, Will Dark!'

It outraged Egg, the way that everyone just seemed to have accepted that Utterly was gone. 'We must wait and see,' Aish had said, and Will Dark and the Skraevelings had all gone along with it. Meanwhile, the Dearloves and everyone else assumed that Utterly was drowned. When Egg reminded them that he had watched her sail away with his own eyes, they just nodded sympathetically and changed the subject, which made him angrier than if they had called him a liar to his face. Only Aish believed him, and it seemed to Egg that Aish cared more about her unborn twins than getting Utterly back from the deep. Of course she must. 'Twas only natural.

Again and again he had told Will Dark they should set out for the Hidden Lands together and rescue Utterly as they had done once before. And again and again Will had replied with annoyingly sensible reasons why they could not. Egg would have gone alone if he could, but the only boat on the whole west coast of Wildsea was the one the sea-witch Thurza Froy had built, and that lay upended and abandoned now among the dunes at Marazea. Even if the frosts and rains of two winters had left it seaworthy, it was much too heavy for Egg to turn right-side-up and drag down into the water on his own, and who else was likely to help him? They were all far too frightened of the Gorm.

Angry at Utterly for leaving, angry at himself for failing to stop her, angry at the world in general, Egg had become crabby and solitary. There was no one he could talk to of his feelings but Tab the cat, and the sea. He went walking sometimes on the beaches, telling his worries to the waves in the hope that Utterly might hear him. Maybe she would come running out of the surf to tell him he was being silly, and challenge him to a race to the hill fort, or the top of Owlsbarrow Beacon, like she used to in the good old days. 'Utterly!' he shouted, standing on the dunes with the west wind flinging salt spray in his face. But if Utterly was out there, she was not listening, or Egg's voice was too small and thin to reach her. Sometimes he thought about running into the sea himself, but he recalled too well how it had picked him up and thrown him on the beach when he had tried to follow Utterly before. The Gorm was stronger than him, and she did not want him in her ocean.

Will Dark and Reverend Dearlove had ended their beachcombing and were starting to make their scrambly way back up the cliff path. Egg, not wanting them to see him, writhed backwards on his belly away from the cliff's edge, then stood up and dusted himself down. As he turned to run back to the house, something made him glance south towards Gull Point and the distant rank of sea-stacks called the Spillikins. There, clear as day on the dark blue afternoon sea, a ship had appeared.

At first, in a great, dizzying uprush of hope, Egg thought it must be the ship from the Hidden Lands, bringing Utterly back home. But that hope died almost instantly. This ship had come from the east, not the west, and as she rounded the Spillikins her mass of sails gleamed white as summer clouds, and the sunlight shone on bright brass fittings and the cheerful chequerboard of gun ports along her side. The ship that Utterly had sailed away on had been black, and even from a distance, Egg had been able to tell her sails were rags and tatters. So this ship was a different one. But she was still a ship, and no ship had ventured upon the dangerous waters west of Wildsea in the whole of Egg's lifetime.

He forgot about not wanting to be seen. He ran to the top of the cliff path and shouted down to Will and Reverend Dearlove, 'A ship!' then stood pointing while they hurried up to join him. 'Look there, Will Dark! Look, vicar! A ship! A ship! A ship!'

# 7

# HMS ACANTHA

The ship sailed past Sundown Watch, and the Darks, Dearloves and Skraevelings followed it, hurrying down the cliff track and through the dunes. By the time they reached Marazea, the ship had dropped anchor in the bay, and the whole village had turned out to gawp at it, loudly wondering who would be foolish enough to set sail upon the Gorm's own sea, and how long it would be before the Gorm noticed them there and dragged them down to their watery doom.

Egg, elbowing his way through to the front of the crowd, found the Dearlove children already there, taking turns to view the ship through Horatio's pocket spyglass. Lucy was currently in possession of the glass and, being the oldest, was reluctant to give it up. But Egg had sharp eyes, and no need of a telescope to see that the vessel had two masts, over which the sailors were swarming like Barbary apes as they furled her sails.

'She is not a true ship,' said Egg, who had made two voyages to Summertide the year before and considered himself an expert on such things. 'She is only a sloop, or brig.'

'That won't be much comfort if she is full of horrid Frenchmen come to capture Wildsea for Napoleon,' snapped Lucy. 'We shall all be murdered, I expect. Or else they shall make us talk French, and eat frogs' legs for dinner. I am not sure which would be worse.'

Little Emily, who felt sorry for the poor frogs, started to cry, but Horatio said, 'You can't see any better with a telescope than without one, Lucy Dearlove. Don't you see that big red flag flapping from her jackstaff? That is the red ensign, and it means she is the King's ship, I mean sloop.'

'Of course I know that,' said Lucy, with great dignity. 'It is only that the sun was in my eyes.'

Egg grabbed the telescope from her, and was able to see that the sloop was named HMS *Acantha*. Her deck was cluttered with crates, hen coops, and a mysterious sailcloth-covered item shaped somewhat like a haystack. A trim white cutter was being lowered from davits on her stern. The crowd of onlookers grew restless. Being Wildsea folk, they were wary of leaving the safety of the

dunes and going any nearer to the fickle sea, but Will
and Aish and a few of the younger and more daring men
strode down to the water's edge to meet the cutter as it
rowed ashore. Egg handed the telescope to Emily and
ran after them.

The cutter ran its white keel onto the sand. The rowers
stowed their oars and leaped out to drag her further up
the beach, until the three gentlemen who sat in her stern
were able to step out without wetting their buckled shoes.
One of them was clearly the *Acantha*'s master, very splen-
didly turned out in his blue coat, white breeches, and
gold-tasselled hat. The second was a small, solid-looking
gentleman dressed all in black, with a white wig; the
little lenses of his spectacles caught the sunlight as he
looked up and down the beach, and glinted like a pair of
silver sixpences. The third was a young man with dark,
curly hair and a pleasant face, which became downright
handsome when he spotted Will among the onlookers.
He gave a delighted laugh. 'Will Dark, old fellow! I was
hoping I'd find you here!'

'Constantine!' said Will, amazed. He stood and
stared, as the young man came hurrying across the sand
towards him. Frank Constantine had been a friend of his
when he lived in London. Indeed, Constantine had been
the most dashing, most devil-may-care, most *Londonish* of
all Will's friends in those days. Constantine the master
of revels, Constantine the would-be poet, would-be

actor, would-be journalist, darting restlessly from one fad to another like a bee determined to sip from every flower. Constantine who never missed a lecture at the Royal Society, and claimed that science would soon transform the world . . . They had exchanged a letter or two since Will came home to Wildsea. Now here stood Constantine himself, large as life upon Marazea strand, making faces to amuse the little children who peeped out at him from behind their mother's skirts. He was so out of place that Will could scarcely believe he was real

'What the Devil are you doing here?' he asked, returning Constantine's firm handshake. 'Don't you know how dangerous the seas are, west of Wildsea? There are reefs, shoals, strange currents . . .'

'Oh, Captain Bulstrode can cope with all those things,' said Constantine, looking Will up and down, and seeming a little perplexed to find him dressed at least twenty years behind the London fashion. 'The *Acantha* is one of the Navy's most modern ships; she has a sliding keel that may be heaved up to let her pass quite unharmed over reefs that would rip the bottom out of less ingenious vessels.'

'But what are you doing aboard her?' asked Will, still mystified at his old friend's presence here. 'You always claimed you could not last a fortnight away from the comforts and delights of London town! When you wrote to me at Christmas you said you were about to take up a position as secretary to some eccentric old bore from the north country . . .'

'Pray allow me to introduce my employer, Lord Langdale,' said Constantine loudly, managing to drown out the 'old bore' and most of the 'eccentric', but Lord Langdale still looked coolly at Will through the tiny lenses of his spectacles as he made his bow.

Will returned the bow, and said he was honoured to meet His Lordship, and Captain Bulstrode too. He reached back towards Aish and she let him take her hand and draw her forward to stand beside him. 'May I present my wife, Aish of the Dizzard,' he said.

Egg saw the three newcomers' eyes widen as they took in Aish's trollish features and the tangle of charms hanging around her neck. Constantine recovered himself first, and murmured that he was delighted to make her acquaintance, but he was too late; Egg had already decided not to like him.

'This is my friend Frank Constantine, my dear,' said Will.

'Then I am glad to meet you, Mr Constantine,' said Aish, 'for any friend of Will Dark's must be a friend of mine, I think. But, Mr Constantine, you have still not told us what has brought you to our island in your sweet little boat.'

Captain Bulstrode looked highly displeased at hearing the *Acantha* called a sweet little boat, but he said

46

nothing. Lord Langdale watched Aish with cold curiosity. Constantine laughed, and said, 'Why Mrs Dark, it is nine-tenths your husband's doing. Will, do you recall that night at the Pleasure Gardens, a few weeks before you left London? You had just lately received word of your poor brother's unfortunate death, and you held all the ladies quite spellbound with your Romantic tales of this place and its quaint legends.'

'I do not recall,' said Will, blushing a little. (In fact he recalled the occasion perfectly, and also that he had been a very foolish young man in those days.)

'"I shall never go back to Wildsea," you said,' Constantine reminded him. 'So you may imagine our astonishment when, within the month, you did! But though you were gone, the stories you had told stayed with us – or they stayed with me, at least. Your account of sea dragons and storm witches exerted such a fascination upon me that I resolved to learn all I could about these Autumn Isles of yours. That was not much, but it was all so peculiar that I made a point of writing of it to Lord Langdale, who takes an interest in such mysteries. He decided at once that an expedition should be got up, and was good enough to offer me employment as his secretary and companion.'

'Aye, these "Hidden Lands" of yours, Mr Dark,' said Lord Langdale, in a creaky, mineral sort of voice. (It was, thought Egg, just precisely the sort of voice one of the carved skeletons on the headstones in Marazea churchyard would speak in if it woke up one day and had something to say.) 'There are too many reports to dismiss out of hand. It is high time they were investigated properly, in the light of the latest scientific discoveries. If there are really unknown lands out there, we must make a landing on them, so that they may be thoroughly surveyed and explored.'

'Indeed,' agreed Captain Bulstrode. 'We must grab 'em, my lord. Claim 'em for King George and dear old England, before the Frenchies or the damned Americans can get their hands on 'em.'

'Mr Constantine,' said Aish, before Will could reply. 'My Will Dark is Watcher on Wildsea, as you know, and I am sure he will tell you the same as I do: that there is great danger out there in the sea, and mysteries that no mortal can ever hope to solve. All those who have tried have come to grief.'

'With respect, ma'am,' said Captain Bulstrode, 'I don't suppose those who tried before had a well-found vessel with a sliding keel, nor one that carried twelve thirty-two pounder carronades. Whatever it is you fear out there in the Western Deeps, the *Acantha* can deal with it.'

'Quite so,' agreed Constantine, and his pleasant smile could not quite conceal his thoughts, which were revolving around the problem of how Will Dark had got himself married to such an outlandish and superstitious woman as Aish. 'Quite so. "What does the Watcher on Wildsea watch for?" I asked you once, Will, and you said, "Most likely for nothing." But Lord Langdale and I are convinced that there is *something* wrapped up inside your tangle of old fishwives' tales, and with the Navy's help we shall puzzle out what it is. Now, we should be much obliged if we could take a look at your family's Log-books, so that we may attempt to plot a course for these invisible lands of yours.'

Will looked helplessly at Aish. 'I suppose . . . Yes, you must come up to the Watch. Egg, run ahead and tell Mrs Skraeveling we shall have guests at dinner.'

'Yes, you should come to Sundown Watch,' Aish agreed. 'You will be safer there. And you should let all your sailors come ashore too, Captain Bulstrode. For if you leave your little boat anchored out there in the bay, I reckon the old Gorm will have dragged it down into her deeps by morning.'

# 8

# THE EXPEDITION

Despite Aish's warning, and somewhat to Egg's annoyance (for he would have loved to see Mr Constantine and the other gentlemen taken down a peg) the *Acantha* was still afloat next morning. She lay at anchor on the blue water as though Marazea Bay were just an ordinary bay, and not the domain of the rampageous Gorm. Captain Bulstrode, who had insisted on sleeping aboard, could be seen strutting about on deck, proud as a peacock in his fine blue uniform. Several boats were going to and fro, ferrying water from Marazea Brook, and pigs and chickens that the Navy had purchased from the local farms.

Lord Langdale had been given the guest bedroom at Sundown Watch. Mr Constantine, much to Egg's disgust, had slept in Utterly's old room. 'What if Utterly comes home tonight?' Egg had said, when he heard Will Dark suggest it. 'What if she sees that light you leave a-burning in the Tower for her, and comes home, and finds a great fool of an Englishman snoring in her bed? What sort of welcome would that be?'

He mistrusted Constantine. The grown-ups all seemed charmed by the young man's good looks and ready smile, but Egg sensed some underlying nervousness in him, and he had noticed that his coat was frayed at the cuffs and collar, and that the linen of his shirt was wearing thin. If Utterly had been there to talk to, he knew she would have said, 'Oh, Egg, it stands to reason a gentleman would not wear his best clothes on a sea voyage. And as for nervousness, perhaps he is fretting over some secret sorrow – an ailing relative, or unhappy love-affair.' But Utterly was not there, and in her absence Egg's imagination was making a villain out of Mr Constantine. What if he was another cunning, treacherous sort of gent like Dr Hyssop, the disgraceful vicar who had tried to do them down on Summertide? Why, then it was Egg's duty to keep an eye on him, that was what.

'Langdale's no fool,' Constantine was telling Will, when Egg came into the breakfast room that morning. 'He is a self-made man, you know. A miner from the hills of Westmorland who used his grasp of natural sciences to set up mills and furnaces and forge himself a fortune, which he now devotes to the study of mysteries. When I told him about your Hidden Lands he guessed at once that they are not hidden by magic, but merely by some natural phenomenon, which prevents us from seeing 'em, except in certain conditions.'

'It is an interesting theory,' agreed Will, politely. 'May I press you to another kipper?'

'Why, thank you, Will. It is a most *elegant* theory, and it explains perfectly why so many ships founder out there in your Western Deeps – the sailors do not see the reefs and rocks until it is too late. Luckily, Captain Bulstrode, though a dull fellow, is a capital seaman.'

'But, Frank,' said Will, passing the dish of kippers, 'what about the Gorm? She is not merely a legend, you know. The reason several volumes of the Log are missing is that they were destroyed, along with the Tower, when she came storming ashore two autumns past. I saw – well, my recollections of it are somewhat vague, but I *saw* her, Constantine. She was a thing of weed, towering, colossal – and then, next day, a woman, cold and beautiful . . .' He turned his eyes to the window, gazing at the blue-grey sea and thinking of his brother, and of Utterly. 'How does the Gorm fit into Lord Langdale's theories?' he wondered.

Constantine looked pityingly at him, and sprinkled pepper on his kipper. 'It is easy for our imaginations to run away with us in wild weather, Will. And in weather wild enough to tear down a tower, I am not surprised you should imagine giants. It is disappointing, I know – nothing would please me more than to find some ancient magic lingering here. But this is the nineteenth century, and modern science has the measure of such things.'

Will met Egg's disapproving gaze across the kippers, and sadly shook his head. He once had been just as certain that the Gorm and her works could be explained away, and just as convinced that he was the man to do it. No one had been able to persuade him otherwise until the Gorm herself came calling. Perhaps Constantine and Lord Langdale would need to meet her for themselves before they too could understand.

Before he could say any more about it, Lord Langdale himself entered, reporting that he slept much better than on the voyage out, when he had been plagued by seasickness. Perhaps that was what made him more agreeable this morning, congratulating Will on his charming house and its excellent views. Will began to warm to the old fellow a little. So did Egg, although Lord Langdale seemed not to notice him sitting at the far end of the table, busily eating kippers and bacon.

'Toast, Your Lordship?' said Mrs Skraeveling, entering from the kitchen. She was all a-flutter to have an actual lord eating at her table. She bowed low as she placed the toast rack beside him, and went backwards out of the room, colliding on the way with a side table, then the doorframe, and finally with Aish, who chose that moment to come in. Aish ruffled Egg's hair as she eased herself carefully into the seat beside him. 'I hope you have saved some kippers for me, gentlemen,' she said, 'for I have two more hungry mouths to feed beside my own.'

She patted her belly, while Constantine and Lord Langdale looked at their plates, the view from the window, the mantelpiece clock, anywhere but at Aish. A London lady in her interesting condition would never have drawn attention to it; indeed, she would probably not have gone into society in such a state at all. But Aish did not realize she had shocked her visitors – or perhaps she did, and did not care. She helped herself to toast and tea and said, 'So are you still intent upon this foolish expedition, gentlemen?'

'Alas,' said Lord Langdale, 'I shall play no further part in it myself. I was worse afflicted by the seasickness on the voyage from England than I had anticipated, and I do not believe my constitution can withstand another voyage so soon. But Constantine here shall make all the observations I need.'

'And I shall leave this very day to begin making them,' explained Constantine. 'Captain Bulstrode is eager to set sail upon the noonday tide, while the wind is blowing so conveniently from the south-east. Were it to set in from the west, we might be stuck in your bay for weeks, and you would grow sadly tired of our company.'

'Oh, I'm sure I should,' said Aish. 'But I could always go to my other house, and I would far rather you were boring us at Sundown Watch than floating in the Gorm's cold deeps all dead and drowned.'

Constantine looked disapprovingly at her. Gentlemen about to embark on a sea voyage do not like to be reminded of the possibility of drowning, and he seemed to think it tasteless of Aish to raise the subject. He murmured again that the *Acantha* was a well-found ship and her master a capital seaman.

Lord Langdale turned to Will. 'Of course, as Watcher on Wildsea, you shall be accompanying us, Mr Dark.'

'Of course he shall not!' said Aish, reaching out to take Will's hand in hers, as if she thought the very mention of such a thing bad luck, and feared the Gorm might reach in through the window and snatch him from the table.

Lord Langdale raised a sceptical eyebrow. Constantine looked embarrassed, cleared his throat, and said, 'Well, here's the thing, Will. I mean to say, you *are* the Watcher on Wildsea, after all, and the acknowledged authority on these Hidden Lands. The crown pays you a yearly stipend for your services and has granted your family this fine house. So the Admiralty rather expects you to do your duty and set sail with us.'

9

# THE LURE

Utterly swam with the Gorm through seas of time. They soared through the sulphurous plumes of undersea volcanoes, through gulfs of ice, and over plains crisscrossed with the tracks of creatures that looked to Utterly like giant, submarine woodlice. They plunged into abysses where all the fish were lit up like Chinese lanterns, and through sunlit summer shallows where sea dragons sported. When they put their heads above the waves they saw shores dense with jungle. Once, a herd of huge animals left off munching the treetops and craned their long necks to watch Utterly and the Gorm as they walked on the wet sand at the sea's edge.

They swam again, and arrived at a lonely beach that was more mud than sand. Mist was tangling in the huge ferns which clad the hills behind. No birds sang among those fern-forests, and no animals moved, but across the beach small shapes were creeping. Frogs, thought Utterly at first, as she and the Gorm left the sea and walked towards them. Her feet sank ankle deep in ooze with every step. She wondered why her mother would choose to bring her to such a slimy place just to show her frogs.

But they were not frogs, those creeping things. They were curious little fish, who were using their fins like limbs to pull themselves laboriously across the mud.

'Look at them,' said the Gorm. 'The little traitors! They have all the lovely gardens of the sea to play in, and yet they choose to crawl up onto land.'

Offshore, a dark and spiny back broke the surface, suggesting to Utterly exactly why the poor fish might prefer to take their chances on shore.

'These cowards are the ancestors of all the creatures of the dry land,' said the Gorm. 'They are not much to look at, but their descendants will become people and horses and those stripy things and those big, grey ones with the noses . . .'

'Then this beach must be *very* long ago . . .' said Utterly.

'The sea is already old,' said the Gorm conceitedly. 'But this is where life on land begins.'

Utterly shivered. For it had suddenly occurred to her that there were no other people in the world at all.

There was only herself and the Gorm, and the Gorm was not exactly a person. Even Adam and Eve had not been created yet. Why, God was probably only just laying out the flowerbeds in the Garden of Eden. And as for Uncle Will, and Aish, and Egg, and the Skraevelings, and everyone else whom Utterly loved, why, none of them would be born for thousands upon thousands of years.

She felt more lost than she had ever felt before. She *was* more lost! More lost than anyone had ever been! Even Robinson Crusoe, cast away upon his desert isle, could console himself that the world he knew was still continuing without him. Utterly, a castaway in time, was altogether alone.

'I want to go home,' she said.

'But you *are* home, Utterly. The sea is your home.'

'I want to be back in my proper time.'

'But all times are yours, to swim in as you wish.'

'Well then, if it please you, I should like to swim in the year eighteen hundred and twelve, and among the Autumn Isles.'

'Then you must use your sea-sense, Utterly,' said the Gorm, sensing a chance to educate her daughter. 'You must sniff out the current that will lead you there, and follow it. But be careful not to go too far.'

Utterly ran through the mud, leaving a line of deep footprints that would one day puzzle gentlemen of science exceedingly. When she plunged into the sea she could sense nothing at first. But as she sank deeper she became aware of different strands and layers in the water, some warmer, some cooler. She had noticed these strands before, but she had been too busy following her mother to pay them much attention. Now she perceived that they could guide her, and their different temperatures and flavours could tell her to what portion of the sea they led. This one seemed to flow from the tropics, scented with the laughter of brown children and the warmth of white sand, while that one issued from the chilly north, where whales sang lullabies and the waves slapped boisterously at the keels of longships. But all these many currents were woven together like the threads of a great tapestry, so that for a moment, Utterly felt quite at a loss. There were so many of them, she did not think she could ever hope to find the one that would lead her home.

But as she hung there treading water in the darkness, she caught a scent upon the water that spoke to her of Wildsea; of its particular cliffs and coves, familiar as a well-beloved face. It did not even take much effort to swim there. She kicked her feet once, twice, and she was surfacing in the straits between Wildsea and the Hidden Lands.

To the gulls riding the night wind above them she looked like a seal, just her sleek dark head bobbing on the waves, lit by the fat orange moon that was rising behind Owlsbarrow Beacon. The night was dark; the sea was calm; the stars of the Milky Way were strewn across the sky like spilled sugar. And along the shores of Wildsea more stars showed, white and amber, twinkling along the edge of Marazea Bay and among the hills.

'What are all those lights?' asked Utterly.

'You have followed the water-paths too far, child,' said the Gorm, surfacing beside her. 'We have swum into the Sea-that-will-be. Come, we must return.'

Utterly was surprised to hear something in the Gorm's voice that had never been there before. If it was not fear, it was at least caution. But what would the Gorm need to be cautious about?

'Oh, may we not swim closer, and look around?' Utterly pleaded.

'We should not,' said the Gorm, in that same uneasy tone. 'I do not swim in the Sea-that-will-be. My power is weakened here.'

'Weakened how?' asked Utterly. 'I thought you ruled all seas?'

But the Gorm only turned and dived, calling sharply for Utterly to follow her.

Utterly was about to do as she was told when she noticed another light, closer than the others. It seemed to come from below the water as well as above it, and it was so silvery and beautiful that she did not think it could do any harm to just have a look.

So she swam nearer, following a curious cool current

in the sea that seemed to lead directly to the light. And when she drew close, she saw that it was coming from a ship, and that the ship was trailing the light beneath it. The light burned even under the water somehow. It did not feel quite like magic, but nor was it quite like anything else Utterly had seen. If she listened very carefully, she could hear that it was softly singing, just a single, low, pleasing chord, infinitely extended.

Utterly went closer, and then closer still, gliding through a shoal of little fish that had been drawn like her towards the light. She saw that the light was encased inside a basket woven from strands of shining metal, and suspended on a long cable. The cable led up towards the surface, where Utterly could see the leaf-shape of the ship's hull. Fishermen, she supposed. But for what could they be fishing, with such a strange and lovely net?

Then suddenly, as she reached out to touch the light, she realized that it was suspended inside a larger structure – a cage with metal bars so dark and lustreless and somehow dead, she had not noticed them until she was inside them.

And by then it was too late, for the cage seemed to know she was there, and as she went to swim away, the opening she had come in by sprang shut, cutting off her escape. She gripped the bars and tried to force the cage open again, but there was something about the touch of its dark metal she did not like; it made her fingers tingle, and the tingling spread up her arms and into her head and made her dizzy.

The sea swirled, and suddenly the Gorm was there in the dark outside the cage, staring in.

'Oh, help me!' wailed Utterly, and, 'I'm so sorry!' – for she felt very remorseful now at having disobeyed her mother's wishes.

The cage lurched, and began to rise.

'Help!' cried Utterly again.

But to her astonishment, the Gorm did not transform into a huge, white shark and tear the cage to pieces with her teeth, nor into a giant of weed and jetsam who could prise the bars apart with stony claws. She remained only a woman, hanging there, woe-struck, in the midnight sea, and as the cage was heaved up towards the surface all she seemed able to do was reach after it with her pale hands and cry out, 'Utterly!'

And then the surface broke around Utterly's cage in white foam and spilled away, and she was dangling in air and being swung, by some strange crane that growled and roared, sideways over a ship's side, and down onto its deck. The deck was made of metal; indeed, the whole ship seemed made of it; big slabs of metal held together with fat rivets. And while Utterly was numbly wondering how such a ship might float, its crew came crowding round, shining lanterns on her between the bars.

The lanterns were so bright, their light so steady, that

Utterly did not think they contained candles, but must be lit by coal gas. She raised a hand before her dazzled eyes, trying to see who these men were who dared to snatch the Gorm's own daughter from the sea like a lobster in a pot.

She could only see the shapes of them, and a few details that the light allowed; spectacles glinting on the face of one; slithery oilskin trousers on the legs of another. But she heard their voices all around her, loud, excited voices, speaking English with an accent she did not know and a lot of words in it she didn't understand.

'We've got her!' one man shouted excitedly. 'See, Nigel? I *told* you those signals weren't just a reflection off the deep scattering layer . . .'

'Don't go too close, she could be dangerous . . .'

'What will she do? Turn us all into frogs?'

A man came closer, and shone his lantern directly into Utterly's face. 'Quiet . . .' he said, and then, sounding surprised, 'This isn't the Gorm! It's just a girl!'

# 10

# BRING SOMETHING BACK

'But Aish,' said Will, 'it is my duty.'

'Duty?' said Aish angrily. 'And what of your duty to me, and to your twins?'

'I shall return to you. God willing, I shall return this very night, or tomorrow at the latest.'

'God no more controls the Western Deeps than I do, Will Dark. *Gorm* willing is what you should say, and the Gorm is *not* willing. I can feel her watching us, even as we stand here in your garden, and it is not a friendly look that she is giving us. Do you really think she will let these foolish men set foot upon the Hidden Lands? She will drown them, Will Dark. She will put them away in the deepest cellars of the sea where they shall moulder and be forgot, and you with them, if you are foolish enough to go with them. Though *I* shall not forget you – I shall mourn you always.'

And she began to weep.

'Oh, come, come,' said Will. 'Who can tell what the Gorm may do? She spared my life once before. And Constantine is not foolish; nor is Captain Bulstrode. As for Lord Langdale, who has proposed this whole expedition, he is a very eminent man indeed.'

'I do not like him. He has an old, cold, stony sort of feeling about him.'

'Nevertheless,' said Will, who thought His Lordship no colder or stonier than other wealthy old men he had met, 'if there is even a chance that he may find the Hidden Lands, it is my plain duty to go with him. For Utterly's sake. Do you not miss Utterly?'

'Of course I do! Of course I do! I miss her with all my heart! But did we not agree Utterly would be safe in her mother's keeping till she decides to come back to us?'

'We did! But Aish, it has been a month. And what if Utterly has forgotten us? The Hidden Lands can play such tricks upon our memories. If I could just go there and see that she is safe, and remind her that we are all thinking of her. It is my duty to go, Aish.'

They were standing on the sloping lawns outside the drawing-room window, looking alternately at each other and out across the blue-grey morning sea. Neither had noticed Egg, who was crouched behind a nearby bush of broom, one of the few plants that thrived on the seaward side of the house.

'I wish I had the old Gorm's power, or even the Hunter's,' Aish was saying. 'I would call my trees to weave a fence around you so you could not go to sea. I would make the timbers of that pretty ship burst into bud and leaf and put down roots so she could never stir from Wildsea. But I am only Aish, and I have not the power to change the world, only to love my little part of it.'

'Perhaps that is why you are not cruel like the Gorm or the Hunter,' said Will gently. 'Oh, Aish, don't cry . . .' He put his arm around her, and they walked together a little further down the lawn, speaking in such soft voices that Egg could no longer hear what they were saying. He did not need to hear any more, though. He had already made up his mind. He reckoned Will Dark was right about this voyage to the Hidden Lands. Rash it might be, and deadly dangerous no doubt, but it was their best and only hope of finding Utterly. Will Dark would go, whatever Aish said. And Egg would go with him, to keep an eye on him, and bring him safe home to her if he could. He even toyed with the idea of asking Will if he could join the expedition. But in Egg's experience it was always easier to ask forgiveness after you did something than to get permission in advance. Besides, Egg was an old hand at stowing away on ships. When HMS *Acantha* raised her anchors and set sail that forenoon, Egg planned to be aboard her.

*

In the event, it was quite easy to slip aboard the sloop. There was so much coming-and-going from the beach, and the strand was so crowded with onlookers from Marazea and its outlying farms and hamlets, that it was no trouble at all for Egg to jump into one of the boats as it was leaving. When the men at the oars asked who he was he just said, 'I'm the Watcher's assistant. I'm to sail with you. His Lordship's orders.' Five minutes later he was scrambling up the *Acantha*'s side, and once he was aboard there was no shortage of places to conceal himself.

The *Acantha* was not a large vessel by the standards of the Royal Navy, but she was by far the largest Egg had ever been on. She seemed to him a whole wooden world, full of men in striped shirts and white duck trousers and hats made black and shiny with tar. They all kept rushing busily about while a man called Lieutenant Sidcup bellowed orders at them through a brass speaking trumpet and Captain Bulstrode looked down from his place on the quarterdeck like God Almighty.

Loitering behind the domed, sailcloth-shrouded object on the deck, Egg saw Will come aboard in the last boat with Mr Constantine. Will even glanced in Egg's direction, but since Egg had taken care to hide his telltale ginger hair under a knitted cap, and since he was by no means the only boy aboard, he went undetected.

Then the gentlemen were hurried below, the boats were swung aboard, dripping water upon the deck, and various sails were raised (some square, others triangular, Egg could not recall their names). Then the *Acantha* weighed anchor and let the fortunate wind carry her out of Marazea Bay, towards the empty reaches of the sea.

Will stood at the stern-rail, waving and waving. Aish was still unhappy at his going, but she had not wanted to let her unhappiness spoil what she feared might be their final hours together. Their parting had been fond, and Will missed her dreadfully. He could see her now, standing upon the lawns of Sundown Watch, waving back to him, a white kerchief fluttering in her hand.

At her side stood Lord Langdale. He did not wave; he simply stood there, motionless as one of the rough granite pillars that the Wildsea folk of old had set upright on the hillsides. 'Bring something back,' he had commanded Will and Constantine before they embarked. 'Observe every detail. The smallest thing may turn out to be the key which unlocks the way into the Hidden Lands.'

Constantine leaned against the rail too. When the *Acantha* was so far from land that even Will had to admit he could not see Aish any longer, his friend turned to him and said, 'You are a lucky man, Will Dark.'

'I should feel luckier still if you had not dragged me

away from my home on this fool's errand, Constantine,' said Will, a little peevishly.

'But at least you have a home to be dragged away *from*,' said Constantine. 'I was a little surprised by the fair Aish yesterday, but that was before I saw how well the two of you agree. And Wildsea suits you too, Will; you seem so much healthier and more wholly yourself than ever you did in London. I only wish I too had somewhere that I might feel at home.'

'Do you not enjoy London any more?' asked Will. He felt surprised. He had always believed Frank Constantine the happiest and most fortunate of fellows. It was a little disconcerting to learn that Constantine now thought the same of him.

Constantine looked a little embarrassed. 'The trouble with London,' he said, 'is that it is so dashed expensive. I am in debt, Will; deep in debt. It is my own fault entirely – too many nights at the gaming table, too many fine dinners, too many fine clothes. None of that rich living brought me any happiness, and now I am ruined.'

'But Constantine, cannot your father see his way to helping you?'

'He has done so in the past, but he has had enough of me, and I cannot blame him. He declares me a wastrel and a libertine, and has cut me off without a penny. That is why I jumped at the chance to accompany old Langdale on this quest of his. If I had stayed in England

I should have been carted off to debtors' prison. I can never go back, Will.'

'Then where shall you go?' asked Will.

'Where indeed?' Constantine turned and gazed out through the openings between the *Acantha*'s various sails at the sea spread out ahead. 'How I hope that we shall find these Hidden Lands of yours.... Perhaps my place is among them somewhere.'

'Oh, do not say that, my dear fellow!' said Will, alarmed. 'The Hidden Lands are not places where anyone would wish to live.'

Constantine laughed. 'Why, Will – that is exactly what you used to say about Wildsea!'

The sun went west and the ship followed it. Egg wandered the dark and stinking spaces down below, and climbed up on deck sometimes to see what was happening. Whenever anyone asked him who he was he told them, 'Watcher's Boy: I'm with His Lordship's party, ain't I?'

The sailors accepted him. They were not unfriendly. But, as Egg moved among them, he realized that the *Acantha* was not a happy ship. England's wars with France had been going on for so many years that the King was short of sailors, and half the *Acantha*'s crew were serving against their will. Some were thieves and poachers who had chosen the Navy instead of gaol or transportation; others were men from merchant ships who had been dragged aboard the *Acantha* by press gangs. A good few were Americans, forced into the British service and decidedly grumpy about it. Even the regular British tars had been unhappy to learn that they were to be sailing on a scientific expedition, for it offered them no chance of capturing French ships and gaining prize money. And now that they had spent some time on Wildsea and heard the stories the Wildsea people told, they had a new reason to be discontented. The whole ship was filled with dreadful rumours of the Gorm.

'I hear Gorm is great sea monster, and Hidden Islands are place of ghosts and wampires,' said a burly Russian, when Egg sat down among some other men to eat skilligallee that evening.

'Well, I 'eard they are the Isles of Plenty,' said a Welshman, 'and King Arthur 'imself lies sleepin' there. Maybe we'll find gold and treasure, mates.'

'If we find gold,' said a gloomy Manxman, 'it will be ten fathoms down, in Davy Jones's Locker, and we shall never go home to spend it.'

'It's outrageous, is what it is,' said one of the Americans. 'Risking our lives in storm and battle is one thing, but risking our immortal souls in these here haunted seas is another. No king and no captain has any right to make a man do that.'

'I had a shipmate once what jumped overboard in the South Seas,' said a sailor named Hard-tack Joe. 'First he took to staring over the side, and after a bit he said he could see fields down there under the sea, and houses, and a pretty girl calling to him to come down and cuddle her. So over he went, and *down* he went, and that was the end of him. The calenture they call it. Sea madness. That's how the rumour of these Hidden Lands got put about, mates, you mark my words. Just poor madmen in the grip of the calenture.'

*Either that,* thought Egg, *or there are Hidden Lands in the South Seas too, and it was the Gorm herself as your shipmate saw a-calling to him. For who knows how far her power extends? She probably rules over as many of the wet parts of the world as King George does over the dry . . .*

It was late by then; the sky cloudless and brass-coloured in the west where the sun was sinking down towards the sea. Captain Bulstrode ordered sails reefed and soundings taken. While Lieutenant Sidcup ran around making sure it was done, the captain and Constantine stood at the stern-rail with their telescopes and scanned the empty sea around them. Will Dark stood with them, and thought of all the times he had studied this self-same patch of sea through his own telescope, from the Tower at Sundown Watch. *If I were there tonight I would have something novel to write in the Log,* he thought. *'The sky clear, the sea calm, and a ship of fools cruising to and fro in the north-west . . .'* And he wished very much that he *were* there, with Aish sitting next to him to keep him company.

They watched until the sun went down, but no islands appeared. In the moments after sunset one man called out loudly, 'Land! I see land! Close on the larboard quarter!' But no one else could see it; the man's mates shushed him and Lieutenant Sidcup cursed him for a drunken fool.

Will turned and looked east. There, almost invisible in the deepening dusk, the hills of Wildsea rose, with the first stars twinkling above them, and one solitary light shining on the shore. That, Will knew, was the lantern in the window of the Tower: he had lit it every night for Utterly, and tonight Aish must have lit it, so it was shining for him as well.

'Blimey!' said the midshipman who had been given the task of repeatedly lowering a lead over the side to check the depth of the sea. Captain Bulstrode glared at him, but Will said, 'Come, sir – what is it?'

The midshipman was no older than Egg, and rather nervous at having to address a gentleman as distinguished as the Watcher on Wildsea. But he pulled himself together and said, 'Sir, the lead touched bottom at ten fathoms. But the strange thing is this, sir. A moment ago it was too deep to touch at all.'

'There must be submerged rock or mountain below us,' said Captain Bulstrode. 'We should proceed with caution.'

'Begging your pardon, sir,' said the midshipman squeakily. 'It ain't rock, nor mud, nor sand.'

'What is it, then?' snapped Bulstrode.

The lead the midshipman held was cylindrical, with slots in it designed to bring up a sample of the sea floor. He held it out so the gentlemen could see the little pale shapes that filled the slots. 'It's flowers, sir. Primroses.'

'They cannot be primroses,' said Constantine, when the gentlemen were all gathered around the table in the captain's cabin.

The primroses – if primroses they were – had been spread on a sheet of paper on the table, and a lantern placed nearby. Constantine said, 'They must be some type of deep-sea weed which simply happens to *resemble* primroses.'

'They certainly look like primroses to me,' said Mr Samuels, the *Acantha*'s surgeon. 'My mother grows primroses just like them in her garden at Exeter. And look here – there is meadow grass mixed in with them. And I believe this is a dandelion.'

'Well, Mr Dark?' asked Captain Bulstrode. 'Have you ever seen seaweed like this washed ashore on Wildsea's beaches?'

Will shook his head. 'Indeed not. But when Davey Froy and his wife sailed these waters forty years ago they found the Hidden Lands underwater. Mrs Froy herself once told me how they saw trees and meadows and the roofs of grand buildings below their boat's keel. She had constructed a diving suit for her husband, in which he descended to explore.'

'But Lord Langdale has given us to understand the Hidden Lands are merely concealed from us by some sort of airy veil,' said the surgeon. 'He said nothing about them being sunk.'

'But he must have suspected they might be,' said Constantine. 'I am sure you noticed that contraption under the sailcloth covers when we came aboard, Will? That is a diving bell. It will allow me to descend to a depth of several hundred fathoms in perfect comfort and safety.'

'I would not recommend it,' said Will.

'What became of your Froys?' asked Mr Samuels. 'What did the brave fellow find, when his wife lowered him down in her ingenious diving suit?'

Will wanted to say, 'He found the Gorm, and she destroyed him.' He wanted to tell them of how the horrible old diving suit had been washed up next to Thurza Froy's drowned corpse at Marazea, the day after the storm, and how it had been still all sealed together as if Davey was inside, but how, when opened, it was found to contain nothing but seawater.

But all he said was, 'Alas, it did not end well. He never returned.'

'Ah,' said Constantine, who was pondering his own descent into the deep, and had been hoping for a happier outcome. 'Still, a home-made diving suit, sewn forty years ago, by an ignorant Wildsea woman . . . It is small wonder it weren't watertight, Will. There is no comparison with our diving bell, which is constructed to Mr Smeaton's design, with a few improvements of Lord Langdale's own. I shall descend at dawn and pick His Lordship a posy of flowers from Madam Gorm's garden.'

# 11

# THE *SEA WITCH*

Grey daylight stained the skirts of the eastern sky, and as the darkness began to fade Utterly crouched on the floor of her cage and looked about her. The strange ship that had captured her was moving swiftly towards Wildsea, not driven by the winds but by some type of engine, which throbbed and pounded beneath the metal deck. It had no masts, just the big metal crane amidships that had winched the cage aboard, and a sort of deckhouse like a metal shed astern. Across the front of this deckhouse was painted what Utterly took to be the vessel's name: RV *Sea Witch*. On its roof a metal basket thing turned endlessly around and around, and from its windows she sometimes heard, over the beat of the engine, the sounds of pipes and drums and singing voices, as if there were a band playing in there, although the deckhouse did not look large enough.

As for the crew, they mostly kept away from her, although sometimes they glanced curiously at her as they made their way from one end of the ship to the other across the flat portion of deck where her cage rested. Once, two of them came and looked at her while they smoked tobacco through small white paper pipes. They were young men; one already balding, the other with long, mouse-brown hair, and round spectacles which gave him a look of permanent surprise. They were well-spoken, despite their shabby clothes – but Utterly supposed gentlemen did not wear their finest clothes when they went to sea.

'Well, we'll have to see what old Stone makes of her,' said the bespectacled one.

The balding one said, 'He'll blow his top when he sees she's just a kid.'

'Perhaps she's the Gorm, though,' said the first. 'The Gorm's supposed to take on different forms, isn't she? She can't be just a kid, that's for sure – not any ordinary kid, not underwater, way out here.'

Utterly was inclined to tell him that she was the Gorm's own best-beloved daughter, and that if he and his mates did not return her at once to the sea, her mother would rise up in fury and drown the lot of them. But then she recalled the look of hopeless horror she had glimpsed upon the Gorm's face as her cage was winched up, and remembered the Gorm saying that her powers were weaker in the Sea-that-will-be, and reflected that perhaps the Gorm could not come to her rescue here. After all, if she could, she surely would have done so by now.

And besides, Utterly felt too small and cold and scared to scold these men, and her tummy seemed terribly empty. She did not recall eating anything since that first breakfast in the Gorm's house, and she could not say how long ago that had been – days, or years, or maybe centuries.

The sailors had lost interest in Utterly and turned away to lean on the ship's rail. Snatches of their conversation still reached Utterly over the chugging of the engine, but they were no longer talking about her. They were discussing an acquaintance of theirs named Muhammed Ali. He was a most pugnacious gentleman by the sound of him, for they had watched him knock out another man in a fight on the *Telly*. (Utterly assumed the *Telly* was the name of some other ship.) She waited for a pause in their debate, then put her face close to the bars and said, 'If you please, gentlemen, I am most exceeding hungry.'

The men looked round at her in surprise, as if it had not occurred to them she would be able to speak English, or even to speak at all. The balding one said to the other,

'Stone said no interfering. We'll be at the Centre soon enough.' But his friend said he did not see what harm it could do, and fetched something out of the pocket of his coat. 'There you go, kid,' he said. 'Have a Penguin to keep you going.'

Utterly had never eaten penguin before, and wasn't sure she wished to start now, for she imagined they would be oily, salty-tasting birds. But she was hungry enough that she took the little oblong packet the man passed through bars. It was made from shiny red paper with a picture of a penguin on it, but when she unwrapped it she found inside a bar of brown stuff that looked nothing like penguin meat, and when she bit into it, it was sweet and crunchy and better than almost anything she had tasted in her life. She ate it quickly, and licked the brown stains from the inside of the wrapper, and said, 'Thank you, sir, that was a most delicious piece of penguin.'

'She's polite, at least,' said the balding young man, walking off to see to something in the deckhouse. The one with the spectacles lingered just long enough to say, quite kindly, 'Don't worry, kid. We'll be at Belfriars Bay soon enough. There will be food there, and dry clothes for you. You'll be OK.'

Then he went off after his friend, leaving Utterly alone to ponder his meaning. What did 'okay' mean? And why should the master of this peculiar ship wish to put in to Belfriars Bay, a steep-sided, empty little cove a few miles south of Sundown Watch, where nobody went for fear of the Gorm?

But in this odd new world that she had come to, it seemed people no longer feared the Gorm, and Belfriars Bay was no longer empty. For soon the cliffs of Wildsea came in sight, and there was Belfriars Head, with a cluster of boxy buildings on the shore below it, where there had never been any buildings before.

What year had she arrived in, wondered Utterly, where boats moved without sails, and people had found time to build what seemed a whole new village down in Belfriars Bay? A sudden fear struck her and she turned and looked the other way, northward up the coast of Wildsea. There, just before the cliffs hid it, she caught a brief, reassuring glimpse of Sundown Watch, still standing sentinel upon its clifftop.

So that is where I must take myself, she thought. I must break free of this cage somehow, and escape these men, and find my way to Sundown Watch and ask the Watcher for help.

For she knew that, even if she was in an age so distant from her own that Uncle Will was very old, or even dead, there was sure to be a Watcher. There must always be a Watcher on Wildsea.

The *Sea Witch*, with much grumbling and snarling of engines, came alongside a little wooden jetty that poked out into the bay. A man and woman were waiting for her there. The woman was plump and pretty and fair haired, and looked a little like Mrs Dearlove, except that she wore trousers, which Mrs Dearlove would have thought very shocking. The man was older, and dressed in a coat with a great many pockets. As the *Sea Witch* bumped up against the jetty he stepped forward and set his foot on her gunwale, peering down at Utterly through tinted spectacles. He was a stocky, square-ish, grey haired man. When he spoke his voice was smooth and gentlemanly, but with something rough beneath it, like water flowing over a bed of gravel.

'She's all you found?'

The man who had given Utterly the Penguin came and stood by the cage and said, 'The instruments picked up something, but when we hauled the rig in she's all we had. If there was anything else down there . . .'

'And you had no sightings of land? Radar picked up nothing, west or north-west?'

'No, Professor Stone. But . . . I mean, she *looks* like a girl, but she was in deep water, miles offshore. The rig was at twenty fathoms when she entered the containment unit. What do you reckon she is?'

Professor Stone looked long and hard at Utterly, but she could not see his eyes, just her own scared face reflected in those tinted spectacles. She had the feeling that he recognized her, although she was sure they had never met. At last he said, 'Cold and tired is what she is,

Nigel. Let's get her ashore and find some clothes for her, and maybe a bite to eat.' He smiled at Utterly, or at least his mouth stretched into the shape of a smile. 'How does that sound, Utterly Dark?'

12

# THE DIVING BELL

April 30th, 1812, wrote Will in his notebook. He felt that as Watcher he had a duty to keep his own record of the *Acantha*'s voyage. Besides, writing helped him to forget his fears; fears which had kept him awake for much of the night. *The sea is very calm,* he wrote, *and quite empty of islands, except that Wildsea is visible in the east, and there is a smudge upon the sky to the north of it, which may be smoke from the mine chimneys on Seapitts. The night passed without incident, the ship at anchor. A sample taken from the sea floor this morning confirmed last night's observations. Constantine has decided to make a descent using Lord Langdale's diving bell.*

The sailcloth coverings had been removed from the diving bell, and it hung by heavy pulleys from the crane which had been fitted to the *Acantha* for the purpose. It looked to a landsman's eye like a vast, wooden barrel, with a few bullseye windows of thick glass set in brass frames, and a long tube emerging from among the brackets and other fittings on its roof. Will knew that the bottom of the barrel was open, and that when it was lowered overboard the pressure of the air inside would keep the sea from filling it, just as the air remained inside a glass pushed carefully down into a bowl of water. He understood the principle, but he felt very glad he would not be the one making a descent. The idea of being deep underwater with nothing to protect him but those wooden staves and the bubble of air they contained filled him with horror.

Constantine seemed to feel much the same way, to judge by the way he had tossed and turned all night in the narrow cabin he and Will shared. Now, in the morning light upon the quarterdeck, he looked pale and unhappy. But then, so did many of the ship's company. All through the night watches men sleeping down below had kept calling out in terror at awful apparitions in their dreams, while some of those on deck claimed to have seen lights nearby, or heard strange music. The ominous name of the Gorm was being whispered all around the ship. Captain Bulstrode, sensing the uneasy mood, had sought to cheer up his crew by issuing a ration of rum to all hands.

'So now they are not only terrified, but drunk,' said Constantine, watching unhappily as some of the sailors swung the diving bell out over the ship's side.

'Are you certain this contraption is safe, Mr Constantine?' asked Captain Bulstrode.

'Of course it is safe!' said Constantine. Anxiety was making him snappish. 'Diving bells have been in use since the time of Alexander the Great, and this one is constructed on the soundest scientific principles. The air your men pump down the tube will constantly replenish the supply inside the bell, and there is a useful rope, which I may pull to signal to you if anything goes wrong.'

'Nevertheless, sir,' suggested Will, 'perhaps it would be as well to send it down empty first, just to ensure that everything is running smoothly and that your fellows know what they are about.'

This managed to offend both Constantine and Captain Bulstrode, for Will had cast aspersions not just on the diving bell but on the *Acantha*'s crew. Constantine glared at him. Captain Bulstrode, marching over to the quarterdeck rail, shouted down to the men on the deck, 'Mr Constantine is feeling uneasy about making a descent in his machine. Here is a guinea for any man who will go down in the bell and take a look about beneath the waves.'

The sailors stared up at him. Egg, standing by the winch that worked the crane, could almost hear the clockwork of their brains at work. A guinea was a lot of money, they were thinking, but what if the Gorm was waiting for them down below? You can't spend money when you're dead and drowned, no matter how much of it there is.

There was a long and awkward silence, during which the diving bell swung gently to and fro like a corpse on a gibbet and the ropes supporting it softly creaked. Then Egg stepped forward and said, 'I'll go, sir.'

*Because the Gorm knows me*, he reasoned to himself, as the babble of voices broke out all around him. The sailors stared at him, and some drew away as if he were already a drowned ghost. *The Gorm and me, we're almost like old friends. She let me visit her place once and come home safe, so who's to say she won't again? And anyway, she ain't down there alone; Utterly's there with her, and Utterly won't let no harm come to me.*

All of which had sounded very reasonable when he volunteered, but seemed rather less so as he made his way to the ship's side and looked up into the diving bell, which dangled above him as if it were a candle-snuffer, and he the flame it was about to extinguish. He pulled off his hat and ran a hand through his hair, nerving himself to climb up inside the bell. And then, of course, there was an anguished shout of 'Egg!' because Will Dark had recognized him.

Egg turned as the men around him parted to let Will

through. 'Egg, how came you here?' Will demanded, and then waved the question aside before Egg could reply; Egg was an old hand at stowing away; indeed, in Will's experience, a boat or ship was as likely to have Egg hidden somewhere about it as not. He gestured at the diving bell instead and said, 'This is no job for you, Egg. It may be dangerous, and what would Aish say if I were to lose you as well as Utterly?'

'But it's Utterly I'm going down to fetch,' said Egg. 'It worked before, didn't it?'

'Then let me go,' said Will.

'Aish'll have a lot worse to say if it's you that don't come home,' said Egg. 'And I'd sooner drown than have to listen to her say it. So you wait here, Will Dark, and make sure they get you back to Sundown Watch if I don't come up again.'

Lifted by rough but helpful hands, Egg clambered up into the bell and perched himself on the wooden seat which stretched across the middle of it. Will appeared below, shouting up at him to come out, but he was pushed aside by Constantine, who started bellowing instructions about air pressure, the rate of descent, which line to pull to signal the ship, and to be sure and bring up plenty of samples. Then, swinging as if it really were a bell, and Egg the clapper inside it, the whole machine was lowered towards the waves, slightly faster than Egg might have wished.

'You've done it now, Egg,' he muttered, as the bell splashed down into the water. 'I don't know why you have to keep letting yourself in for these things,' he scolded himself, as the lead weights hanging from the bell's sides dragged it down. Blue water rose up past the glass of the lower porthole, then the higher one, and he was underwater. 'It's only for Utterly's sake I'm doing this,' he reminded himself. 'Because Utterly would do the same for me.'

He had been sceptical when he heard the bell would stay full of air but, sure enough, it did. The sea surrounded him above and on all sides, but it stayed obediently in the opening where the floor should be, lapping and sloshing a little, but showing no sign of swirling up to fill the bell. The light from the portholes dimmed rapidly as the bell sank. Egg made a swift inventory of the various buckets, bags, and tools which hung from pegs around the walls. A piece of paper had been pasted beside the signal cord, bearing a list of the different messages he could transmit to the ship – one pull for *safely down*, two for *all's well*, three for *winch me up!*

Egg had barely time to read them before the bell settled, with a gentle bump, upon the bottom.

He looked down, expecting either mud, or the grass and primroses the *Acantha*'s soundings had found. Instead, he saw that the diving bell stood upon a perfectly dry chequerboard floor of black and white marble tiles.

*Odd*, thought Egg. But he had learned it was best to expect the unexpected where magic was concerned, and there was no point wasting time on being surprised. He stood up on the bench and peered out through a porthole.

Outside, a pillared hall stretched away from him into infinite distances, like a demonstration of perspective in one of Will Dark's books on drawing. Egg tried the other portholes, but the view was the same from each. No fish swam between the towering pillars; no anemones or corals waved their fronds from the ornate finials. The light that slanted in through the high windows was no more dim and blue than a summer's twilight on dry land.

He pulled the cord once, and after a moment felt the bell jerk as it rose a little; Constantine had declared it must be held a few inches above the sea floor. Egg watched carefully as it rose, but no water rushed in beneath it, so when it steadied again he pulled the cord twice to let the ship know all was well, then jumped down off the bench.

There was just enough space between the floor and the bottom of the bell for a small, determined person to wriggle out. Egg wriggled, and soon found himself standing outside the bell, which hung incongruously in the centre of an immense and apparently deserted palace. The cables and air-tube rising from its top stretched up through dim air to the far-off ceiling, which had been painted with a picture of the sea, complete with fish,

90

mermaids, sea-serpents, and the underside of a ship, to which the air-tube and the cable led. Nearby, another cable descended from the painted ship, and at the bottom of it was HMS *Acantha's* main anchor, its flukes deeply embedded in a patch of shattered tiles.

It was very quiet. Salt water dripped from the diving bell into a spreading puddle that had formed beneath it. From far off came another sound, which might have been the sea, or just the noise of the blood pumping through Egg's own body. And beneath that, very faint, he caught a third sound.

Somewhere in this twilit palace, some poor soul was sobbing as if their heart had broken.

'Utterly?' called Egg.

His voice came echoing back at him. The sobbing continued. He looked around, trying to gauge which direction the sound was coming from. It seemed risky to leave the diving bell. How could he know when the Gorm would grow weary of maintaining this illusion, and these grand halls would turn back abruptly into a deep-sea canyon or a sunken cave?

*But if that is Utterly crying her heart out*, thought Egg, *then I must go to her. And if it ain't, I still have to go anyway.* For Egg was not the sort of boy who could leave someone in distress and not at least *try* to comfort them.

So he set off towards the sound of sobbing, and his footsteps rang out eerily upon the black and white tiles.

Statues watched him pass from alcoves. They were all statues of goddesses, and all the goddesses were some tribe or nation's notion of the Gorm. Sometimes he passed windows, and looked out through them into a twilit country where soft shafts of sunlight came down through the clouds. The vast building he was in seemed to stand at the centre of a maze of yew or box hedges, and the tops of the hedges had been clipped into the shapes of leaping dolphins, sharks, and whales. Beyond the hedges, lawns of grass, speckled with primroses, stretched away to an uncertain horizon.

He was not sure how long he had been walking when he came to a sort of crossroads where four halls met. There in the centre, with the light spilling down on her through windows high above, a woman sat on the tiles. She sat like a child with her legs stuck out in front of her and face raised to the light and her mouth wide open, and she wailed. Her hair, in black entanglements, ebbed and flowed around her bawling face like weed on a current.

Egg was disappointed to see no sign of Utterly, and frightened enough of the Gorm that he almost ran back to the diving bell before she knew he was there.

*But she must know I'm here,* he reasoned, *because why else go to the bother of conjuring up this whole great palace to impress me?* Anyway, in spite of everything, he felt sorry for her.

He went gingerly towards her. On the tiles at her side lay a small embroidered bag which he recalled Utterly carrying sometimes on trips to Merriport. The Gorm seemed to have upended it, spilling out a comb, a hair-brush, a pocketknife, and a useful-looking length of string.

'Gorm?' said Egg.

The Gorm stopped crying, and looked at him. Egg thought how like Utterly she was; like an older and more beautiful Utterly. He had never noticed their resemblance before, but now it made his heart skip a beat, the two of them were so alike.

Perhaps the Gorm had thought he was somebody else. A wild hope was in her face as she turned to look at him, and then faded when she saw he was only Egg. She began crying again, louder than ever.

Egg put out a hand and gently touched her shoulder. 'What is the matter, Gorm?' he said. 'I'm Egg. Utterly's friend. Remember me?'

The Gorm's eyes were ice-white, as if they had frozen over. 'Utterly!' she wailed.

'I came looking for her,' said Egg. 'Is she here? Those are her things, aren't they? I gave her that bit of string myself. So where's Utterly got to?'

The Gorm drew a shuddering breath and let it out as small whimpering noises. She drew another, and looked at Egg again, and said, 'Utterly is gone!'

She was frightened, Egg realized. Grieving too, but mostly frightened. That made him frightened too, for what could frighten something as mighty as the Gorm?

'*Where* has she gone?' he asked.

'Into a place I cannot see,' snivelled the Gorm. 'She swam there, I followed, and something happened, and now she is not here nor anywhere in all the sea's long dream. She is lost in the Sea-that-will-be, and there I cannot go. I cannot see her, and cannot help her.'

'What was the thing that happened?' Egg asked.

'I DO NOT KNOW!' bellowed the Gorm, buffeting him backwards the way the west wind sometimes did when it came roaring off the sea and rushing up the cliffs. 'I CANNOT SEE!' she howled.

'Where is this place?' asked Egg. 'Where is this Sea-that-will-be? Cos wherever it is, Mrs Gorm, we can't just leave her there.'

'I left her in the deeps that lie west of Wildsea, in an age that has not yet dawned,' whispered the Gorm. 'I cannot go there again.'

'Let me go then,' said Egg. 'I'll fetch her back.'

'You?' said the Gorm, disdainfully.

Egg shrugged. 'If Utterly is there, I'll find her, and if she can be brought back, I'll bring her. And if I can't, at least I can help her. Be company for her, like.'

'I could send you there,' said the Gorm, as if the thought had just occurred to her. 'To help.'

'That's what I just said!'

'But no. I am the Gorm. Why should I, who swim through the aeons and hold the lives of millions in my hand, why must I rely on the help of a . . .' (Here the Gorm paused for a long time, as if she could not think of any word contemptuous enough to describe Egg.) '. . . the help of a *boy*,' she sneered at last.

'Well, if you've got a better idea, good luck to you,' said Egg, and he turned and began to walk away.

'STOP!' said the Gorm.

Egg stopped. He did not turn, but he saw the shape of her shadow on the tiled floor beside him change and lengthen as she rose to her feet.

'I got one condition,' said Egg. 'Will Dark's up there aboard that ship, and Aish'll have forty fits if he don't come home, so if I'm going to help you, you got to promise you won't drown him or shipwreck him. And you got to send some sign up to let him know I am all right.'

The Gorm did not answer. She just went on rising, up and up, taller than a woman now, taller than a house. Her growing shadow engulfed Egg, and all the halls around him echoed to the sounds of her transformation; the slither and the squelch and the wet, flapping, knotting noises of forests of seaweed slithering over marble floors, moving with a purpose.

*

'He has been down there for almost five minutes!' said Will, leaning out over the *Acantha*'s side and watching the place where the diving bell's cable led down into the sea. 'It is time you pulled him up!'

'Don't fret, Dark,' said Constantine. 'The air we are pumping down means there is no danger of suffocation. Well, almost none. The boy will be all right.'

'If he isn't, it will be your doing, Constantine!' said Will. 'It should be you down there!'

'Bring him up!' commanded Captain Bulstrode, at a surprising volume. 'The lad has had time enough to make all the observations he can, Mr Constantine,' he added. 'And if he has proven the machine safe, you may make a further descent yourself.'

The sailors heaved, the tackle creaked, the pulleys slowly turned. Will stayed at the gunwale, watching as fathom after fathom of thick rope rose, squirting water, trailing slimy pennants of weed. At last the bell itself emerged, and was swung in over the deck.

'Egg!' Will shouted, running through a rain of seawater to peer up into the bell's interior.

Which was as dry as it had been when it descended, but entirely empty.

'Egg?' said Will, with a faint, desperate hope that Egg might be hiding somewhere.

'There is something on the seat . . .' said Captain Bulstrode.

He reached up for the thing, and it fell on the deck at Will's feet. It was a little driftwood mannikin, lashed together with strands of weed. Two shells had been pressed into its wooden face for eyes.

## 13

# NO DIRECTION HOME

How very strange it was, this world that Utterly had come to. As strange in its way as the Hunter's woods, or the Hidden Lands, but all the strangeness here was the work of people, who seemed to have grown exceedingly clever in the years that had passed since Utterly's own time.

Five buildings had sprouted in Belfriars Bay. The one nearest the quay looked like a gigantic boat house, built from some form of smooth, grey stone. Another building of the same material squatted at the foot of the cliffs. The three in between were unlovely-looking things, square and flat roofed, more like sheds than houses, although they seemed well-made and had surprisingly large panes of glass in their many windows. In the one to which

Utterly was taken there were lamps that lit up by electricity when you pressed a little toggle on the wall. Music jangled out of a box on a shelf, and a voice sang that all she needed was love, la la la la la. Outside the window a number of brightly coloured carriages were drawn up, but there were no horses to be seen, and no apparent need for any, for these ingenious machines were able to move about at great speed without them. (Judging by the noise they made, and the blue smoke which emerged from flues at their rear ends, Utterly presumed they must be powered by little steam engines.)

The men who had been on the ship went off to wash and change, and to sleep, no doubt, for they had been out at sea all night. Utterly was put into the care of two young ladies. One was the plump, fair-haired person who had come to meet the boat, who said her name was Jill. The other was a black lady who wore tortoiseshell spectacles as big as windowpanes and whose hair was trimmed into a perfect globe. Her name was Harriet.

'You are quite safe with us,' Jill promised, in the small room where they took Utterly to strip off her sodden dress and wash herself. There was a sort of porcelain cupboard which she had to stand in, and when Harriet reached in and turned a handle warm water gushed out of a thing like a watering-can rose which poked down through the ceiling.

Jill handed her a cake of scented soap. 'You're very

important, Utterly. We are scientists, and we're helping Professor Stone study the Western Deeps. The Prof has a theory that there's a whole other reality out there, hidden from ours by a sort of wrinkle in space-time. It'll be so cool if you can help us prove it! A whole other world . . . It would change everything – like getting a message from outer space.'

Utterly understood very little of what she had said. 'What are scientists?' she asked.

'In your time we would probably have called ourselves natural philosophers,' said Harriet.

The way she said 'your time' made Utterly feel uneasy. 'Please,' she said, 'what year is this?'

'We're not supposed to tell you' said Harriet. She turned off the flow of water, and Jill wrapped Utterly in a towel as soft and white and fluffy as a summer cloud. 'Professor Stone will have a lot of questions for you. He's afraid it might change your answers if we tell you too much.'

A nasal-sounding gentleman in the music box was wailing something about a rolling stone that did not know in which direction its home lay. Utterly asked if he was singing about Professor Stone, and Harriet laughed and said maybe he was, but Utterly thought she was joking. Then Jill brought her a pair of the blue trousers everyone in this era seemed to wear, and Utterly, who had never worn trousers before or even imagined wearing trousers, spent some time struggling to get them on. They were far too big for her, but a belt around the waist kept them up, and Harriet rolled the bottoms up to stop them dragging on the floor. They also gave her a short-sleeved tunic that was called a 'tea shirt' for some reason. It was made from yellow cotton and on the front was drawn a picture of a grinning sea-serpent with the words, *I've seen the Gorm on Wildsea Island.*

'They sell those at the shop in Marazea,' said Jill. 'I bought it for a joke, but it's too small for me.'

'But the Gorm does not look anything like this!' said Utterly, staring at the picture. 'I have never seen her be a serpent at all . . . And there is no shop in Marazea.'

'Nobody believes in the Gorm nowadays,' said Harriet. 'It's just an old legend. I suppose the Wildsea Tourist Board thought they could bring in some visitors with it, like the Loch Ness Monster. It didn't really work though – Wildsea is too far for most people to come, and hardly anyone has heard of the Autumn Isles.'

'There used to be a holiday camp in Marazea,' said Jill. 'But it went bust a few years back . . .'

Utterly pulled the shirt on. It was remarkably light and loose-fitting, and quite comfortable. When it was on Jill smiled at her and said, 'There, now you look like a twentieth-century girl,' and Harriet shushed her, so Utterly knew that she must be in the twentieth century, which meant that at least eighty-eight years had passed since she left Sundown Watch.

'Oh!' she said unhappily.

'What is it, Utterly?' asked Harriet.

'It is just that after all these years Uncle Will must surely be dead. And Egg and the Dearloves are dead too, unless they have grown very old. And they must have spent all their lives thinking that I had just abandoned them . . . And what of Aish? Does Aish still live on Wildsea? Aish surely could not grow old, or die, for what would Wildsea be without her?'

Jill and Harriet looked blankly at her. They seemed not to have heard of Uncle Will, or Egg, or the Dearloves, or even Aish. Harriet handed her a handkerchief to dry her tears, but it turned out not to be a proper handkerchief but only a square of soft paper. Jill patted her arm and said, 'I expect you'll feel better when you've had some breakfast, Utterly.'

They took her into another room, where she sat at a white table and ate things called cornflakes, and drank the juice of an orange. Then there was toasted white bread with marmalade, and tea in a glass cup. While she ate, Professor Stone sat at the far side of the table and watched her. When she had finished, he said, 'So, Utterly, you are probably wondering how I know your name.'

Utterly had been wondering no such thing. With so many other marvels to distract her, it had seemed quite natural that he should know who she was. But now that he came to mention it, it did seem curious.

'I've been studying Wildsea and the Western Deeps for a long time,' said Professor Stone. 'A *very* long time. I've read everything there is to read on the subject. The Watchers' Logs, the Marazea parish records, the Admiralty report on the loss of HMS *Acantha*. I know that a girl with the unusual name of Utterly Dark vanished from these shores in the spring of 1812. I know that she had some connection with the entity called the Gorm. I have even seen your portrait . . .'

He slid a piece of paper across the tabletop so that Utterly could see it. Printed there in shades of grey was a portrait of herself, wearing her best sprig-muslin dress. How strange, thought Utterly. The only time she had sat to have her likeness taken was when Mrs Dearlove made a drawing of her in watercolours. Perhaps this picture had been made from Mrs Dearlove's sketch after her departure, so that Aish and Uncle Will and Egg might have something to remember her by? The idea made her start to weep again. Harriet passed her another paper handkerchief.

Professor Stone slid the picture back to his own side of the table. 'So you see, I recognized you at once, Utterly. Now, I thought to myself, how could a girl who left Wildsea in April 1812 be found swimming in deep water ten miles off its western shore in September 1971?'

So that was the year in which her accident had stranded her, thought Utterly; nineteen hundred and seventy-one. Since she had been washed up on Wildsea as a baby in the year 1799, she supposed she must now be one hundred and seventy-two years old, which made her very ancient indeed.

'How did you come here, Utterly?' asked Professor Stone.

'My mother brought me,' said Utterly.

'Your mother?'

'Yes.' Utterly blew her nose on the flimsy handkerchief. 'My mother is the Gorm,' she said, 'and all the seas are her domain, in all the different ages of the world.' She looked down at her chest, where the cartoon sea-serpent still grinned like a loon on the tunic they had given her. 'Oh, sir, the Gorm does not look anything like this. She is very ancient and very powerful, and she is able to take on a great many different shapes. I am afraid that if you do not let me go back to her in the deeps, she will grow angry and storm ashore, and do great execution here.'

'As she did once before, in the autumn of 1810,' said Professor Stone, nodding. 'I always guessed the Wildsea Hurricane was no mere storm. But I must tell you, Miss Dark, your mother has turned her back on our world since then. Few people nowadays even know of her as a legend. It is only in recent years, with the development of radar, satellites, and so forth, that we have been able to detect certain anomalies in the Western Deeps. That is what has allowed me to persuade the government there might be something out here worth investigating. That's what this research centre was set up to do. We've had some interesting results from our instruments, but you're the first solid proof we've found that we are on the right lines. So we are going to make a careful study of you, Utterly. And when we are done with that, we will see about getting you home.'

'Home, sir?' asked Utterly. She thought of Sundown Watch, and how sad it would be without Uncle Will, and Mr and Mrs Skraeveling, and Egg, and Aish. But perhaps Professor Stone and his young friends, being such eminent philosophers, might know a way to return her to her own proper time? 'I should very much like to go home,' she said.

'And so you shall,' said Professor Stone, pushing back his chair and standing up. 'But first, I want you to show us how we too may swim through time, and visit your mother's Hidden Lands.'

# 14

# EGG

The Gorm gathered up Egg in her great weedy fist and strode through the deeps of the sea to where the roots of Wildsea rose. She carried him through time as well, although he did not know it, curled up tight and terrified in the bubble of air which lingered uncertainly between her weed-woven fingers. ('I wasn't scared,' he would boast later. But he was.)

The fist opened at last, and dissolved into a shapeless, drifting mass of weed, but it still had enough of the Gorm's fierce will left in it to push Egg, wet and spluttering, through the shallows and up onto the sand.

He was in Marazea Bay. His first thought as he crawled out of the sea was that he was hungry and that he would run up to Sundown Watch and ask Mrs Skraeveling for a bite to eat before he set about looking for Utterly. Then he noticed there were lights showing everywhere, as if there were far more houses in Marazea than there should be, and each house had lit a bright lamp in every window – a shocking waste of lamp-oil. There were lights that moved too, like huge glow-worms racing along the coast path, or up the tracks that led over the hills. Above the murmur of the sea, Egg's sharp ears detected other sounds; roarings and snarlings, as if a pack of wild animals was loose.

It was unnerving, even for a boy as brave as Egg. He turned to ask the Gorm's advice, but the sea was empty of her. The waves just kept rolling in, flopping limply on the sand as if they had never so much as heard of the Gorm.

'I'll find Aish,' he told himself. 'Because this is a pickle, all right, and if there's one person who knows how to get us all out of pickles, it is Aish.'

He started walking north along the edge of the sea, keeping a wary eye on the lights inland. A cluster of light-less, box-like buildings had been built among the dunes. Nearby, small fires were burning, and dark figures sat or stood around them, or danced to a wild, loud, pounding, shouting sort of music. 'Like a parcel of bloomin' Red Indians,' said Egg, but he did not mean it in a disapprov-ing way: Egg had always liked the sound of Red Indians, and felt he would get on very well with them were he ever to find himself in the wilds of America. He thought the pounding music was thrilling. It got inside of him somehow, and he swaggered along the sand in time to its beat.

He was less impressed when some of the dancers left their camp fires and came sprinting down the beach, running past him and throwing themselves with whoops and howls of laughter right into the sea. He stood and watched them for a while, wondering how they could be so rash and whether he should warn them about the Gorm. But the Gorm showed no interest in drowning them, and Egg was on a mission, so he shook his head and went on his way, leaving them to splash and holler in the surf.

Wherever he went, he found his island strangely altered. The coast path had become a road, paved with some hard, flat material he could not name. From time to time, as he stomped along it, there would come a blaze of light and noise, and he would have to throw himself down into the heather to hide as a fierce shape sped past. An animal, he thought, the first time it happened: a great, fearsome animal with round, glowing eyes. But the things ignored him, and pretty soon he realized they were just wagons and carriages with bright lamps affixed to them, moving without any horse or ox to draw them. Each time one passed, it filled the air with a strange, oily scent, almost as thrilling as the music on the shore.

The road turned inland in the lee of the old hill fort. A metal sign announced TROLLBRIDGE, as though folks on this new Wildsea were too dim to know the names of their own villages. The Trollbridge Inn was shut up and dark, with a lot of the shiny carriages drawn up on a paved place beside it where the orchard ought to be.

Egg crossed the bridge, and started to climb through the woods, calling 'Aish! Aish!', just as Utterly had been doing on that long-ago morning when he first met her. But it seemed things had changed even on the Dizzard. It was getting light by this time, and Egg could see that the woods had been tamed somehow; the old stony path was gone and in its place the same road of flat grey stone continued, climbing the hill in patient zig-zags.

'Well how did this get here?' Egg wondered. 'They must have had to move a load of the old stones to make it. And cut down trees too, and Aish wouldn't never allow her trees to be cut down . . .'

For the first time it occurred to him that Aish might not be here after all, or that if she were, she might be as powerless in this strange era as the Gorm was.

He followed the road, stopping every few yards to shout Aish's name, until he came out onto the broad, bald top of the Dizzard where the houses of Dizzard Tor stood below the rock called Aish's Lookout.

Or where they *had* stood. For they had all been cleared

away entirely, and replaced by bigger, newer houses of brick and cut stone, with roofs of thatch or slate instead of turf, and brick chimneys instead of smoke holes, and big glass windows, and painted front doors, and more of the curious carriages waiting outside, like little houses themselves, but set on wheels.

Egg turned around, not quite able to believe he was in the right place. But there was the tor itself, and there the old, familiar view where the land dropped away and away and you could see out over the tops of the trees to the white surf breaking on the Knacker's Kniferack. There had been dragons sporting out there, that day when Utterly first came up here.

'Aish!' he shouted, as loud as he could, in desperation. But Aish did not answer, and he knew she would never answer, for she was gone from Wildsea. Instead, a dog began barking in the new house that stood where Aish's house had been. A window opened, and a man stuck his head out and said, 'Hey! What's all the noise about? Hop it! Get back to your caravan site or wherever you come from. Don't you know what time it is?'

'I don't even know what bloomin' year it is,' grumbled Egg, as he turned and ran, away from the houses, off the road, out into the rough, rocky heathland on Mawgan's Head.

But the tide of change had reached even there. Set into a hollow at the cliff's edge was a tiny building with such thick walls and tiny slot-like windows that Egg could tell at once it was a fort. A winding path led through the brambles to it. It had no door, just a door-shaped opening that led into a single, dim, unfurnished room. The narrow windows looked out southward, giving him a view over Trollbrook Mouth towards Marazea Bay, with St Chyan's Head beyond it.

'What have you got me into, old Gorm?' he said, watching the surf roll in far below, and the carriages go creeping along the roads like tiny, shiny beetles. 'What's become of Wildsea? And how am I supposed to find Utterly, with everything so queer and mucked about with?'

But no one answered him, and after a while, exhausted, he lay down upon the hard floor and fell asleep.

15

# BAIT

Professor Stone asked Utterly a great many confusing questions, which she answered as well as she was able. He placed a peculiar sort of crown upon her head, from which a festoon of coloured wires trailed, leading to boxes with brightly glowing windows. While she did her best to answer everything she was asked, Jill, Harriet, and the bespectacled young man, whose name was Nigel, and the balding one, who was called Jim, peered into the windows of the boxes, and wrote notes in notebooks, and made clattery sounds with the trays of little grey and blue blocks that lay on the tabletops in front of the boxes.

Later, they made other experiments. They shone lights into Utterly's eyes, and peered through instruments into her ears, and pricked her with pins to which glass vials were attached, in which they took away samples of her blood. They drew the blinds and used a clattering magic lantern to show her astonishingly realistic pictures which moved somehow. She saw flying machines, and cities with tall towers, and far more of those horseless carriages than she would have thought could possibly be needed. She watched a man in a white garment not unlike Davey Froy's old diving suit go bouncing around in a grey, desert-ish sort of place beneath a black sky. He bounced so slowly that Utterly assumed he was beneath the sea, but they assured her that he was actually walking on the surface of the moon.

Utterly was not sure what to think. Were they making game of her? It was hard to know what to believe in this new world.

For instance, Nigel's corduroy jacket had a badge on the lapel which said *Save The Whale*, but when Utterly asked him which whale it meant, and why it needed saving, he told her it referred to all whales everywhere, for they were being hunted in such numbers that very few remained. Yet Utterly remembered swimming among schools of hundreds, sleeping upright in the deep like great stone pendants. She could not believe that *all* of them could have been hunted down. And if they had, why had the Gorm not done something about it?

But perhaps she had misunderstood. It was often hard for her to understand what Harriet and Gill and

Professor Stone and the others were saying. Their manner of talking was so strange, and so encumbered with words Utterly did not recognize. Sometimes, because the walls were thin, she overheard them discussing her, but it was never as interesting as she hoped, because what was she to make of it when Harriet said she seemed 'remarkably healthy psychologically' or when Nigel announced that her 'platelet count' was 'normal'? She supposed it was better than being remarkably unhealthy psychologically, or having an abnormal number of platelets.

It was as if they spoke a foreign language. Gradually Utterly learned to translate some of it – 'okay' meant 'yes', 'cool' meant 'good', the 'rig' was the cage they had used to capture her, and when they talked about 'the thaumaturgic entity' they meant the Gorm. But so much of the rest was incomprehensible to her, Utterly suspected she must be missing a great deal.

*This must be how a rare fish feels,* she thought, *listening to the philosophical gentlemen who have netted it discussing it while it swims around its bowl.* And she shivered a little, for she believed that when philosophical gentlemen had finished discussing their rare fish they would often kill them and pickle them in alcohol, as scientific curiosities.

But Professor Stone and his people showed no sign of wishing to kill or pickle Utterly. Indeed, they behaved kindly to her. On the afternoon of her arrival, Jill and Nigel drove to Merriport in Nigel's motor carriage, and returned with socks and undergarments for her, a quilted coat, and a pair of red leather shoes called sandals – they had round toes with patterns of little holes cut in them, and did up with a strap and a silver buckle.

She was given a little room to sleep in, in the same building where Harriet and Jill slept. As she lay on her narrow bunk that night, waiting for sleep to come, the moon rose over Belfriars Head and peeped in at her through the window. There was no sign that anyone had been walking about on it.

Nigel and Jim had their rooms in another of the buildings, alongside Professor Stone's. The sailors who worked aboard the *Sea Witch* were Wildsea men who drove their carriages home to Merriport. So was Mr Kennett, the enormous fellow who sat guard each day in a little sentry box beside the gate. Utterly was astonished that such people could afford carriages – even Uncle Will had not owned a carriage, and you would think a philosophical carriage which went along without any need for horses would be far costlier than the old-fashioned sort. But in this world of wonders it seemed that even working people could afford such things.

She quickly grew to like the food they gave her; shepherd's pie; fish fingers; Angel Delight; tinned peaches. She learned that Penguin biscuits came in three different coloured wrappings, red, blue, and green, but they were all the same underneath. The brown stuff that covered them was called chocolate, but it was nothing like the chocolate she was used to, which was a rather bitter, purplish, hot drink. Chocolate in this era had been very much improved: it was sweet and flavoursome, and melted most deliciously on your tongue. How she wished Egg were there with her, for she knew he would appreciate it. One afternoon, after a long session with Professor Stone, Harriet brought in a tray of chocolate cakes made by a person named Mr Kipling, and to Utterly's amazement, they tasted even better than one of Mrs Skraeveling's cakes. But the comparison was unfair, she decided, for this Mr Kipling was able to use the improved new chocolate as an ingredient, and Mrs Skraeveling was not. Perhaps, if Professor Stone and his companions could puzzle out a way to return her to her own age, she would take a recipe for chocolate with her.

Each day, Professor Stone would question her further about her travels with the Gorm. He had spent a long time asking her exactly how she found the currents which the Gorm followed to and fro through the ages. Here on dry land, Utterly found it hard to explain. She remembered being in one place and then in another, but of the journeys themselves she recalled almost nothing.

'Then if you can't tell us,' said Professor Stone, one afternoon, 'perhaps you can show us.'

They took her to the building on the shore, next to the quay where the *Sea Witch* was moored. Inside the building was a pool, into which the sea swirled at high tide. The tide was high when Utterly entered. The water lapped at the edges of the pool and made wavering reflections on the roof and walls, which were otherwise quite featureless. The smell of the sea was very strong, and Utterly realized how much she had missed it. *Slop* went the little waves, smacking at the pool's sides. *Glop*. Utterly listened carefully in case her mother's voice was in those waves, but it was not. She felt a sudden longing to dive in and swim away, but the openings at the pool's far end where the sea came in were screened by metal grilles, and Jill kept hold of her arm while she stood on the poolside.

Nigel and Jim placed the crown of wires upon her head again, and linked it to a box that stood on a wheeled trolley at the side of the pool.

Professor Stone said, 'Now, Utterly, show us how you command the sea. Can you sense any of those currents that you told me of? Can you smell the Hidden Lands?'

Utterly shook her head. She knelt on the poolside and put her hands down into the water and tried to find the water-scents of other lands which had seemed so clear when she was with the Gorm. But all she felt was the cold sea.

Professor Stone made a rumbling noise in his throat, which Utterly took to mean he was losing patience with her.

'I am very sorry, sir,' she said.

He did not answer, but went to a panel on the wall and pressed some lever there which caused the whole seaward end of the building to open up, the wall there splitting in half and sliding aside to reveal a vista of the sea. It was evening, and the sun was sinking towards the horizon, gilding the tops of all the little waves.

'Utterly,' said Professor Stone, returning to her, and squatting down so that his face was on a level with her own. 'Out there somewhere are the Hidden Lands.'

'I know, sir. I have seen them often.'

'But I have not. I have been trying to get a sight of them for longer than you might credit. I used to believe they were simply hidden from our eyes by some optical illusion, but plenty of ships have sailed those waters now, and planes have flown over them, and no trace of land has been found. So I have come to realize that the Hidden Lands are not part of our world at all, but fragments of another reality which intrudes sometimes into our own. In the past, the Gorm made them appear at will: the accounts of the Watchers on Wildsea attest to that. Now she has gone quiet, and sightings have dwindled away almost to nothing – just some strange readings detected by the radar station on Gull Point in 1942, and a confused account by an airline pilot in '57. It seems the Gorm no longer chooses to open the passage to the Hidden Lands. So you may be our only hope of reaching them, Utterly. You are the only person on earth who has a connection both to our world and to hers.'

Which, Utterly supposed, was just a twentieth-century way of telling her what Aish had told her long ago, when she had said, 'You are of the land *and* the sea, Utterly Dark.'

'So do your stuff, Utterly,' said Professor Stone. He stood and helped her up, then put his hands on her shoulders and guided her to some shallow steps that led down into the water of the pool. Utterly went down one and then the next, the sea rising to her knees then her waist. Professor Stone was careful not to let the water touch his shoes, but he kept his hands on her shoulders, and aimed her like a weapon at the western horizon, where the sun lay on the sea's rim like a red-hot penny.

'Open a way for me, Utterly,' said Professor Stone. 'Show me the Hidden Lands.'

And Utterly tried. Not because Professor Stone had asked her to, but for herself. Because if she could make the Hidden Lands appear it would mean there was still magic left in this peculiar new world, and if she could see the Hidden Lands then maybe she could go to them, and find the Gorm there, and the Gorm would show her the way home to her own time.

The small waves rolled in, wetting the hem of her T-shirt. Professor Stone let go of her and stepped back out of their reach. Utterly tried to feel the currents, as she had so easily when she was swimming with the Gorm. She breathed in deeply the salt smell of the evening sea and tried to scent in it the elusive musk of the Hidden Lands.

And in the west the sun went down like a foundering ship until only one last ember showed above the sea, and then even that was gone. The sky grew gorgeous with the afterglow. Wraiths of high cloud, which had looked dowdy a moment earlier, put on bright raiments of rose and gold. Then their brief glory faded, and the light dimmed, and the first stars appeared above the sea, and still there had been no sign of any land out there.

'Nothing at all,' said Jim, turning from the machine he had been studying.

'Nothing,' agreed Harriet, lowering the binoculars she had been watching the horizon through.

Professor Stone did not speak, but Utterly could sense his anger. The others felt it too; they watched him nervously as he paced to and fro on the poolside. Jill came to help Utterly back up the steps. She started to take the girl's wet trousers off, and wrapped a towel around her, and that was when the explosion came.

'She does not *want* us to reach the Hidden Lands!' roared Professor Stone, and the echoes of his voice boomed from the low roof and rolled to and fro above the sea-pool, while his people stood like scolded children trying not to meet his eye. 'She is as proud as her mother. She thinks we are not fit to venture in her realm.'

'I'm sure Utterly was only doing her best,' said Jill. 'We could try again tomorrow . . .'

'Please sir,' said Utterly. 'It is not that I don't *want* to help. It is only that I don't know *how*. When I swam with the Gorm I was just beginning to learn my way around the threads of the sea, but now I am here I have quite forgot how it was done. I am not even sure the Gorm and the Hidden Lands are there any longer. The sea just feels like water now. All the magic is gone out of it. Perhaps the Gorm is gone too.'

'Oh, she is there,' said Professor Stone. He glared down at Utterly. He had taken off his tinted spectacles and she saw for the first time that his eyes were grey, with flecks of green in them, and other colours too, so that when she looked into them she felt she was seeing deeper and deeper until there in the very deepest distance there shone a sudden spark of red-gold, like a fire igniting.

Then the spark faded, and Professor Stone looked away. 'She's out there, isn't she, Kerr?' he said. 'The instruments on the *Sea Witch* detected her the night you brought Utterly aboard.'

'There were certainly two readings,' said Nigel. He took off his spectacles and polished them on the sleeve of his corduroy jacket. 'One was Utterly: the other was stronger, but we were only able to track it for a few seconds.'

'The Gorm,' said Professor Stone. 'She swam into our sea, into this world. And why?'

Nigel put his spectacles back on and stood looking sheepish, like a schoolboy who suspects his master is asking him a trick question. But Jill said, 'She came to call Utterly back. She came here for Utterly. Because she loves her.'

Professor Stone snapped his fingers and pointed at her. 'Bingo,' he said. His temper had subsided. 'Tomorrow night,' he said, 'we'll try something new. This child is clearly not capable of opening a sea-way for us, but she can serve us in a different way.' He smiled at Utterly, and she saw that ginger light flare up again in the depths of his eyes. 'After all, what do you do when you catch a little fish? You use it as bait, so you can catch a bigger one.'

## 16

# THE MUTINY

News spreads quickly through a vessel as small and crowded as HMS *Acantha*, and bad news spreads more quickly still. Within five minutes of the diving bell being brought up, every man and boy aboard knew that Egg had not come up with it. That in itself might not have troubled them much, for sailoring was a dangerous life, and they were used to losing at least a few shipmates on most voyages. What worried them more was learning that the boy had not simply been drowned. *Something* down there in the dark waters beneath *Acantha*'s keel had taken him out of the diving bell, and replaced him with a sinister little dolly . . .

Captain Bulstrode bellowed for order as men left their stations to discuss the dreadful occurrence. The boatswain hurried about lashing sailors with a rope's end, but he lashed half-heartedly, for the terror of the Gorm had gripped him too. Even Lieutenant Sidcup seemed half inclined to take the sailors' side: he had dreamed of deep, dark water in the night, and believed his dream had been an omen.

The wind had died away to nothing. A curious, unnatural haze lay all around, reducing the whole universe to a disc a few hundred yards across, with the *Acantha* at its centre, sitting with limp sails upon a glassy sea. From time to time a cry of 'Land ho!' would go up as the haze lifted for a moment and seemed to reveal an island, but the island was always in a different place, and the men who sighted it made wildly differing reports. Some described barren rocky shores, others verdant, wooded hills. One said he saw a city of white buildings, and a bonfire burning in a temple on the beach.

'What is this Gorm person playing at?' demanded Captain Bulstrode, summoning Will and Constantine to his cabin late that afternoon. 'Land comes and goes, our compasses and chronometers are all confounded, and every time we take a sounding the bottom seems to lie at a different depth – now less than three fathoms, now deeper than we can tell. What sort of a way is this to carry on? What does she want of us?'

Constantine had no answer. Will said, 'It is impossible to say, sir. The Gorm is not governed by reason, but by her moods and fancies, which may change in a twinkling. The fact that we are still afloat suggests she is not feeling unfriendly towards us.'

'She drowned your boy, though.'

Will shrugged unhappily. 'We must hope not. Egg and I have wandered in her realms before. She is quite capable of making air for him to breathe beneath the sea, or setting him safely ashore on one of these islands which come and go.'

'Well, it is dashed bad form,' blustered Bulstrode. 'If she is friendly she should let us see these Hidden Lands of hers instead of flaunting 'em and then whisking 'em away. And if she ain't friendly, she should come up and fight fair, like a good English sea-monster. She is behaving worse than a Frenchman! Oh, what now?'

For a great confusion had broken out on deck, with shouting and a thunder of running feet. The cabin door opened to reveal a quivering midshipman who stammered, 'S-sir, Lieutenant Sidcup's compliments, and he says to tell you the Devil himself is come!'

Will and Constantine followed the captain to the quarterdeck. The strange, hazy sunshine was growing golden, and seemed to cast no shadows. All around men cowered and trembled, gawping up between the sails at something that circled the ship on wide wings.

'It is just a bird . . .' said Constantine.

Captain Bulstrode snatched a brass speaking trumpet from his lieutenant. 'Back to your duties, lads,' he bellowed. 'These gentlemen say the brute is nothing but a bird. You're not afraid of a bird, are you?'

'Or possibly a bat,' said Will.

'Or possibly a bat,' boomed Bulstrode. 'A harmless flittermouse.'

But the bird – or bat – seemed angered by Bulstrode's voice. It uttered a bone-chilling screech and plunged towards the quarter deck. Will, as he leaped out of its path, caught a glimpse of wide, leathery wings, and a long beak lined with vicious little teeth. It snatched Bulstrode's hat from his head and soared out over the sea astern.

'It is a sort of lizard,' cried Mr Samuels.

'A flying lizard!' said Constantine. 'Lord Langdale must certainly have a specimen . . .'

'My hat!' spluttered Bulstrode.

The bat-bird-lizard let the hat fall into the sea and swung back towards the ship, rising as it came, as if it intended to resume its circuits of the *Acantha*. Will wondered if it had mistook the ship for an island, and the masts for trees, and planned to roost up there among the topgallant shrouds. But as it passed over the quarterdeck there was a flash beside him, and a bang. Constantine, drawing a pistol from his coat, had taken a shot at the creature, and his aim was true. It crumpled in mid-air and fell, bouncing from various spars and ropes on its way down before landing heavily in the ship's waist, one broken wing draped over the diving bell. The sailors there drew back from it with cries of woe. 'What have you done, you gurt lummox?' shouted one, as Constantine went running to examine his prize. 'You have brought bad luck upon us all! 'Tis worse than shootin' an albatross!'

'Silence!' thundered Captain Bulstrode.

But many other voices were shouting too, as if the pistol-shot had triggered a storm which had been brewing all day.

'That leather-bird was the Gorm's own pet, and now she shall have her revenge!'

'The ship is doomed!'

'This is the Gorm's own sea! We never should have come here!'

'Sidcup!' roared Captain Bulstrode. 'Call these mutinous curs to order! Forty lashes for the next man who speaks out of turn!'

'I am sorry sir,' said Sidcup, turning on the captain as the men came swarming aft. 'But I agree with them. This is no place for decent folk. These men would follow you gladly into battle, and trade broadside for broadside with a French seventy-four, and so would I. But we draw the line at unreal islands, and giant bats, and things that steal boys out of diving bells. We must leave this awful place.'

'That's right, sir,' agreed a burly sailor. 'These are accursed waters, and if us die here, our souls shall never find their way to Heaven.'

'Aye! Aye!' agreed a score of voices.

'And how do you propose we leave?' demanded the captain, looking aghast at this rebellion. 'There is no wind. We are becalmed.'

'The Gorm will send us a wind if we rid ourselves of those who've angered her!' shouted a sailor.

'Aye! Aye!' shouted others. 'The Gorm's a great lady and it stands to reason she don't want no philosophical busybodies a-poking and prying in her sea . . .'

'Why, Will,' said Constantine, returning to Will's side, 'I believe they are talking about you and me. . .'

'T'ain't natural!'

'They be Jonahs!'

'Overboard with them, and then the Gorm will send a wind to waft us home!'

As if it had heard them, and approved their sentiments, the wind breathed softly on the sea, ruffling it into little waves. The mainsail stirred. A cry of triumph went up from the sailors.

'Cast 'em overboard!'

'Give 'em to the Gorm!'

'No man is going overboard while I am in command,' declared Captain Bulstrode.

'Then, sir,' said Lieutenant Sidcup, 'I fear I must relieve you of command.'

'This is mutiny, Mr Sidcup!'

'In any normal waters it might be,' said Sidcup. 'But I do not believe your authority extends here, sir.'

The crew, emboldened, came rushing up both stairways onto the quarterdeck. One man took Constantine's pistol from him, and pointed it at the captain. Others had drawn cutlasses, or snatched up heavy wooden belaying pins, which they wielded like cudgels. Captain Bulstrode, accepting that he and his supporters were outnumbered, reluctantly handed Sidcup his sword.

'So are we all to go overboard?' he asked. 'Like heathen sacrifices to this Gorm, of whom not one of you had even heard till we touched at Wildsea?'

'Yes!' cried some of the men, but the rest looked shamefaced, and one said, 'No need for that, mates. We'll lower the cutter, and provision it, and the captain and these gentlemen and any man who wants to go with them can take their own chances with the Gorm.'

'And we'll set a course for America,' shouted another. 'Where a man can live free, and not be sent against his will to annoy no sea-monsters!'

And so it was decided. Within moments Will found himself gathering his few possessions and climbing down the ship's side into a boat that looked impossibly small to sail upon such a sea. It looked smaller still when Constantine was in it, and Captain Bulstrode, and Mr Samuels, who had elected to come with them because he wished to get home to his family in England. They were joined by a brace of young midshipmen who felt the same way, and an able seaman named Hard-tack Joe, who had been born a slave in Virginia and said he would sooner take his chances with the Gorm than go back there. Provisions were lowered down – a barrel of water, a crate of salt beef and another of ship's biscuit – and stowed beneath the thwarts, which made for even less room. Into a second boat went a half-dozen other men under the command of the *Acantha's* second lieutenant. And while all this was happening the wind increased. By the time the boats were cast off it was blowing hard enough to set the *Acantha* moving quite rapidly, and after a very few minutes the haze swallowed her entirely.

Captain Bulstrode ordered the cutter's little sail to be rigged, and consulted the pocket compass that the mutineers had been good enough to leave him. The needle spun wildly, as the needles of all compasses had since the expedition entered these waters. But the haze that had swallowed up the *Acantha* was turning reddish-gold, which he deduced was the glow of sunset, so he had the cutter go about and began tacking as accurately as he could in the opposite direction, hailing the other boat and telling them to follow. 'We should strike the Autumn Isles by morning,' he said. 'And if we miss 'em, why, we shall reach England after a day or two more.'

Will, crammed miserably into a small space near the boat's bows, reminded himself that Bulstrode was a capital seaman, and tried to console himself with the thought that he would see the hills of Wildsea by dawn, and be back with Aish for luncheon. But as the light faded, the haze around him seemed to fill with islands, and none of them was an island that he knew.

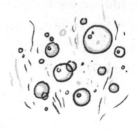

17

# DANIEL AND MIM

Egg slept dreamlessly on the floor of the little clifftop fort until mid-morning. Even then he did not wake until someone started licking his face. Opening his eyes, he discovered the someone to be a cheerful ginger-coloured dog of the spaniel sort. Since Egg liked dogs, and this dog liked him, he spent a happy minute or two scratching it behind the ears and making a fuss of it, glad to have friendly company at last.

Then, recalling his situation, he started to wonder who the dog belonged to. For it clearly belonged to someone – there was a collar about its neck, and a silver disc dangling from the collar with the dog's name, *Tess*, and a number.

'Well, Tess,' said Egg, getting stiffly to his feet, 'it's

time I was on my way, for I have to find some breakfast, and then Utterly.'

But Tess, thinking he had got up in order to play with her, began to bark, and the barks rang so loudly from the walls and low roof of the fort that Egg had to cover his ears with his hands. 'Hush, girl,' he said. 'Somebody'll hear!'

But somebody had already heard. A moment later a shadow blocked the sunlight in the doorway, and a man came in.

Egg made a desperate attempt to escape. He put his head down and charged, hoping that a good butt in the breadbasket would surprise the stranger sufficiently that Egg would be able to dodge past him and get away. But although the man was not young, he seemed surprisingly fit; he stepped sideways to avoid the collision and snatched hold of Egg's shirt-collar before he could get past.

'Now then, Tess,' he said. 'What have we here?'

He held Egg at arm's length, and they looked at each other. Egg saw a suntanned, Wildsea-looking man of fifty or so, with blue eyes and a long, lined face. His white hair was cut very short, but he looked less outlandish than the people on the beaches had. Not only that, Egg realized, as he stood there wondering how to slip free, this was the same man who had leaned out of a window at Dizzard Tor a few hours earlier and angrily told Egg to hop it.

'You again!' said the man, recognizing Egg at the same moment Egg recognized him. 'You're the lad who woke us up, shouting under the window in the middle of the night.'

Egg nodded reluctantly.

'What are you doing up here?' the man asked. 'You're not from Trollbridge or Marazea, are you? And the schools went back last week, so I don't reckon you're a holidaymaker. Where are your parents?'

Egg shrugged.

'It was someone called Ash you were yelling for last night. Who's he then?'

'She,' said Egg. 'Aish. She's a good friend to me. Mrs Aish Dark.'

The man shook his head. 'There's no one of that name round here,' he said. And there haven't been any Darks on Wildsea for years. You sure?'

Egg shrugged again, and hung his head. Hearing that Aish was not just gone but forgotten filled him with a dreadful despair, and a longing for his own Wildsea. Tess seemed to sense it, for she came to nuzzle his hand and look up lovingly at him.

'Tess is a good judge of character,' said the man. He let go of Egg's collar and stepped away from him. If he had wanted to, Egg could have run out through the doorway then. But Egg did not want to, not quite, although he stayed ready to run. He figured that if he was to find

Utterly at all on this mad new Wildsea he would have to talk to someone sooner or later.

The man watched him with a sort of amusement, as if he had an idea what was going on in Egg's mind. He sniffed, and glanced around the inside of the little fort. 'They put this up during the war,' he said. 'There's another in the dunes at Marazea, and tank-traps all along behind the beach. Supposed to stop the Germans landing. They were a waste of time though, cos it turned out old Hitler didn't know the Autumn Isles existed. But we didn't know that back then.'

Egg listened, and tried to look as though he understood.

'I'm sorry I woke you, sir,' he said.

'Ah, that's all right, lad. I'm sorry I shouted at you. I'm old and crotchety is all. And there's no need to call me "sir", though it's good to know there's still some kids left with a bit of respect for their elders. Dan's my name. Dan Smy. What's yours?'

'I'm Egg.'

'Egg, is it? Well, I was just thinking I could do with one of those, or maybe two, scrambled. You had any breakfast, Egg? I reckoned not. Why don't you come back with me; my missus'll be just putting the kettle on about now.'

Ten minutes later Egg was sitting at the table in the Smys' cluttered little kitchen, while Dan's wife, Mim, cooked scrambled eggs and sausages and golden triangles of white bread fried in butter. A small, round, cheerful woman, she was as friendly as her husband, although she could not conceal her surprise at Egg's strange clothes, or her curiosity as to who he was and where he had come from.

'Are you on holiday, dear? Where be you stopping, then? I thought all the children was back at school by now. Are your people some of them hippies, maybe?'

'Now then, Mim,' said Dan. 'Let the poor lad catch his breath.'

Mim brought the food to the table and dished it out onto three big plates with a pattern of orange and yellow flowers on them. Dan poured three cups of tea from a matching teapot. The plates and teapot looked expensive, and as Egg looked around the kitchen he saw glass-fronted cupboards with more crockery in, and shelves of books, and a painting of boats in a harbour. There was a small music box on one of the cupboard tops that played beautiful tunes and never seemed to wind down. He supposed the Smys must be very rich, even richer than Will Dark, perhaps. But they did not talk like gentlefolk, and they seemed to have no servants. It was a mystery, and Egg had no time to puzzle it out, because the smell of sausages was reminding him how long it had been since he ate.

When he'd had second helpings, and then third, Mim suggested he should take a bath. 'And while you're at it, I'll look out some of our Stevie's old clothes for you,' she said. 'He's off at university in England,' she added proudly. 'But I'm terrible at throwing out his old things. I reckon some of them will fit you. They're not the latest fashions, of course, but that won't bother you, will it, Egg? I haven't seen anyone wearing knee breeches since I was a girl.'

Egg usually did his best to avoid baths, but even he had to admit that he was in a shocking state of filth. He was covered with the dust of the clifftop fort, and his hair and clothes were stiff with salt. Anyway, the Smys' bath was not a normal tin one, but a luxurious pink porcelain affair. It stood in its own room, along with a matching pink sink and an indoor privy, which seemed an insanitary idea, except it did not smell at all. Egg stood and gawped at it all for a full minute before Mim showed him how to turn the two silver handles on the bath so that jets of hot and cold water gushed from silver spigots. HOT said letters printed on the top of one spigot, and COLD said the other. Egg felt pleased now that he had let Utterly teach him how to read; it had seemed a silly undertaking at the time, but in this new world it seemed reading had become important.

Mim squirted stuff from a pink bottle into the bath water, which caused it rise up in clouds of foam. She put a pile of clean clothes for egg on top of the lid of the privy. 'These are some of our son's old things. He's been gone two years, and don't we miss him! I don't suppose he'll be coming back to Wildsea neither. He's got a girlfriend now in Manchester, and a job lined up. Still, young people have to find the world that suits them best, don't they?'

Egg agreed. He felt this world suited him very well. He had never known such luxury. When Mim had left he stripped off and submerged himself in the steaming water, making snowballs out of the scented foam, and scrubbing himself with a cake of pink soap that smelled like all the flowers of spring.

As he lay there afterwards, luxuriating in the steaming water, he heard the Smys talking in a neighbouring room. They were trying not to be heard, but the walls of the house were thinner than the granite walls which Egg was used to, and his ears were sharp.

'Well, where do you reckon he's come from, Dan?'

'I couldn't say. He's not a Wildsea lad, I'd lay money on that. Over from England maybe?'

'What, all that way on the ferries, all alone? And what about those funny clothes?'

'Well, they wear all sorts in England nowadays. 'Tis fashion, ain't it. Like them pop stars on the telly.'

'The poor scrap looked half starved, the way he wolfed his breakfast down. And he looked round our bathroom like he'd never seen a bathroom before. I had to show him how to turn the taps on! You think maybe he's run away from somewhere?'

'I don't know, love. I suppose . . .'

'Cos we ought to call somebody. The police or Social Services or that.'

Egg tensed. He did not know what 'police' meant, nor what a Social Service was, but he had the feeling she meant *busybodies*; vicars and beadles and charitably minded ladies and other sorts who did not like boys like Egg doing what they wanted. They had been bad enough in his own world, and he certainly could not afford to have them prying into his business in this one. For he did not know enough about it yet to pretend that he belonged here, and if they found out where he *did* belong, there'd be no end of bother. They'd probably stick him in a zoo in London, with a label on his cage to say, *The Boy Who Fell Through Time*. And he hadn't time for that, not when he had Utterly to find.

So he lay there in the water listening hard, and eyeing the bathroom window. It was only a small window, but Egg reckoned he could slip out through it easy enough if he needed to.

'He's not much more'n ten, judging by the size of him,' Mim was saying (which made Egg indignant, for he reckoned he was twelve at least). 'Somebody might be missing him,' she went on. 'We need to tell somebody he's here.'

There was a pause. Then Dan said, 'If he has run off, Mim, maybe he had good reason. I had trouble enough myself when I was a lad, and no policeman or teacher or Social Services ever helped me much, though I daresay they meant well enough. No, the best thing we can do for the boy, I reckon, is just let him stay on here a bit and get his bearings. It'll be nice to have a kid about the place again. And once he's settled in a bit, well, maybe he'll let us know where he belongs.'

## 18

# 20TH-CENTURY BOY

Egg was someone who adjusted easily to new places and new people and he was quickly starting to feel at home at the new Dizzard Tor. When he had finished his bath he helped Mim feed the chickens, which lived in a coop out back. Then he went to watch Dan at work in a big shed next to the house, which smelled of oil and metal and the sweetish scent of cut grass. Half of the shed was taken up by an outsized sort of motor carriage which Dan called 'the van': it was grey, and along its side were written the words, *D. Smy, Gardening & General Maintenance*. In the other half there was a workbench, a grey metal chest of drawers, and a wall where tools hung on hooks just like in Mr Skraeveling's shed at Sundown watch, except there were many more tools, and some which Egg didn't know the words for.

That morning, Dan was stripping down a lawn mower. Lawn mowers were what people used now instead of scythes, it seemed, and Egg thought they looked a great deal more trouble – the one Dan was working on was a great oily tin contraption, and when he got its lid off it was filled inside with all kinds of pipes and complicated clockwork-looking goings-on.

'What's all that then?' Egg asked.

'Well, that's the engine, Egg.'

"Tis a marvellous small one,' said Egg. The only engine he had ever seen was the Trevithick steam engine which powered the pumps at Wheal Tizzy tin mine over in Stack. But that had a whole big granite barn to house it. If you could fit an engine in this little tin box, it explained how all those carriages went rushing about so fast.

Egg leaned in closer, trying to make sense of it. 'Where does the coal go in?'

'Coal?' chuckled Dan, who thought Egg was having him on. 'They don't teach you kids much at school these days, do they? 'Tis petrol he runs on, and it sits in this tank here, see? And here's the filter, and the fuel line, and this here, he's the carburettor, which I reckon is what's causing the trouble, so I'm going to strip him down . . .'

Egg watched him work, and passed him a rag or a spanner from time to time when he asked for one. He didn't ask any more questions, because he was afraid of revealing how little he knew about this world, but Dan told him things anyway, showing him how the fuel-filter worked, explaining how the engine wouldn't run properly if there was too much air mixed in with the petrol, or too little. Egg didn't follow it all, but he followed enough that he started to feel fascinated. The bits of the dismantled engine lay spread out on an old sheet on the floor, and Egg understood that he was looking at the power that made this new world run. It was as wonderful in its way as any magic, but it was better than magic, because there were rules and reasons to it, and Egg reckoned if he had a bit of time he could learn them.

Dan cleaned and reassembled the engine and let Egg pull the cord to get it started. The mower woke up with an ear-splitting roar and a splutter of blue smoke, and Egg laughed with triumph.

After dinner – shepherd's pie – he helped wash up. Then he took Tess for a walk on the cliffs, marvelling at the new houses whose roofs poked up here and there all over the top of the Dizzard. He lay on the shingle in Gull Cove and watched mysterious silver arrowheads scratch long white lines across the blue sky. Slowly he worked out that the arrowheads were machines of some sort too, and the rumbling sound like lazy thunder, which rolled all around him when they went over, was the sound of engines like the one he'd helped Dan clean, but much bigger. Perhaps they were mowing the sky . . .

'Well, Gorm,' he said, sitting up and looking at the sea. 'This is a strange new place you've brung me to, and I ain't sure exactly how I'm supposed to find Utterly in all of it. You got any bright ideas?'

But the sea said nothing. Tess brought a stone for him to throw, and he went back up the cliff tossing it ahead of him and letting her bring it back, thinking how easy it would be to get used to living in a world like this.

At teatime there was bread and jam and a sort of dance of questions, with Dan and Mim gently trying to find out where Egg had come from and who his parents were, and Egg carefully not telling them the truth. 'Their name's Dark,' he said, because that was easier than explaining that he had no parents. 'Mr and Mrs Dark. William and Aish.'

'There used to be Darks at Sundown Watch, down the other side of Marazea,' said Dan. 'Maybe you're related? But old Mr Edward was the last of them. The house is shut up now mostly. There's just a lady comes over from the mainland for holidays sometimes, and I don't know if she's family or not . . .'

'You got any brothers or sisters, Egg?' asked Mim.

'I got a sort of sister,' said Egg. 'Her name's Utterly.'

'Utterly?' said Dan. 'That's not a name!'

'Hush, Dan,' said Mim. 'Everything's a name if someone calls themself by it. Where is Utterly now, Egg?'

Egg shrugged. He had hoped they might have heard some word of her, but he could see they hadn't.

'And Aish is an unusual name, too,' said Dan. 'Wasn't that what you were shouting outside our window last night, when you woke me?'

'Aish,' said Mim thoughtfully. 'That's a Wildsea name. The rock at the end of our garden used to be called Aish's Lookout in the olden days, and I remember my granny telling me about a sort of witch called Aish who used to live up here. A nice witch, mind.'

'What happened to her?' asked Egg. 'She still about?'

'Who, Aish? Oh no, love. This must have back in Queen Victoria's time. Aish'd be long dead now.'

Aish couldn't *die*, Egg wanted to say. But perhaps she could? Perhaps she had? Perhaps, in this new world of machinery, there was no room at all for old things like Aish?

'Mim's made you up a bed in Stevie's old room,' said Dan. 'You can kip here tonight. It's Saturday tomorrow, so we'll go down to Merriport and maybe see about letting someone know you're here.'

Egg didn't like the sound of that, but he was too tired to argue, so he decided to let tomorrow look after itself. He sat with the Smys in their cosy living room and they lit up a sort of magic lantern box that showed them scenes of other countries, and the antics of funny men who made Egg laugh like a drain. Later, while he was cleaning

145

his teeth with a little brush and some minty-tasting stuff Mim gave him, he heard Dan say, '. . . and maybe if he ain't got no one he could stop on here with us. We've got plenty of room now Stevie's gone . . .'

Egg knew that he could not stop there with them, but he thought it was proper nice that Dan would say that. It made him cry, almost. It was good to know that, for all the changes the world had been through, people had not changed much, and there were still some who were as good-hearted as Aish or Utterly.

When the Smys' son went off to university in England he had left behind more stuff than Egg had ever owned. The shelves and cupboards in his bedroom were filled with books, clothes, big toy animals, small toy cars, and boxes full of miniature soldiers. Model flying machines dangled from the ceiling on pieces of almost invisible thread. A raggedy-looking fellow stared down from a big picture stuck to the back of the door; he wore a hussar's jacket so Egg supposed he was a military man, but instead of a sword or pistol he carried a funny-looking fiddle.

Under the table beside the bed was a pile of old newspapers. They weren't dull newspapers like the *Island Post* or the London *Times*, which Will Dark took at Sundown Watch; they had bigger writing, and there were pictures too. Egg spent some time looking through them while he worked up the nerve to switch off the electric light. He puzzled over headlines about strikes and astronauts and Vietnam until he began to yawn, and was just about to stop when the front page of the *Merriport Argus* brought him suddenly awake. For there, staring up at him, was a face he knew.

*MYSTERIES OF THE DEEP* said the big black writing above the picture. The story below, in smaller type, was about something called an Ocean Research Centre. *Professor Stone of Cambridge University (pictured above) is the brains behind the project. The professor and his team will spend the next two years living and working on Wildsea's west coast, and exploring the Western Deeps in their research vessel, a converted minesweeper called* Sea Witch . . .

But the man in the picture was not Professor Stone. His hair was cut differently to how it had been in 1812, and he wore big square spectacles now instead of little round ones, but Egg would have known that glum face anywhere.

It was Lord Langdale.

# 19

# AISH AND STONE

Aish was watching the western sea as she walked alone upon the cliffs at Mawgan Head. (She did not know it, but she was on the very spot where the concrete pillbox that Egg had slept in would one day be built.) She watched the sea in the hope of seeing the HMS *Acantha* sailing home, for it was three days now since the ship had set sail.

She wondered if she should go down the hunter's paths to the beach and beg the old Gorm to spare Will Dark and Egg and their friends (for Egg had been missing since the day the *Acantha* departed, and Aish had no doubt he was aboard). But the Gorm's moods were so unpredictable that mentioning Will Dark to her might only make her even more inclined to drown him. Besides, the sea was in an odd state that day, shivering with odd little plashy waves and uneasy swells, as if it could not make up its mind whether to be rough or calm. Aish could not tell if the Gorm was watching her or not.

But someone was. Aish turned, and there was Lord Langdale, lounging among an outcropping of clifftop rocks as if he were a rock himself. Could he have been there all the time, and she had failed to notice him? She did not think so, but she could not be sure. She drew her shawl about herself a little more tightly.

'And what are you, I wonder, ma'am?' Lord Langdale said, leaving his place among the stones and making her a stiff little bow.

'I am Aish of the Dizzard, as I believe you know. And I am Mrs Dark of Sundown Watch.'

'The yokels of this island may believe that,' said Lord Langdale scoffingly. 'But you are no ordinary mortal, Aish of the Dizzard. You are a thing of the woods and the high hills, I'd say. I wonder if Dark knows it?'

The stony feeling Aish had noticed before came off him like a bad smell. She sensed an air about of him of violence, well-suppressed, but ready to be taken out and used when necessary. She recalled Will Dark or maybe Constantine saying that this lord had been a miner once. She could imagine the pleasure he must have taken in swinging a pick and smashing the rocks apart.

His spectacles shone with the clear, cold light of frozen puddles on a winter's morn.

'Will Dark and I have no secrets from each other,' said Aish, and felt herself redden with anger and unease.

'So it is love,' Lord Langdale said. 'I see it in your eyes, my dear, and in that becoming flush upon your cheek. But how can you love something that will pass away? In a few score years Will Dark shall be dust and you shall still be as you always have. You are setting yourself up for a broken heart, old thing of the woods and hills.'

She guessed then what he was, and felt ashamed she had not seen it earlier. How could he have hidden it so well? 'You are of the land, like me,' she said. 'But your land is far away, and you have cut yourself free of it some-how, and come a-wandering in the world. Where was your home, I wonder? What woods or waters dreamed you into life?'

Lord Langdale laughed – a quick little sharp sound, like the call of a stonechat. 'No woods,' he said. 'I began my days upon the summit of one of the highest moun-tains in Westmorland. It was a beautiful, terrible place. Nothing grew there but stone. I watched rivers of lava flow across the pure stony world below me. I heard the voices of the Oldest Ones, Mrs Dark. They were still singing their songs in those days, down in the fiery deeps which lie beneath the crust of the earth. I was happy upon my mountain for many centuries, listening to those songs . . .

'But slowly the Oldest Ones sank deeper, down towards the world's hot heart where I could no longer hear them. Grass and trees grew over the earth like mould on a loaf. People appeared, and began to build their huts and villages and then their cities. I sensed the magic starting to fade out of the world. *It is a time for men and their ways*, I thought. So I became a man, and set about making myself a rich one.'

Aish laughed. 'But why would you want riches, Lord Langdale?'

'Please, Mrs Dark, call me Stone. That is the name by which I have always called myself. When I moved into the world of men I became Jack Stone, or Tom Stone, or Sir Upland Stone, changing my name every twenty years or so, moving from one spot to another before any could suspect my true nature. Lord Langdale is merely another in a long line of names; they grow on me like lichen. As for why I should want riches, your innocence surprises me. A rich man has the ear of kings and governments. So when, for example, I heard young Constantine's talk of Wildsea and realized that the Gorm herself was still awake out here, I was able to arrange this expedition to her Hidden Lands.'

'And what will you do if you find them, Stone?'

'I will catch the Gorm, and make her teach me her secrets,' said Stone. 'For I believe the Gorm's realms extend throughout time itself. If I could move among the ages as she does, I might achieve anything. I might be able to return to the times when I was happiest. How I long to hear once more the songs of the Oldest Ones, and walk again upon stones still warm with the heat of the world's creation . . .'

Aish looked at the sea and considered this. She could not blame Stone for mourning the world he had lost. She felt the same sense of loss herself, whenever she recalled the great woods which had covered all Wildsea in her youth. But when people arrived and the woods retreated she had found other things to delight her. Stone had not. He just wanted to return to his old world. But if he found his way back through time to it, Aish feared he would still not be content. Not until he had set his foot upon the first green thing that began to grow upon the earth, and ground it back into the dust. Then all might be changed, and the world would never bring forth grass, or flowers, or trees, or animals, or any of the things Aish loved.

'I have wondered sometimes,' she said, when she had pondered for a while, and come up with a plan, 'if there might be an easier way to the Gorm's old Hidden Lands than sailing there. For the ocean is an exceeding wet and inconvenient element, and as soon as you set out upon it the Gorm sees you, and knows where you are bound.'

'That is why I dared not sail with the *Acantha*,' said Stone. 'But what is this easier way you speak of?' Behind his spectacles a faint red-gold light flared, so Aish knew that she had interested him.

'Why, through the Hunter's Wood, of course,' she said. 'It had its entrances all over this world once, and in the Gorm's realms too, I reckon. If you could find your way into one you could pass through the labyrinths of the trees and emerge in the Hidden Lands. The Gorm would never see you coming, and you would not need to bother with ships and the sea. I wish I had thought of it before the gentlemen sailed away.'

'But all the entrances into the Hunter's Wood were stopped up long ago,' said Stone.

'Not here on Wildsea,' said Aish, with a smile. 'This is a queer, old-fashioned sort of place. I believe there is a way into the Wood not above two mile from where we stand. Perhaps, while we wait for our friends to come home from the sea, you should like to see it?'

## 20

# THE GORM SANDS GANG

Egg had opened the curtains before he went to sleep, so he woke at first light. For a moment the strange surroundings confused him, but he soon remembered where he was, and what he had to do. In the half-light, Lord Langdale's face looked bleakly up at him from the newspaper on the bedside table. He dressed quickly and went out through the window rather than risk creeping downstairs, where Tess the dog was sure to wake and want a walk.

Egg had thought hard before he fell asleep, and decided it would be best to leave alone. His first instinct had been to wait and ask Dan and Mim about Lord Langdale, but it would be hard to ask much without letting on how he knew the man. Anyway, Dan had said something last night about taking Egg to Merriport. Egg didn't have time to go to Merriport. He had a trail to follow now. Because if Lord Langdale had somehow got himself across the years to this place, then maybe he'd know something about Utterly.

Nowhere in the newspaper had there been any mention of where on Wildsea's western coast Lord Langdale's Ocean Research Centre actually was. The only clue was the photograph, in which a few squarish, flat-roofed buildings were visible behind His Lordship's head. They reminded Egg of the dark buildings he had seen from the beach when he first arrived. Set among the dunes, between Marazea and the sea, they seemed a likely place for ocean research.

Walking down to Trollbrook Mouth in the sunrise, he could almost imagine himself back on the Wildsea that he knew. But when he had crossed the river he had to negotiate a whole fenced-off town of wheeled white huts, which had sprouted on the seaward slopes of the old hill fort, and when he reached Marazea he found there were twice as many houses as he recalled, and all of them were ten times nicer. There was even a shop; an Aladdin's cave of brightly coloured spades and buckets, whirling windmills, hats and clothes, and a hundred other things Egg did not know a name for. *Lost Your Car Keys On The Beach?* asked a hand-written placard outside. *Get Some Here – Just 50p Each!*

Opposite the shop, a new lane led off towards the sea. The boxy outlines of the buildings Egg had seen two nights ago showed among the dunes, surrounded by a high fence. He walked towards them. But long before he reached them he could tell this was not Lord Langdale's research centre. These buildings looked abandoned and unloved, and sand had drifted against the fence. The lane ended at a gate secured with a big, rusty padlock. A faded sign bolted to the fence beside it showed a comical sea-serpent squirting water from a hole in her head, like a whale. Two pink children were sporting happily in the fountain it made. Above them, almost erased by the sun and wind, were the words *Gorm Sands Holiday Camp.*

Egg thought about heading back to the shop and asking the shopkeeper where he could find Lord Langdale. But he was wary of talking to more grown-ups, and the abandoned camp seemed like a good place to rest unseen while he decided his next move.

He made his way along the fence, following a narrow little path which wound through the nettles and clumps of mallow and sea cabbage. The path had been made by children, judging by the footprints he saw here and there in the sand. It led him to a place where a section of the fence could be shifted aside, opening a gap that was easily wide enough to squeeze through.

Why the place was called a camp, Egg could not imagine. There was no sign of any encampment; just a lot of little cabins and a few larger, barn-like buildings, all with pink and pale blue paint peeling from their walls and their tar-paper roofs growing ragged in the sea wind. All the windows he could see were broken. Crumbs of glass littered the mounds of sand that had blown into the empty doorways, making them glitter like snowdrifts.

Wandering along the little roads that snaked between the buildings, Egg worked out that Gorm Sands must have been a sort of pleasure garden. There was a big rectangular hole lined with blue tiles which he guessed had once been a bathing pool. It still held a pool of greasy water in its deep end. Old handbills peeling from walls and windows advertised swimming galas and glamorous grannie contests from summers past, coach trips to Wheal Tizzy Tin Mining Museum, and a band called Davey Jones and the Lower Third who had come 'all the way from Swingin' London!'. This place had been busy and exciting once, thought Egg, but the years had moved on and left it behind. How many different Wildseas there must be, all piled up on the memories of each other, stretching back from this September Saturday to Egg's own time, and then back again beyond that, into the deep past that Aish had sometimes spoken of, when the island had been all woods, or surrounded by a frozen sea . . .

It made him feel giddy just thinking of it.

On the door of a locked building he found a big map of Wildsea, faded almost to transparency. He was studying it, hoping to find Lord Langdale's Ocean Research Centre marked somewhere, when voices reached him on the wind.

They sounded too close to be coming from the dunes outside the fence. Egg turned in alarm, and the voices' owners came into view almost at once. Three boys, hurtling towards him on spindly machines. The machines looked like bad drawings of thin horses, but with a big wheel front and back instead of legs. The riders held on to shiny metal horns at the front end, and propelled themselves along with pedals fitted to a small third wheel between the two big ones. Egg blinked in the cloud of fine sand they threw up as they skidded to a halt in front of him, penning him against the wall where the map was.

'Who are you?' demanded one of the boys.

'What are you doing in our base?' asked another.

'You're not supposed to be here,' said the third, whom Egg thought might actually be a girl, though it was hard to say since they were all dressed alike in those short-sleeved shirts and blue trousers, and all had the same shaggy shoulder-length hair. The girlish one and the older boy looked like brother and sister; round freckled faces and sandy hair. The other boy was shorter and stockier; *Planet of the Apes* said the slogan on his shirt, and Egg thought he looked like an ape himself, with that dark fringe falling over his eyes.

'We're the Gorm Sands Gang, and this is our secret hideout,' said the oldest boy. 'How did you get in?'

'Through the loose bit of fence by the gate,' said Egg, clenching his fists and bracing himself for a fight. 'It's not *that* secret,' he added. 'Anyone could find the way in.'

'Well, you'll have to leave. And swear not to tell another living soul about this place, or . . .'

'Or what?' asked Egg.

"Well, we'll have to kill you, probably."

Egg shrugged, unimpressed. He had been alarmed at first, but he saw now these were just children, and only playing at being tough. But since they *were* just children, and in a place they probably shouldn't be, he saw no harm in talking to them. 'I'm looking for a bloke named Lord Langdale,' he said. 'Only he calls himself Professor Stone these days. He's got a place called an Ocean Research Centre somewhere round here. My friend Utterly's gone missing and I reckon he might know where she is.'

"Utterly's not a name," said the older boy.

"Anything's a name if someone calls themself by it."

'What, you mean this Lord has – he's *kidnapped* her?' asked *Planet of the Apes*.

'I didn't say that, did I? I just said he might know . . .'

'Where have you come from?' said the girl. 'You're not from round Marazea.'

'Dizzard Tor,' said Egg, and then, deciding to try honesty for a change. 'But I'm from Dizzard Tor as it was, not as it is.'

'What do you mean?'

'I mean it was eighteen hundred and twelve when I left home, and now I'm here in nineteen hundred and seventy-something, so it's a bit confusing, is all.'

The gang gaped at him. 'You mean you can travel in time? Like Doctor Who?'

'Who?'

'Where did you park your time machine?'

'What time machine? I don't need no time machine. The Gorm brung me here. You've heard of the Gorm, ain't you? You named your flamin' gang after her.'

'We just named ourselves after this place – Gorm Sands,' said the older boy. 'The Gorm's a monster in old stories. She's not *real*.'

'You can believe that if you want, but don't let *her* catch you saying it.'

The gang looked at Egg some more. They assumed he was lying, but it was the sort of lie that, if they went along with it, might turn into a game that would keep them entertained all weekend. They were impressed.

'What will you do when you find Lord Langdale?' asked the girl.

Egg shrugged. 'Ask him if he knows where my friend is, I suppose. And how he got here – cos he's from the same time I come from, see? And I can't think it was the Gorm brung him here. She's not generally very obliging.'

'OK,' said the older boy. 'I'm Luke, and this is Splodge, and that's my sister Sharon.'

Egg nodded. 'I'm Egg. Now, you heard of this centre place or not? It was in the paper. There was a picture.'

'There's some scientists down at Belfriars Bay,' said Splodge. 'My dad did a bit of work for them, building a jetty.' He got off his machine and came to poke a grubby finger at the map. 'They got a boat down there.'

'The *Sea Witch*,' Egg remembered. He looked at the map, at the long, wriggling line of the coast road winding its way up and down over all the cliffs and coves. 'But Belfriars Bay is half-way to the Spillikins. That's two hours walk.'

'Won't take long on bikes,' said Luke.

'What's "bikes"?' asked Egg, in a way that made the three children think, just for an instant, that he really *might* be a traveller from another time. But Egg had already worked out that they meant their wheeled machines. 'You'd let me borrow one?' he asked.

## 21

# BIKES TO BELFRIARS BAY

The gang's bikes were precious to them, and they weren't about to go loaning them to strangers. But Egg was glad of that, because he didn't understand how the machines balanced on their two big wheels anyway, and he doubted he could have stayed upright. Instead, he sat on the saddle of Luke's bike with his arms around Luke's waist while Luke stood on the pedals and drove the bike along. With Sharon and Splodge speeding on ahead they rattled back down the pitted lane to Marazea and turned along the coast road, past the new vicarage (which looked old now) and the little church (which looked exactly as it had always done). The island had woken up by that time, and carriages kept rushing past them. 'Cars' the Gorm Sands gang called them, so Egg did too. They did not scare him so much now he knew about the carburettors and things working away inside them.

Beyond the church the road climbed steeply up onto St Chyan's Head, and they had to dismount and push the bikes. At the top stood Sundown Watch, looking sad and shabby and shut up. Big, unkempt bushes filled half of Mr Skraeveling's gardens, and the other half had been flattened and covered with weed-speckled gravel. Egg stood and looked at it all, and a wave of sadness came over him. He knew now how ghosts must feel, hanging around the places they'd loved in life, watching them get changed and mucked about with, and not being able to do a thing to stop it.

'I used to live there,' he said.

'I thought you said you lived at Dizzard Tor?' asked Splodge.

'Yes, but this is where Utterly lives, and I can come and stay whenever I like.'

'It's empty now,' said Luke.

'It's always been empty,' said Splodge.

'There's a lady called Miss Brightling comes and stays there sometimes,' said Sharon. 'Our mum says she's a nutcase.'

'She's just eccentric,' said Luke.

'What does that mean?' asked Splodge.

'It means she's a nutcase,' said Sharon.

'We should break in,' said Luke. 'We could make it

our new hideout. It would be better than Gorm Sands because anyone can get into Gorm Sands. Those kids from Owlsbarrow are always poking about.'

They stood looking thoughtfully at Sundown Watch, imagining what it would be like to camp in its dusty rooms. But Egg could tell they weren't really house-breakers. 'I know a better hideout,' he said. 'There's an old sort of fort thing up on the Dizzard cliffs.'

'A pill box? Will you show us?'

'Yes,' said Egg. 'Well, if I'm still here. I don't know how long I'm staying. I got to find out about Utterly first.'

They rode on. The bikes got up speed on the long downhill stretch south of St Chyan's Head, and the sadness that had settled upon Egg blew away. *Tick, tick, tick* went the flickering wheels, and *whirrr* went their tyres on the smooth new road. The sun shone, and the cloud shadows on the moor tried to keep pace with the bikes and failed. It felt to Egg as if he were flying.

Someone had planted a whole new wood on St Chyan's Great Common. Hundreds of drab green pine trees were lined up in tidy rows like cabbages, each as tall as the mainmast of a man o' war. The children stopped in the shade, flung down their bikes, and drank startling fizzy stuff from a red and white can Luke fetched out of his saddlebag. It made Egg sneeze and stare.

'Ain't you ever tasted cola before?' asked Splodge, taking the can from him.

'Course he hasn't, Splodge,' shouted the others.

'He comes from times before it was invented,' said Sharon.

They almost believed it, thought Egg. But only in the way that he and Utterly and the Dearlove children had almost believed they were explorers or castaways when they were playing their games in the dunes. The sadness rose in him again as he recalled that those games had been a hundred years and more ago. Then the half-empty can of cola came back to him and he took another swig and sneezed some more and laughed with his new friends, and felt glad of them.

Opposite the southern end of the wood a gravel track branched from the coast road and led down steeply into the cleft of Belfriars Bay. *Her Majesty's Government: Ministry of Agriculture and Fisheries* announced a red sign. *No Unauthorised Vehicles Beyond This Point*, said a blue one. *Trespassers Will Be Prosecuted*, added a third, in black and white. The gang lay on the grass verge in the shade of the signs and looked down the track at the cluster of boxy buildings on the beach below. The buildings had a high wire fence around them, as if they might wander off if they weren't penned in.

'We'll need wire cutters,' whispered Luke.

'Or a laser cannon,' Splodge hissed back.

'Have you got those things?' asked Egg.

'Yeah,' said Splodge, and demonstrated the laser cannon, but it was only imaginary.

Egg stood up. 'I'm going to go and ask if Lord Langdale's in,' he said, and started walking down the track.

Luke walked with him a little way. 'Is your friend really down there?' he asked.

'I don't know,' admitted Egg.

'We ought to go back. All those signs. We don't want to get prosecuted. This place is proper top secret I reckon. For real, I mean, not like our hideout. We could probably get arrested.'

Egg shrugged. 'I'm just going to go and ask if Lord Langdale's around, and if he's seen Utterly. I've come all this way, so I've got to ask, haven't I?'

He turned and looked at Luke, and Luke felt the oddest little chill run through him, as if he really were talking to a time traveller. Then Egg shook his hand and said, 'Thanks for the bike ride. Better than ponies those things are, and nothing like as much trouble.'

'Should we come with you?' asked Luke.

'I don't see why.'

'Should we wait here then?'

'If you want.'

'How long will you be?'

'I don't know.'

Egg stomped on down the track. Luke stood watching

for a moment, then turned back to join the rest of his gang, sprawled in the grass beside their bikes where the track joined the road.

At the foot of the cliffs, a metal bridge spanned Belfriars Brook. Egg strode across it and walked up to the gate in the wire fence. As he reached it, a big man came out of a sentry-box affair just inside and said, 'Oi! What do you want, kid?'

'I want a word with Lord Langdale,' said Egg.

'Who?'

'Lord Langdale. Professor Stone, he calls himself now.'

The man looked Egg up and down and made it clear that nothing he saw impressed him. He shaded his eyes with one hand, squinting up the track to the cliff top, where sunlight glinted on the chrome of the Gorm Sands Gang's bikes.

'Hop it,' he said.

'Lord Langdale!' Egg yelled at the top of his voice. There was a quay down at the water's edge, with a grey ship moored at it: the *Sea Witch*. Some men were working on her, and Egg saw them look up as his voice came ringing off the cliffs on each side of the bay. 'Lord Langdale!'

'I said hop it!' shouted the sentry-box man. 'This is government property, this is. Sling your hook, kid, or I'll have the police on you.'

'It's all right, Kennett,' called another voice. A man had emerged from one of the buildings and was making his way between a line of parked cars to the fence. He stopped when he reached it and stood staring at Egg through the grid of dusty wire.

Egg had been having second thoughts all the way from Marazea, wondering if Lord Langdale and Professor Stone could really be the same person or if his imagination had been playing tricks on him. But now that they were face to face, he was more certain than ever. The last time he had seen this man he had been eating kippers at Sundown Watch while his sloop waited in the bay to sail off to the Hidden Lands.

It was clear that Lord Langdale recognized Egg too. He scowled, and a faint but fiery gleam ignited in the depths of his eyes. 'I know you, boy. How did you come here?'

'I could ask you the same thing,' said Egg. 'Cos you're Lord Langdale, ain't you, large as life, and don't you try denying it.'

'My name is Stone.'

'All right then, Mr Stone. How come you're here, when you should be dead a hundred years or more? And have you seen Utterly? Cos she's lost here in this funny century, and I've come to fetch her home. Do you know where she is?'

Langdale or Stone or whatever he was smiled his

stony smile. 'Ah! The Gorm sent you here, didn't she? She dares not come in person to find the girl so she is reduced to using proxies.'

'I ain't a proxy,' said Egg, who wasn't sure what a proxy was but thought it sounded insulting. 'I just want to find Utterly, is all. Have you got her in there?' He reached out and rattled the wire fence.

'Everything all right, Prof?' asked Kennett, standing uncertainly beside his sentry box.

'Quite all right, Ted,' said Stone. 'Let this boy in. I think he and I need to have a little talk . . .'

Up on the cliff, Luke, Sharon, and Splodge all watched in astonishment as the gate swung open and Egg walked into the research centre. He glanced up at them just as the gate closed behind him. Then the man he had been talking to led him away into one of the buildings.

'Well,' said Splodge. 'What now?'

## 22

# EGG AT BELFRIARS BAY

'You'll be coming out with us aboard the *Sea Witch* tonight,' Professor Stone had told Utterly that morning at breakfast. 'The Gorm is too wary to be lured by the lights and harmonics we used the night we found you. But if we send *you* down in the cage, and make her believe you are in danger – well, what mother would not risk herself to save her child's life?'

'I'm not exactly sure that's ethical, boss,' said Nigel.

'And I'm not exactly sure you wouldn't be better off finding yourself another job, if you don't approve of my methods, Mr Kerr,' snapped Stone.

Utterly, who found she had quite lost her appetite for the cornflakes she had been enjoying, said, 'I knew a real sea-witch once, Professor Stone. Her name was Thurza

Froy and she too tried to use me as bait to make the Gorm do her bidding. And the Gorm came in answer to her call, but things did not go as Mrs Froy hoped, for they found her drowned on Marazea strand next day.'

'Ah,' said Stone, 'but you're forgetting something, little Miss Dark. Namely, that I am not some mad old biddy living in the nineteenth century. I have all the power of modern science at my command. Believe me, I am more than a match for your Gorm.'

He turned his back on her and began allotting chores to the members of his team, which they set off to do with varying degrees of enthusiasm. Jill was told to take Utterly back to her quarters, which she did, but once Utterly was shut in and the door locked upon her she heard Jill saying to someone in the corridor, 'You were right. It's *not* ethical. I think Stone might be going off his rocker.'

'Shhh! He'll hear you!'

'I don't care. I came here to do serious research, Nigel, not kidnap children.'

'She wasn't exactly *kidnapped*, Jill . . .'

But Jill was right, thought Utterly, as their voices faded, moving away along the corridor. She *had* been kidnapped, and it was no use just sitting here and waiting for someone to rescue her, because no one in this year of nineteen hundred and seventy-one even knew that she existed. *So, she thought, I must conceive some means of escape for myself.*

She sat on her bunk and thought for a while, but before she could settle on a plan there was a commotion outside her room. People were hurrying along the corridor, and she heard Harriet say, 'Another one! A boy this time!'

Intrigued, Utterly knelt on her bunk to peer out of the high window. Harriet and the other scientists had come out of the canteen building to watch as Professor Stone crossed the dusty gravel area where their motor-carriages were parked. There was a boy with him. She thought for a moment, as the sunlit caught the boy's ginger hair, that he looked just like Egg, only she knew he couldn't be, not here in 1971, not in those clothes. But then the boy glanced up at something Professor Stone had said, and it *was* Egg.

Of course! she thought, laughing and weeping at the same time. Of course Egg would come to rescue her! And of course he would not be deterred by the inconvenient span of years that separated the age he lived in from the age where Utterly was trapped!

'Egg!' she shouted, hammering with the flat of her hand on the window. She thought he heard her, for he looked round, but he did not see her, and a moment later Professor Stone took him gently but firmly by the arm and led him into the building where she had sat through so many tests and examinations when she first arrived at Belfriars Bay. The others hesitated outside the canteen, talking together in voices that did not reach Utterly.

Nigel glanced towards her window, and Utterly turned away quickly and pretended she had not been looking.

She felt afraid. She was not so much fearful for herself, but for Egg. It was clear that whatever plan he had devised to rescue her had gone awry, and he had been captured. As for her own half-formed scheme, it rather depended on her being able to run to the sea, dive into it, and find the current that would lead her to the Gorm. She had not been able to do that in Professor Stone's sea-pool, but perhaps if she were alone and in the actual sea, she might. But Egg could not. Poor Egg could not swim under the sea. Egg was not the Gorm's own child. Egg was just a boy.

'You are just a boy,' said Professor Stone, when he had led Egg to his office and settled him in a chair. 'How did she bring you here?'

'Don't remember,' said Egg, mostly truthfully.

'Let's see if we can refresh your memory. The log of HMS *Acantha* records that a boy named Egg went down in the diving bell and was lost.'

'Oh, I remember that part,' said Egg. 'There was some underwatery kind of palace down there, and the Gorm was in it, in a right old taking because she'd lost Utterly and couldn't go to where she was. So I said send me then, and . . . and here I am.'

'You arrived today?'

'Night before last.'

'Who gave you the clothes?'

'I stole 'em, didn't I?' said Egg. He had a feeling that if he mentioned Dan and Mim it would be more likely to get them into trouble than get him out of it. 'I took 'em off somebody's washing line,' he said. 'Now what about you? What are you doing here?'

Stone's face took on a look that could have been pride or pain. 'Oh, no sea magic brought me here, boy. I moved through the years as I have always done; one slow day at a time. I made the crossing between the centuries in the old-fashioned way, by simply living for a hundred and fifty-nine years.'

'You never!' scoffed Egg. 'That'd make you about two hundred years old, and you don't look a day over sixty. Or seventy, maybe.'

'Oh, I am *much* older than that,' said Stone. 'I am as old as the hills. Two centuries is nothing to me. They passed in the blink of an eye.'

*So either he is a madman, or he is not a man at all,* thought Egg. *And either way, I don't trust him.*

'After the *Acantha* was lost . . .'

'What do you mean, lost?' demanded Egg. 'What happened? What became of Will Dark? And Mr Constantine? The old Gorm promised me she'd keep 'em safe.' (Although, now he came to think of it, he realized that the Gorm had not exactly *promised* any such thing.)

'After the *Acantha* was lost,' Stone repeated, 'I gave up on my attempts to reach the Gorm's realm by sea. I turned to other methods, under other names. But now technology has advanced to the point where I believe I am the equal of the Gorm. I would have snared her the other night if your friend Utterly had not taken the bait instead.'

'Then Utterly is here!'

There was a knock at the door. A young woman opened it and said, 'Professor Stone, we're wondering . . .'

'Jill,' said Stone, cutting her short, 'I want a full range of tests run on this boy. He has made the same temporal transition as Utterly did. And tell Nigel and Harriet to check through the logs from the instruments in the bay. The Entity was here, in our world, two nights ago, and those damn fools missed her . . .'

'But, Professor,' said Jill, staring at Egg, 'he's just a boy. I mean – we didn't fish him up out of the sea like Utterly. Where has he come from? Have we got his parents' permission to keep him here? We can't just . . .'

'He has come from the year 1812.'

'Are you . . .?'

'Am I what?'

'Well, are you *sure*, Professor? I mean, is there actual evidence that's where he comes from?'

'Evidence?' shouted Stone. 'There's the evidence of my own eyes! I have seen him myself, right here on Wildsea, eating kippers in 1812!'

Jill looked astonished, then started to smile as if Stone had been joking, then realized that he had not and looked confused. 'But you . . .' she said, and Egg realized that Lord Langdale had blurted out a secret. These folk who worked for him did not know what he was, nor how old.

Jill started to say something else, then decided it would be easier to talk to Egg. 'What is your name?' she asked, with a nervous little reassuring smile.

'Egg,' said Egg.

'And when were you born, Egg?'

Egg glanced at the calendar on the wall above Lord Langdale's desk to remind himself what year he was in, counted quickly backwards, and said, 'Nineteen fifty-nine.'

'The boy's lying,' said Lord Langdale. 'Take him away. Run the tests. And send Jim Graham to see me.'

'Right, right, yes,' said Jill, flustered. She smiled again at Egg and asked him to follow her. As she left, Egg turned quickly to Lord Langdale and said, 'The Gorm will sort you out, whoever and whatever you are.'

'The Gorm is no match for me now,' said Lord Langdale. 'I shall deal with her as easily as I dealt with your poor friend Aish.'

## 23

# THE TRAP

There was a narrow cleft between the crags at the end of High Tarn, where the water tumbled loudly away down a series of small cataracts, as if excited to reach Three Sisters Cliff and plunge spectacularly to the sea. Towards this cleft Aish now led Stone, and when they neared it, she held back and gestured for her guest to go ahead.

'Look inside,' she said. 'You'll be surprised.'

Stone went forward, intrigued. He studied the carvings which the folk of ancient times had left upon the rock faces on either side of the cleft, but as he started to go deeper into the cleft itself he suddenly cried out and drew back. The way was strung across with a cat's cradle of strings, and the strings were decked with bird's skulls, twigs, holed stones, and dozens of curious little bags and bundles.

Stone backed out of the cleft and looked searchingly at Aish. 'This opening is deeper than it seems, and so are you, I think. You must have known I cannot pass your wards.'

'I am sorry,' said Aish. 'I had not thought my little webs would trouble one so wise; here . . .' And she squeezed into the cleft herself, nimbly untied the strings, and begged His Lordship to follow her inside.

The cleft was indeed far deeper than it looked, and it opened into another world entirely; the endless, timeless wood that had once been the domain of the Hunter himself. Even Aish was astonished by how much bigger and sort of *tree-ier* the trees were there, and by how richly the air was scented with the mingled fragrances of growth and decay. On her previous visits the trees had all been in full summer leaf, but now they stood bare and sere, and a winter sky shone through their naked branches. A light snow was falling, whispering as it settled on the seas of withered leaves that lay in the hollows between the trees' vast roots.

'So this is the Hunter's realm,' said Stone, sounding awed despite himself as he followed Aish along the winding ways between the trees. The cleft they had come in through, with the summer sunlight shining on High Tarn beyond it, was quickly lost to sight. 'Is the Hunter here? I should like to meet him, the old villain.'

'You are too late,' said Aish. 'He's gone away. He brought himself to the attention of the Gorm, and the Gorm destroyed him.'

'And you think that because the Gorm destroyed him, she will destroy me too?' Stone's laughter echoed in the winter woods like cold stones sliding down a scree. 'My dear, it is almost touching, how very stupid you are. I declare, you have no more brains than the trees that dreamed you into being.'

Aish laughed too, for she was glad there was no more need to keep being polite to Stone. 'I may not be as clever as you,' she said, 'but I have an advantage over you, my lord, and it is this: *I know my way out of this wood, and you do not.*'

And with that she turned, hitched up her skirts, and, springing like a deer over a fallen trunk that barred her path, ran away uphill, quickly vanishing in the shadows between the trees.

'Stop!' cried Stone, struggling to follow and finding his frock coat caught on a hundred brambles. He shouted other things as he stooped to tear it free; wordless shouts that sounded to Aish as she ran like anger and despair.

Aish was a kindly thing, and it hurt her to leave even a disagreeable creature like Stone behind in such a place. But needs must, she told herself. Stone was a danger to her and the place and people that she loved. If she could, she would have fetched her spear and thrust it through

179

his heart. But perhaps a spear would not kill him, and this way seemed surer. For had not she not already seen with her own eyes that he was quite incapable of entering the Underwoods past her barrier of charms? Which told her that, once she had put the barrier in place again, with even stronger knots and spells, he would not be able to leave. He would be trapped in the Underwoods for ever, and either he would learn to thrive and be content there, or he would fall victim to one of the dreadful things that were said to dwell among the ancient trees. For Aish did not for one moment believe that he could find another way out of those woods.

There was the cleft ahead of her; a slice of summer sunshine on the cold air. She ran towards it laughing – and stopped short.

'Did you not think I could find my own way back?' asked Stone. He stood just outside the opening, shading his eyes with one hand to study Aish. 'Did you not think I could smell your Wildsea stone, such a sharp, clean smell among the mould-stench of the Hunter's midden? For shame, Mrs Dark; you have underestimated me.'

*Well*, said Aish to herself, *he may have outwitted me, but he does not outweigh me. I shall throw him in the tarn, and push him underwater, and sit on him. And we shall see how he likes that, for all his cleverness.*

But as she barged through the narrow exit from the Underwoods, Stone raised his hand and snapped his fingers as if summoning a servant. And from the crags that overhung the cleft a rain of small stones came clattering down, driving Aish back into the woods' chill shade. Then, as she made another attempt to get out, still larger stones fell, throwing off sharp splinters and driving her back again. And finally a huge slab of granite, which had balanced there above the cleft for as long as even Aish recalled, lost its footing and pitched forward, bringing down half the hillside behind it, and closing the entrance to the Underwoods as neatly as a door.

In the dark behind it, Aish stood shocked, with the blood starting to trickle down her face from cuts the flying shards of stone had made. She reached out her hands and pushed at the fallen stone, but it was the size of a small house, and she could not begin to shift it. Behind her, the trees of the Underwoods creaked and whispered, and unknown creatures went rustling through the thickets between them.

It was starting to snow in earnest now.

# 24
# ESCAPE

Around noon, Jill brought Utterly's dinner to her room on a tray. 'The Prof doesn't want you to go to the canteen today,' she said. She set the tray down on the table beside Utterly's bunk, started to leave, then turned back and said, 'There is a boy here.'

Utterly wasn't sure if it would be best to say she that she knew Egg or that she didn't, so she said nothing.

'Professor Stone says he's come from the same place as you,' said Jill. 'From the same *time* as you, I mean. But he's not like you. He won't tell us much; he seems like just a normal boy. Stone thinks the Gorm brought him here, and he's furious that we missed her. But he says it proves the Gorm is out there somewhere, watching us, so he's insisting we go ahead with tonight's experiment, even though the rest of us don't want him to. He says if we don't he'll give us the sack, and make sure no other researcher will ever hire us, so we can't afford to leave and even if I could, I couldn't, because – well, I don't want to leave you here all on your own.' She shrugged unhappily. 'I think he's developed a bit of an obsession with the Hidden Lands actually. Sometimes when people get very focused on making some great breakthrough, they start to think it justifies . . . well, almost *anything*.'

'Even kidnapping?' asked Utterly.

Jill did not answer that. She went to the door, and worked the knob which locked it. 'These locks are very unreliable,' she said. And then: 'Your friend is in the room at the end of this corridor.'

She left, and closed the door behind her, and it was a little while before Utterly realized why she had said those things. Then she understood. Jill was helping her, or at least giving her a chance to help herself. She tiptoed to the door and tried the handle. It opened easily. The corridor outside was empty. She slipped out and ran to the room at the end. There was a glass window set into it, and when she stood on tiptoe she could look through it and see Egg sitting disconsolately on an orange chair. She tried that door too, and sure enough, it was unlocked.

'Oh, Egg!' she whispered, darting in. 'I am so happy to see you!'

She could tell he was happy to see her, too, because

Egg did not like hugs at all, yet when she closed the door and ran over to him, he submitted to hers without the least complaint. 'I thought they'd locked me in!' he said. 'I didn't even think to try the door . . .'

'They are on our side,' said Utterly. 'At least Jill is, and Nigel, I think. Come, we must escape, though I do not know where we can go . . .'

'Away from here would be a start,' said Egg. 'You know that Stone ain't all he seems? He's some sort of old thing, longer-lived than normal folk.'

'I am sure you mistook, Egg. He seems just a man, although a very clever one.'

'Then how come he was poking about on Wildsea the year you went away, looking not a day younger than he does now? He called himself Lord Langdale then, and . . .'

He was about to tell her about the *Acantha*, but stopped himself. Those ugly things Stone had said about the *Acantha* being lost and Aish dealt with had shaken him deeply, but he did not want to burden Utterly with them yet. He would rescue her from Stone's clutches first. 'Oh, Utterly,' he said. 'Where have you been? I thought we'd never see you again!'

There was no time for Utterly to explain her adventures with the Gorm. She knew that any moment Professor Stone might come to check on them.

'Egg,' she said, 'we must make an escape.'

'All right then. We're good at that. Remember how we got up that chimney on Summertide to escape from Doctor Hyssop?'

Utterly frowned. '*You* got up it, Egg. I did not. And Professor Stone is a far more dangerous adversary than Doctor Hyssop, so please take this seriously.'

She put a finger to her lips to quiet Egg's objections, then went and peered out through the door. There was still no one in the corridor, so she whisked the door open and they both hurried out, the thin carpet muffling their footsteps as they ran to the door at the far end which led out into the sunshine. Keeping low, they crept behind the row of parked carriages drawn up outside. But when they reached the end of the row they stopped. Yards of empty gravel stretched between them and the gate, and the gate was closed, and in the sentry box beside it Mr Kennett sat picking his nose and reading his newspaper.

'I do not see how we can both get past him,' said Egg. 'We must make a dash for it, and I shall distractify him while you climb the fence. I have some friends waiting at the top of the track there – at least, I hope they're waiting. They have things called bikes that can go like the wind, and if you tell 'em I sent you, they'll get you safe away.'

'But *how* shall you distractify Mr Kennett, Egg?' said Utterly. (She did not think that 'distractify' was really a word, but felt this was no time to criticize Egg's grammar.)

'I shall punch him on the nose, of course.'

'But you are just a boy, and he is a man, and built like a prize fighter.'

'That is why it will be such a distractification, see? He will not be expecting it, and while he stands amazed, he will not notice you scaling the fence.'

Utterly did not feel this proposal numbered among Egg's better plans. For one thing, once he recovered from his amazement, Mr Kennet was liable to do Egg an injury. For another, she feared Egg was overestimating her fence-scaling abilities. But while she crouched there trying to find some way to voice these doubts without hurting her friend's pride, she heard footsteps approaching.

She hissed at Egg to keep quiet, and they crouched still lower as Harriet walked past, apparently without seeing either of them. Strolling towards the gate, Harriet called out loudly, 'Ted, open up. I need to check the monitors out on the headland before the tide starts coming in.'

Mr Kennet put down his newspaper and, without getting out of his sentry box, did something that made the gate unlock itself and swing open. But instead of going through it, Harriet leaned against Kennett's little window and started talking to him.

'Quickly!' said Utterly, realizing what was happening and pushing Egg towards the gate. 'That lady is called Harriet. I believe Jill must have told her of our escape, and she is helping us! She is our distraction, Egg!'

186

They ran towards the gate, and through it. They were beyond the fence and across the bridge before they heard Kennett's voice behind them raised in an indignant bellow. 'Oi! You kids! Get back here!'

Utterly and Egg kept running. The track steepened, leading up towards the clifftops and the road. When they were half-way up, Egg glanced back and saw Professor Stone emerging from a building down there, and Kennett pointing wildly up the track. When they were two thirds of the way up they heard the engine of Professor Stone's carriage roar into life. They looked back. There seemed to be some confusion in the carriage park – Nigel had started his own vehicle, and it was blocking Professor Stone's way to the gate; Professor Stone was leaning out of his window and gesturing angrily at Nigel.

'They are confounding him!' said Utterly happily.

But Egg knew how fast the carriages could move, and had no doubt that Professor Stone could overtake them, especially now they were breathless from the steep climb. He urged Utterly on towards the top of the track. The Gorm Sands Gang might still be waiting there, he thought, ready to whisk them away by bike. If not, perhaps there would be a carriage passing by on the road whose driver they could flag down and ask for help.

But the gang and their bikes were gone, and the coast road in both directions was empty. Beyond it, the trees of the new plantation stood guard on the slopes of St Chyan's Common like a regiment of foot.

Professor Stone's carriage snarled, climbing the track.

'Quick!' said Egg. 'Into the trees!'

## 25

# THE WILD WOODS

Aish was shoving her way through the thickets and thorn-breaks of the Underwoods. Initially, she had done her best to stay in sight of the entrance, even though she feared Professor Stone had blocked it up for ever. But things had come creeping through the undergrowth around her; unseen things that never quite showed themselves but prowled and growled and made alarming rustlings. So there was nothing she could do but move away, in search of shelter and perhaps a weapon she might use to defend herself. She was not as easily disconcerted by the woods' old magic as a mortal would be, but even so, it was not long before she had no idea which way she had come from, and even less where she should go.

The snow blew around her, and fell on her, and melted, soaking through her summer dress. Ice crackled under her feet, and the wind moaned through bare branches.

'Aish,' she said, 'you have been a great fool, for thinking you could outwit that wicked creature. I suppose you have been taught a useful lesson, but it is a hard one, and I do not in all honesty see how you are to profit from it, if there is no way out of these trees . . .'

There was no way out of the trees. The path she followed twisted and darkened, winding around buttresses of holly and over the roots of oaks so large she found it hard to scramble over them. In the shadows beyond the path toadstools grew; small slimy crowds of them like tiny onlookers with wet brown hats, and big solitary ones the size of dinner plates. And always, from behind her and from either side, there was the soft prickle and whisper of prowling paws.

She came to a black pool and stopped there to drink. And when she raised her head she saw that one of the prowling things had gained the courage to show itself at last. It stared her from among the dead leaves on the far side of the pool; a huge grey wolf with yellow eyes and a growl bubbling behind its fangs.

'Nice doggy,' said Aish, climbing cautiously to her feet. There had been wolves on Wildsea once, and she had been on quite good terms with them. But the wolves of the Underwoods were larger and crueller than the wolves of the outer world: they were the sort of wolves who ate people's grandmothers, and lay in wait for lost children. They were like the idea of wolves turned into flesh and fur and muscle, and Aish was their idea of prey.

The one that had shown itself growled louder. Its yellow eyes shone, and all around it in the shadows of the woods other sets of yellow eyes lit up, and other pointy ears were laid flat, and other hairy haunches hunched, ready to pounce.

'Well I can't outrun them,' said Aish, putting one hand to her belly and thinking of the babies asleep in there, whom she must keep safe if she could. 'And they do not seem inclined to be friendly. So I shall have to fight them, I suppose.'

She drew from her belt the knife she always carried. She had seldom used it for anything more violent than peeling an apple or cutting a switch of wood. She was not sure how many wolves she could dispatch, but she hoped that if she could kill one the others might fall to eating it instead of her, and give her time to climb a tree.

The chief wolf shrugged his way out of the undergrowth and swaggered around the edge of the pool. Some of his followers came the other way, to cut off Aish's escape. Her mouth went dry. She gripped the knife so tightly that the birch-bark strips she had bound around its handle dug painfully into her palm. But before the wolf could spring, something fell with a splash into the pool, and a noise erupted in the branches overhead; such a hooting and a hullabaloo that the wolves lost their nerve and fled as if the Hunter himself was upon them.

*Which he can't be*, thought Aish, who was almost as startled as the wolves had been. *Because I saw him gobbled up myself by the Gorm in the shape of a great big fish.* But she recalled that when something like the Hunter dies it leaves a vacancy, which some other thing will seek to fill.

She looked up. Above her, the trees were full of faces.

'I'm Aish,' she told them hopefully. 'Hello . . .'

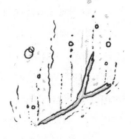

# 26

# THE STONES

The two thousand acres of pines which the Forestry Commission had planted on St Chyan's Common after the war were as unlike the Hunter's realm as it was possible for two woods to be. In this forest the trees were of all the same type, and much the same size, and stood in ordered rows, with wide level tracks leading through them for the forestry workers' vehicles to drive on. There was not even much undergrowth between the trees, just a carpet of dead pine needles laid over the rough ground. Even so, Utterly and Egg could not help being reminded of their adventures in the Underwoods, as low branches whipped at their faces and they tripped and stumbled over roots. Utterly's new sandals, of which she had been so proud, turned out to be not so good for walking in as she had imagined; the straps hurt the tops of her feet, and the backs pinched her heels.

After they had gone half a mile or so they came to one of the forest tracks, and were just about to step out onto it when Egg heard a car approaching and pulled Utterly back with him into the shadows under the trees. Crouched there, they saw Professor Stone's red carriage come racing up the track, jolting over ruts and potholes. They flattened themselves into the pine needles and prayed he would not see them, but he went past at such speed it seemed clear he was not searching for them. The sound of the engine moved uphill through the trees, then stopped. A door slammed.

'What is he doing?' wondered Egg.

'I do not care,' declared Utterly. 'Let us go quickly, before he returns.'

'We ought to find out,' Egg said. 'If he's not hunting us, what was he in such a hurry for? It might be important.'

They crept through the trees until they reached the edge of a circular clearing. The red carriage had been abandoned on the track there, parked at a careless angle with its door hanging open. Beyond it, where the sunlight lit up a patch of pallid grass, an old granite pillar stood pointed at the sky.

''Tis the old Longstone,' whispered Egg.

The Longstone had always been one of the few landmarks on this part of St Chyan's Common; it used to stand alone on the bleak, boggy skirts of Merriport Hill, but now this new wood had swallowed it whole.

'What is Professor Stone about?' Utterly asked.

The professor was walking round and round the stone. His mouth was moving, but neither Egg nor Utterly could catch the words he whispered. His hands worked too, waving about in careful patterns, as if he were tying invisible knots in the air.

They were so busy watching him that they did not notice at first what was happening to the standing stone.

'It is moving!' said Utterly suddenly.

The stone gave a lurch. Slowly, it rose, with earth and gravel falling from the lower part where it had been thrust for so long into the ground. It lifted clear of the hole where it had stood and hung there in the sunlight, impossible, while the professor went on with his whispering. He reached out and stroked the stone's rough flank, as a man might stroke a dog.

'Egg, let's go,' whispered Utterly, wriggling backwards on her tummy. There was old land magic working here, and she mistrusted it.

Suddenly, as if an invisible string supporting it had snapped, the longstone plumped back down into its hole and stood there looking just as it always had, except perhaps that it leaned over at a slightly different angle. Stone took off his spectacles and rubbed his eyes. Then, as if he had heard a noise, although neither Egg nor

Utterly had made one, he turned and looked straight towards their hiding place.

They slithered backwards down the slope, then gathered themselves up and ran. The carriage engine started up again, but Utterly was certain the red machine was too large to pursue them through the pines. Sure enough, the sound faded, as Professor Stone turned and drove back down the track towards the coast road. Utterly and Egg kept running, flashing through the shadows of the trees and the sunbeams shining down between until they were giddy with the flicker, and flung themselves down to rest.

'I *told* you he was something magical,' said Egg, when he had breath enough to talk.

'And I should have believed you, Egg; I am sorry for doubting it. He is so good at concealing it. Now I come to think on it, I did notice a sort of gleam in his eyes, but in all other respects he seems a perfectly ordinary man.'

'T'ain't your fault,' said Egg, generously. 'Aish herself didn't see it when he came to Wildsea. A hundred and fifty-nine year ago that was, and no magic helped him across the gap of years from then till now – he just lived that long, and stayed unchanged. He must be as old as Methuselah!'

'Yet I don't believe he is a creature like the Gorm,' mused Utterly. 'If he were, I think he would not be so desperate to learn her secrets – he would already know them for himself. And I do not think he is as terrible as the Hunter, who had a whole world of his own to rule. I reckon this Stone is someone more of Aish's station. Except Aish is content to love the world, and he is not.'

'What do you think he was doing with that old longstone?'

'I cannot conceive. But it was something very wicked, I am sure.'

'So what are we going to do now?' asked Egg.

Utterly turned around, scanning the rows of trees for any sign of Professor Stone. 'I think we must keep out of his way,' she said. 'He means to use me as bait to snare my mother, so all we need to do to frustrate his plans is simply not let him take us.'

'But we cannot hide from him for ever, Utterly. Wildsea ain't a big island, and he has men and cars to help him hunt for us.'

'We must find our way home to the age we belong in,' said Utterly.

'How?'

'I do not know. Did the Gorm not give you any sign, when she brought you here, of how you were to return?'

'She did not. I asked her, but instead of answering she only turned herself into a big weedy giant and cast me ashore.'

'She is like that,' agreed Utterly. 'I do not think she

197

*means* to be thoughtless, it is only that she does not really think of anyone but her own self. Well, we must find her somehow, or at least send word to her, and we can do neither in this dry wood, so far from the sea. We must make our way to the shore, Egg.'

They moved on. It was almost pleasant to be walking together through the trees. It was easy enough to find their way, for the ground sloped downward towards the coast road, and between the branches they could sometimes glimpse the far shimmer of the sea. But each time Utterly started to enjoy the sunlight and the resin scent that filled the air, she would hear a car go by on the road, or the sky-filling rumble of one of those machines in the sky, and remember where she was, and *when* she was.

Neither she nor Egg saw how some of the stones that lay here and there among the trees seemed to move as they went by, turning with small, deliberate movements to watch them pass. Beneath the pelts of moss and lichen that had grown on them, flakes of quartz embedded in the stones caught the light and gleamed like little eyes.

At the edge of the woods was a most inconvenient fence. It was not high, but it was topped with strands of wire that had been twisted into vicious metal thorns, and they spent a great while casting to and fro to find a place where they could climb over it without cutting themselves. Even so, Egg tore his trousers. 'Which don't belong to me, and ought to be took back to Mr and Mrs Smy by rights,' he said ruefully, examining the rent.

A narrow strip of grass and weeds separated the forest from the road, which was luckily empty at that moment. They hurried across, although Utterly had to pause to examine the black surface. 'I believe it is made from tar," she exclaimed. "What a curious innovation!'

'Well, they have all manner of innovations here now,' said Egg, 'and one of them will come swooshing along and squash you flatter than a cow-flop if you don't stop wool-gathering there in the middle of the road!'

Utterly ran to join him in the ditch on the seaward side. 'Oh, Egg,' she said. 'This twentieth century is interesting to visit, but I am glad I do not have to live here always. The world has grown very loud and strange, and I hate seeing Wildsea so changed and so tamed. I liked it well enough as it was.'

'Well, I like it better as it is now,' said Egg. 'It is exciting, and life is more convenient than before – there are lights that just come on when you want them, without the trouble of fetching tinder and kindling a flame, and there is music whenever you want it too, and pictures that move, and good food and fine clothes for everyone, and bikes and cars to whisk you about. Dan and Mim have got a thing they call a *fridge*, which is like a little wardrobe full of winter: there is actual *ice* inside it, Utterly, and it keeps milk and meat and suchlike fresh for days. Why, I reckon the common folk these days live better than dukes and princes do in our time.'

'You sound as if you prefer it to our own age, Egg.'

'Well, perhaps I do,' said Egg. 'I have made some friends already – there's Dan and Mim, and Tess, who is their dog. And there's the Gorm Sands Gang, although they ain't a proper gang, just kids. But I do wish Aish was here.' And he fell quiet, remembering what Professor Stone had said about Aish, and wondering again what it could mean.

They were about half-way between Belfriars Bay and St Chyan's Head by this time, and they both knew the cliffs there were far too high for them to reach the sea.

'We'll push on to Sundown Watch,' said Egg, 'and see if we can get down the old path into Blanchmane's Cove. The poor old place looks all shut up and abandoned, and Dan Smy says it's only used for holidays now, so I reckon we can sneak round through the gardens to the cliff path easy enough.'

They went north along the clifftops, dropping into the roadside ditch or hiding behind gorse bushes whenever a car passed, and keeping a watch for Professor Stone's red one, though they never saw it. Utterly kept looking wistfully at the horizon in the hope of making out the Hidden Lands, but she did not expect to see them, and she did not. She recalled how, in former years, she had sometimes felt the Gorm's gaze alight on her from far out there in the Western Deeps. It had frightened her in the past, but how glad she would have been to feel it now.

They were walking quickly, for they were well used to walking, and it did not take them long to come to St Chyan's Head. There Utterly stopped, dismayed. Egg had said that Sundown Watch was shut up and abandoned, but she had not prepared herself for the shock of seeing it in such a sorry state. The old house that had been home her whole life had a sad, neglected air. An ugly new stovepipe sprouted through the roof where Mr and Skraeveling's quarters had been, and the windows of the Watcher's Tower were hidden by heavy boards, making it look as if it had gone blind. The garden wall had largely fallen down, and the garden beyond it had been abandoned to a lot of big, sprawling shrubs with glossy, dark green leaves.

They scrambled over the fallen wall and went across the patch of gravel that had presumably been laid there for carriages to park on. On the granite lintel above the front door the ancient command. *Atte Sundown, Watch* had weathered almost into illegibility. Even the door itself was not the old oak door Utterly remembered but something newer and cheaper. A tarnished brass flap was set in it with LETTERS embossed upon it. She pushed this open and peered through into shadows and a smell of damp.

'Oh, Egg, it has all been changed about! The hallway is too big, and the kitchen door is not where it was!'

'Come on, Utterly,' said Egg. 'We don't belong here. Let's go and find your ma.'

Utterly turned away from the sad scene, and noticed something strange.

'The wall, Egg – the wall we just came across – does it look *closer* than it was?'

Egg looked, and saw that it was so. The line of tumbled granite stones that had once been the wall seemed to have crept towards the house while they'd had their backs to it. And it occurred to him that, while Utterly had been peeping through that slot, there had been some noises going on – crispy, sneaky, rattly, stony sorts of noises, which he had assumed were just cars passing on the road. But now he realized that they had been precisely the sort of noises a tumbledown wall might make if it were sneaking up on a person. And it also occurred to him that those stones had a sort of watchful look – you wouldn't think stones could look watchful, what with them having no eyes and all, but somehow that old wall managed it.

He reached out and groped for Utterly's hand and tugged on it. 'Utterly,' he said. 'Run.'

But as they started to move, the wall moved too. The stones rolled and tumbled across the ground all together with a rushing, rattling sound, and the northern end of the wall curled inward to block Egg and Utterly's way. They turned and ran the other way, but the southern end was just as lively; it writhed across the garden like a stony snake, and soon the two ends met, forming a ring of stones with Egg and Utterly inside it.

'We can climb over!' Utterly suggested.

But they couldn't, for the stones on each section of the wall they approached bristled upright, and champed together, and generally gave the impression of being quite able to break children's bones, and quite willing, too. Not only that, a bright red car had pulled up on the track that led from the old house to the road. Out of it, with an air of triumph, stepped Professor Stone.

'Children,' he said, walking towards them and observing them across the wall with a look of satisfaction. 'As you see, I do not rely entirely on technology. I have some power of my own. I put my thoughts into one of the stones which was set up here long ago to honour some other person of my sort, and through it into every boulder that lies upon the hill. I have sensed you through every pebble you trod underfoot, and watched you through the dim quartz eyes of each rock and gatepost you passed upon your way. They let me know precisely where to find you.'

'You old villain!' shouted Egg, clenching his fists. 'Come here and fight fair! I'll black your eye for a farthing!'

Professor Stone did not reply. Perhaps he thought Egg's shrill challenge did not warrant one. The trick with the wall seemed to have exhausted him; his face was greyish, and shone with sweat, and he looked old – old enough, Egg hoped, they could outrun him easily. Perhaps he wouldn't even be able to work his magic with the wall again if Egg and Utterly took their chance now and made a run for it. But before he could put his theory to the test, another of the red car's doors opened and Kennett climbed out.

'Grab them, Kennett,' ordered Stone.

Kennett had the slightly crumpled, irritable look of a large man who has been crammed into a car too small for him, but he nodded grimly and came scrambling over the wall, which seemed to rearrange itself to make the process easier. Egg and Utterly backed away from him, but the stones that walled them in behind moved and grated in a warning way, and as they hesitated, Kennet jumped down and closed his beefy hands around their arms. 'Now then,' he said, 'you come along nice and quiet.'

Stone stood dabbing at his face with a white handkerchief while Kennett led his captives back over the wall. 'Well, Utterly,' he said, 'you have led us quite a chase. Did you have help leaving Belfriars Bay, I wonder?'

Utterly shook her head, not wanting to betray Jill, Harriet and Nigel.

Professor Stone laughed. It was a hard, clattering sound, like rocks falling on a mountainside. 'Well, it hardly matters any more. You are here, and your mother is out there somewhere in the seas of time, and we are going to bring you back together.'

Kennett let go of Utterly's arm, but Stone seized hold of her before she could think of escaping. 'Take the boy back to Belfriars Bay,' he said.

Kennett nodded grimly and started dragging Egg to where the red car waited, while Egg kicked and punched him and called him names. Then Stone led Utterly around the side of Sundown Watch and down the seaward-facing lawn, which was just a rough slope of grass and rabbit-burrows now. And as she reached the cliff edge she saw that her plan of sneaking down into Blanchmane's Cove would never have worked, because there in the cove the *Sea Witch* rode at anchor, with a little primrose-yellow dinghy waiting on the shingle to carry Utterly out to her.

The sun was beginning to go down towards the sea. And just for a moment, as she looked out along the path it made upon the waves, Utterly felt a familiar prickling between her shoulder blades, and knew the Gorm was watching.

27

# THE ISLAND AT THE
# EDGE OF THE WORLD

Captain Bulstrode, finding that his compass behaved whimsically here in the Gorm's seas, had hoped the stars might be a better guide. But when night fell, the stars that hung above the boats were like no stars any of the castaways had seen before, either in the northern hemisphere or the antipodes.

The men in the cutter slept uneasily. Every half hour or so Bulstrode would call out to the other boat, whose light could be seen across the water, and an answering hail would come back. But sometime after midnight the light faded, and Bulstrode's hails went unanswered, and when dawn came the cutter was all alone upon an empty sea.

Will sat near the bows with Constantine, eating his small share of the rations, which Bulstrode had divided among the crew. The wind had died. The little sail hung limply from its mast. Low patches of mist crept over the glassy face of the sea all around, looking almost solid, like restless white hills. From time to time one of these patches would part to reveal an island – or perhaps the mist turned into islands, Will thought uneasily. The islands were certainly unusual. One seemed to be made of glass. Another stood clear of the sea on four immense pillars. 'It is like the false paradise which King Hiram built, to convince his people that he was a god,' said Mr Samuels. But the pillars were so encrusted with barnacles and limpets that it was impossible to know whether they were the work of man, or Gorm, or mere geology.

'Well, it seems you were right, Will, and I was a fool to doubt you,' said Constantine. Alone among the cutter's occupants, he did not seem discomfited by their strange surroundings. Indeed, he was happier and more light-hearted than Will had seen him since their first days together in London.

'I find I do not mind being proved wrong at all,' he confided. 'When I was a small boy I always had this sense that there was something hidden just beyond the world we see; a sort of fairyland that I longed to visit one day. Of course, school knocked it out of me: I learned to scoff at such fancies. But the longing never really left me,

Will. I see that now. It is why your story of the Autumn Isles struck such a chord in me. It is the reason I was never happy in England. And now I am here at last, in the world I dreamed of, or something very like it. How I should love to make landfall upon one of these isles, and meet with the inhabitants . . .'

'You should be careful,' Will warned. 'Not all who live in such places look kindly upon us.' But he could see his friend was not listening. Constantine looked like a man sleepwalking and dreaming of miracles. And anyway, it hardly mattered, for despite the absence of any wind, the cutter was moving steadily past the strange islands, too far from their shores to attempt a landing. It was as if a powerful current were drawing it through the straits between them.

'These must be the Isles of the Blessed, where good Saint Brendan sailed,' said one of the midshipmen, a lad from Donegal.

'I daresay this is how the legend of Odysseus started,' said Mr Samuels. 'Homer had him wandering the isles of Greece, but no doubt the *real* Odysseus got himself lost among the Hidden Lands on his way home from Troy. I wonder if we shall meet with Sirens and one-eyed giants?'

Towards noon, Hard-tack Joe sighted a bank of cloud on the horizon ahead. Soon they could all see it. The cloud did not move, it just hung there, like a pale wall standing on the sea's brim. A few islands showed darkly

208

against it. The cutter was borne towards it at increasing speed. Slowly the castaways became aware of a faint rushing sound, which seemed to emanate from the cloud-wall. No one spoke of it, each trying to convince himself that it was merely his own imaginings, but it grew louder and louder as the day went by, until at last, Mr Samuels said, 'It sounds like a great waterfall,' and everyone had to admit the sound was not within them but without.

'A whirlpool, maybe,' muttered Hard-tack Joe. 'But it must be a mighty deep one to set up such a hullaballoo.'

'Well, we shall find out soon enough,' said Bulstrode.

And indeed they would, for there was nothing to be done. The current that held the cutter in its grip was dragging it so quickly through the water now that foam was starting to ripple under the keel. The sea was starting to grow agitated, breaking into steep, choppy waves like the tide race at the mouth of a great river. Mr Bulstrode trained his telescope upon the wall of cloud, then lowered it with a look of shock.

'I think Mr Samuels was correct,' he said. 'We are approaching some sort of cataract.'

'It is the edge of the world,' said Will, scrambling forward and peering over the bows. The horizon seemed too near, and the mysterious band of cloud hung just beyond it. 'That is not cloud,' he said. 'It is spray, thrown up by all the waters of the earth tumbling off the edge!'

'But tumbling into *where*?' wondered Constantine,

raising his voice over the sound of roaring water. 'The Earth is not flat, Will! It is a globe! Everyone knows that!'

'Perhaps the Gorm does not,' said Will. 'Or perhaps this is an illusion she has made to entertain us.'

But it did not feel like an illusion, as the boat was buffeted by the waves, and twirled about like a twig in a mill race. The horizon drew closer and closer, and it was clear to everyone aboard the cutter that there was nothing beyond it. The sound of falling water was a constant thunder now, so loud that Bulstrode had to shout with all his might to make himself heard.

'That island there! We must reach it, or be swept over . . .'

The island he pointed to stood right on the horizon, which now lay no more than two miles ahead of them. It looked a pleasant sort of isle to Will, with swards of grass stretching up from a beach of white sand, and some sort of rocky outcrop among the trees upon its heights. But he did not see how Bulstrode ever hoped to reach it, since the current seemed set on carrying the cutter past it with half a mile of sea room. We are doomed, he thought, wondering how long the fall over the earth's unexpected edge would take, and what would be at the bottom of it. Would he be drowned in the cataract, or just fall for ever, till he slowly starved? Neither prospect was very attractive, and the worst of it was, he would never see Aish again, and she would never know what had happened to him, although he hoped she would know that he had been thinking of her, here at the end.

But Captain Bulstrode was not about to admit defeat. Red faced and bellowing over the bellowing of the sea, he made his little crew fetch out the oars and fit them in the rowlocks. 'Pull boys, pull!' he shouted, and he was so commanding that Will put away his misery and took up an oar. Constantine and Mr Samuels did likewise, the young midshipmen shared an oar between them, and Hard-tack Joe set the pace while Bulstrode pushed the tiller hard over and shouted encouragement from the stern sheets.

For a time they seemed to make no progress whatsoever. Then, slowly, Will came to realize that the cutter was creeping crabwise across the current, and that although it still looked sure to carry them past the little island, they would not miss it now by quite such a wide margin. He redoubled his efforts, grunting with the effort each time he swung the oar back, feeling his hands rubbed raw by the wood. Waves slopped over the gunwales and the cutter began to fill with water, but everyone was too busy at the oars to bail. The din of the cataract was so loud and steady now it had almost passed beyond hearing: Bulstrode went on shouting, but his voice was drowned out entirely. But Will could see his mouth opening and closing, and knew that he was saying, 'Pull! Pull! Pull! That's it boys! Another twenty yards! We're there!'

Something loomed out of the sea behind him. Will thought for a moment that some monstrous octopus was reaching up to snatch the cutter down, but it was only a tree; a huge old tree, which had fallen from one of the Gorm's islands and was being carried whole towards the falls. It swept past the cutter with so little room to spare that one of its branches tore her mast away. A moment later, as its roots went by, a rock loomed up on the other side, and suddenly the cutter was among a whole scattering of rocks, and then she was in calmer water, and then the oars were striking sand, and Constantine in his confusion missed his stroke and went backwards off his seat.

'Ship oars!' shouted Bulstrode, and Will could hear him now, because the noise of the water was a little muffled by the cliffs of the island they had come to.

The cutter ran ashore on the same white sand beach he had noticed from afar. He scrambled out with the others and pulled her further up the shore. There, some threw themselves down upon the sand. But Will was too curious to rest yet. Wobbly on his sea legs, stiff as an old man from the effort of rowing, he limped his way up the beach and the grassy ridge behind it. Constantine came with him, and Mr Samuels too, and together they reached the ridge's summit and stood there, gazing at this place the Gorm had brought them to.

The island jutted up from the brink of a dreadful

212

precipice, which stretched away from it in either direction for as far as the castaways could see. Over this precipice, like a world-wide waterfall, the ocean went thundering in cataracts of foam. As they watched, the tree that had almost struck the cutter was swept over the brink and fell, turning over and over as it went, vanishing into the falling columns of water and then reappearing, flickering through the eternal rainbows that hung there in the spray, until it was lost among the mists below.

'It is sublime!' Constantine shouted.

'I am glad you like it,' replied Will. 'For I do not see any way off this rock. We are trapped here.'

## 28

# THE TEMPLE ON THE SHORE

Captain Bulstrode announced that the island should be named after the King, and insisted that it must be explored before nightfall. But the exploration did not take long. King George Island was no more than three miles wide, and consisted mostly of grassland, with a forest of low oak trees. In a sheltered cove not far from the landing place the midshipmen found a crumbling structure, which might once have been a sort of temple, but whether it was a sign that the island had once been inhabited, or whether it had been raised by an earlier group of castaways, it was impossible to say. On the island's highest point there stood a mass of granite rocks which put Will in mind of the tors at home on Wildsea. Constantine, peering into a cleft between them, startled a small deer which almost bowled him over. 'So at least we shall not starve,' he said, as the deer went crashing away through the undergrowth.

'How curious,' said Will, 'for the island is not large, and we have seen no other deer.'

'Hiding, no doubt,' said Captain Bulstrode. 'We shall flush them out tomorrow.'

They ate salt beef that night, and ship's biscuit, and slept in the grass at the top of the beach. But although Will was wearier than he had ever felt before, he lay for a long time awake, thinking of Wildsea and wondering how he was ever to get home. At last, tired of turning the same gloomy thoughts over and over in his brain, he rose and took a walk over the headland and down into the cove where the old temple stood.

It had been built below the tideline, the feet of its crude pillars shaggy with bladderwrack and scabbed with barnacles. Perhaps a statue of the Gorm had stood there once, Will thought. If it had, the sea had long since carried it away. But that did not matter. Because there, in front of the temple, waiting for him by the light of the strange stars, was the Gorm herself.

The stars did not, in truth, cast very much light, faint as they were behind the drifting spray. The Gorm shone mostly with her own light, eerie and submarine. She was very beautiful. Will could see how his brother Drewe had fallen in love with her when he first met her walking in this form on the beaches of Wildsea.

He bowed. 'Your servant, madam.'

'You are far from home, Watcher,' said the Gorm.

'I am, and it is your hand that brought me here, I believe.'

'It is. I have brought you here because there is a doorway on this island. It leads into the forests of the Hunter.'

'A way home?'

'Not for you, Will Dark. The entrance on Wildsea has been shut up, and your wood-wife has been shut up inside it.'

'Aish? But how –?'

'She is in the Hunter's Wood, and she shall not get free of it without your help, Will Dark.'

Will, whose strength throughout this whole ordeal had come entirely from knowing that Aish was safe at home, collapsed on the damp sand at the Gorm's feet. 'What must I do?'

'Go into the wood. Find her. Come out again. I shall do the rest.'

Will glanced up at her. 'Why would you help me?'

Her eyes, which had been a cool grey till then, became for just a moment the colour of sunlight on a summer sea. 'Because Utterly would wish it.'

'And where is Utterly?'

'She is lost to me.'

'And where is Egg?'

'He is with her.'

'I must help them too . . .' said Will, starting to rise.

The Gorm, reaching down, put a fish-cold finger to his lips. 'Shhhh. They are in the Sea-that-will-be. I am afraid to go there again.'

'Afraid? You?' Will almost laughed. 'Of what can the mighty Gorm possibly be afraid?'

Her eyes grew grey again. Will thought he had angered her, but perhaps she was only ashamed.

'If Utterly is in peril,' he said, 'you must go to her.'

'Even though my power is faded there and I may be ensnared by the same creature that caught her, and trapped your Aish in the Hunter's Woods?'

'She is your child,' said Will. 'Of course you must. It is your duty, Gorm.'

The Gorm sighed, and then she was gone. Cold water swirled around Will's feet and rushed back down the sand into the sea. He had the strangest feeling that what he had thought was a woman had only been a wave, which had reared up over him in the moonlight and then withdrawn. Even the words she had spoken were fading from his memory. But he remembered the most pressing of them. He turned and ran from the temple, back across the beach, over the low headland to the landing place.

'Constantine,' he said, shaking his friend awake. 'There is a door here somewhere – a door into the Underwoods. That is why the Gorm has brought us here . . .'

'A door?' Constantine rose, rubbing the sleep out of his eyes. Around them, the men from the *Acantha* slumbered on like so many logs washed ashore by the tide.

'That deer,' said Will. 'I thought at the time a deer seemed odd, just one solitary deer, alone on such an island. It came out of the Underwoods, I'll warrant. Let us find our way back to the opening from which it emerged . . .'

## 29

# THE WOODLINGS

'Lord, Will,' said Constantine, as they climbed away from the sea. 'We used to think you rather a dull fellow when we lived in London. But what a life you lead! Sea goddesses. Land goddesses. Secret doors. Unearthly woods. The whole world flat instead of globular . . .'

'I am sorry you are tangled up in it all,' said Will.

'Oh, do not apologize. I am envious, if anything. You have seen so much more of the world than I have. So much more of *several* worlds, indeed. These Underwoods, for instance. You say they are ruled over by a very dreadful fellow?'

'I said they *were*,' said Will, and crossed his fingers, hoping it were true. 'The Hunter is gone. The Gorm destroyed him. But I suppose his woods may have come under new management, and are now the domain of some other evil thing.'

'Well, let us find out,' said Constantine. 'For look, we are come to the very spot where we surprised that deer.'

Dawn had begun to break while they were climbing the slopes of the island. The rocks towered over them in the gathering light, and from the wooded cleft between the two largest, a little laughing stream emerged. Will made his way to the cleft and peered in. It did not seem very deep, and yet a smell came out of it that was the smell of growth and decay and the endless intricate life of great trees. It told him, as clearly as if a sign had been posted there, that he stood at one of the lost gateways to the Underwoods.

'Is this the place?' asked Constantine, craning to see over Will's shoulder.

'I believe so. And if the Gorm was telling me the truth, Aish is in there, and I must go in after her, though I am not certain how I am to find her in such a maze of trees. Constantine, you should go back to the boat and tell Bulstrode and the others where I am.'

'No, indeed!' declared Constantine. 'I am eager to see these Underwoods for myself.'

Will started to protest that the Underwoods were no place for a holiday, that they were, indeed, a dreadful place – but he did not protest too much, for he was very afraid, and very grateful for Constantine's company. So he reached out and patted his friend's shoulder by way of thanks, and then together they crept deeper into the cleft, where oaks and grey willows spread their shade over them, until Will looked up and found that they had crossed the threshold to the Underwoods without noticing, and its huge, shaggy trees stood all around them.

'Uncanny!' whispered Constantine. (For the Under-woods were like a cathedral; it was difficult to speak in anything but whispers there.)

'It is unsettling at first,' Will whispered back. 'And then, when you grow accustomed to it, it is still more unsettling.'

'But beautiful,' murmured Constantine, leaning back to gaze up at the forest canopy.

'Aish!' called Will, breaking the age-old quiet.

There was no answer, except that the trees seemed to lean in a little closer, and some unseen thing went scampering along a branch above his head. Looking up, he noted that the trees were bare, but bore a first faint flush of green where new leaves were waiting to unfurl.

He stooped and gathered a handful of white stones from the bed of the stream, filling his pockets with them, and encouraging Constantine to do the same. 'This place is a labyrinth,' he said, 'and we must leave ourselves a trail through it. The Hunter may no longer rule these thickets, but Aish said once that there were worse things than the Hunter here. If we meet with any of them, we shall need to find our way back to the entrance in a hurry.'

Carefully dropping a stone every few paces, they began picking their way deeper into the trees.

'You have slandered this place, Will,' said Constantine when they had been walking for an hour or so. 'You spoke of it as Stygian and oppressive. But it is nothing of the sort! These ancient trees are glorious, and there is such a feeling in the air . . .' He set his hand against the mossy flank of an immense oak, and fancied that he could feel the beat of its tree-ish heart as it drew water up through its roots, and pumped sap out to the green tips of its crown of branches. He recalled more clearly now the world that he had dreamed of when he was small: it had been a wood much like this, infinite and wonderful. He felt as if he had come home. 'I declare,' he told Will, 'if I lived among these trees, I would never have needed wine or wild parties to divert me. That scent in the air, and the sound of the wind in the branches, they would be entertainment enough.'

'And you would dine upon acorns, I suppose? And when you lay down at night, the birds would tuck you up under a coverlet of leaves, like the poor babes in the nursery tale . . .' Will felt immune to the beauties and wonders of the Underwoods himself. When you have been pursued through a place by the forefather of all hunters, it tends to lose quite a lot of its appeal. The only feeling that came to him when he looked into the gloom between the trees was an increasingly urgent desire to find Aish and be gone as swiftly as possible.

'Aish!' he called, for perhaps the two-hundredth time.

By way of answer, a flint-tipped arrow came chirring down out of the maze of branches overhead and stuck quivering in a tree just inches from his face. It was so bright in its featherings, and so swift and singing in its flight, Will thought it was a bird at first, and stared at it dumbly for a full two seconds before he realized that he was under attack.

'Arrow!' he squeaked, and then, finding his voice again: 'An arrow, Constantine! Take care!'

Swift scamperings were going on up in the canopy. Sticks and acorns rained down, and enough of them hit Will and Constantine to make it clear they had been aimed deliberately. Squinting upwards, they glimpsed small figures scrambling about among the branches, and leaping like lemurs from one tree to the next.

'What are those?' Constantine said, shielding his face as more twigs fell on him. 'Monkeys?' Another arrow whirred past and stuck in the earth between Will's feet. 'Monkeys with bows and arrows?'

'When Miss Inshaw told us of her sojourn in this world she spoke of people she termed "woodlings"' recalled Will. 'She said they made their home among the trees. Doubtless we have alarmed them. She did not speak of them as being unfriendly . . .'

He leaned out from beneath the heavy bough he had taken shelter under and called, 'Hello! I say, there! We mean you no harm, good woodlings. We have only come looking for Aish.'

A few more sticks fell, but no further arrows. There was movement overhead, and Will thought he heard some hurried whispers. Then, down the trunks of the trees, the woodlings came creeping, as wary and bright-eyed as wild animals.

They were a small people, and went mostly naked, except for lengths of ivy, which they wore as wreaths around their heads. Their hair was the colours of autumn leaves, and their faces were silvery pale, like masks of birch bark. A few had bows, and quivers of arrows hung from ivy belts around their waists. Others carried knives of knapped flint, which they held out in front of them as they advanced upon the newcomers. 'Aish shall stay,' they hissed. 'You shall not take her. Aish is ours. This place is hers.'

'This is good news, Will,' Constantine whispered. 'They have heard of Aish!'

'But it is bad news too,' Will whispered back, 'for I believe they mean to murder us . . .'

The woodlings indeed looked very fierce. Their eyes glinted as sharply as their flinty blades. The ones with bows had set arrows to their strings and seemed to be waiting only for the order to shoot Will and his companion where they stood. But before matters could grow any worse there came a commotion and another band of woodlings appeared running through the trees, calling out in birdlike voices to the hunting party. And behind these newcomers, towering over them like an adult surrounded by eager children, came Aish.

'Oh put away your arrows now, and all your fearsome knives,' she said, 'for these dear folk are friends of mine. Look, here is Mr Constantine! And here is my own Will Dark!'

# 30

# FAREWELL TO THE UNDERWOODS

'These good woodlings have looked after me,' said Aish, leading Will and Constantine to a dell between two massive oaks where a sort of shelter had been built for her. 'They are the people of this world, though they were too scared of the Hunter to show themselves last time we visited. Now he is gone, and they have grown less shy. I should have been lost without them. They drove off a troop of wolves who had grown impertinent without the Hunter to keep them in check. And look, they have made me this pleasant house, from branches and bark and deerskins, and they have found me food, even in the depths of winter. It is much like the tale of Snow White and the Seven Dwarfs, except there are far more than seven woodlings, and I am rather too large to be Snow White.'

Indeed she was. Will, now that he was over his first joy at seeing her, was quite astonished by how enormous she had grown since the last time he saw her, which had only been two days before, or maybe three. But time moved quite differently in the Underwoods, and it seemed that for Aish several months had gone by.

'We must return to Wildsea with all haste,' he said, 'or our children will be born here in the Underwoods.'

'But how can we return?' asked Constantine. 'We would be better staying in these delightful woods, for the only exit we know of will let us out onto that nubbin at the world's edge where Bulstrode and the others are marooned. I can see no way home from there.'

'Perhaps the Gorm will find a way for us,' said Aish. 'Her kindness brought you here to me after all.'

'It is curious to think of the Gorm as kindly,' said Will.

'And yet she is, Will Dark. It is the Gorm's great seas which brought forth fish and birds and people, and governed the weathers which made the plants grow. Her angers and her cruelties frighten me, yet without her kindness, the world would be but a sad place. That is why I fear Lord Langdale more, for he is a thing of stone, and there is no kindness in him at all. As I learned when he entrapped me here.'

'I curse myself that I did not see through his disguise,' said Constantine. 'He seemed just an eccentric and dis-agreeable old man to me.'

'And to me, Mr Constantine,' said Aish, reaching out to pat his hand consolingly. 'But we must not sit here a-blaming ourselves. We must find our way home to Wildsea, and frustrate his knavish tricks.'

The woodlings had been watching them talk all this while, and whispering among themselves. Now one, slightly bolder than the rest, who wore a necklace of fir-cones and rabbit skulls, which Will thought marked her as their queen, came forward and said, 'Aish, you must not go. This is your own place now. Winter fell when the Hunter went away. Then you came to us and spring returned.'

'Aish stays,' whispered the others. 'This is her place now. You shall not take her.'

'But, my dears, they are not *taking* me; I go of my own accord,' said Aish. She looked around at the earnest faces of the woodlings who surrounded her, and then up at those of the many others who clustered in the branches above her little camp. 'I have told you often and often that I have a place I love already. It is my own place, and it is far from here, on Wildsea, and I shall be sorely missed if I do not go home.'

'But if you go, spring will go with you,' the woodlings whispered. They reached out their small hands and touched her. 'If Aish goes, it will be winter always.'

Aish smiled sadly at them. 'Never. It is not me who has brought spring back to this place, but you yourselves. Old things like me sprang into being when the world was new, for how can a thing become itself if there is nobody there to see it? So the first sea rolled, and the Gorm was born, to exult in its wildness and dream strange fishes into being in its deeps. And the first trees grew, and the Hunter awoke; the idea of a forest made flesh. And even on Wildsea, when the wind blew through the oaks, some-one was required to watch and listen and to love them, and that was me. But there is no need for us old things any more, not with so many other sorts of people in the world to witness it. The Hunter has been cast down, as all tyrants are eventually, and his forest is yours now. Guard it carefully, and love it well, and spring will come, and all the other seasons in their turn.'

'Stay, Aish stay,' some of the woodlings wept. But Aish took off the twig-crown they had made for her, and placed it with great solemnity in the wood-queen's hands. Shy woodlings ran to her and hugged her, and woodling children wrapped their skinny arms around her legs. She returned their hugs, then gently pushed them away, and looked at Will. He held out his hand to her, and she took it.

'Look after your trees for me,' she told the woodlings. 'And if ever we can move the great huge rock that seals the entry-way on Wildsea, I shall come back and visit you.'

The woodlings, though sorrowful, seemed satisfied by what she said. Aish, still holding Will's hand, turned to leave. But Constantine, having come with them a little way, stopped and stood looking crestfallen.

'Why, whatever is the matter, Mr Constantine?' asked Aish.

'You may be ready to leave this place,' said Constantine. 'But I am not. It is a very Eden you have brought me to, Will. Having seen it, I cannot just turn my back on it and leave, never to return.'

'But, Frank,' said Will, 'we cannot delay! Bulstrode and the others will be wondering what we are about, and there is Lord Langdale to deal with, and Aish's time is drawing near . . .'

'Oh, you must go, of course!' said Constantine. 'But I will not. You warned me that these woods were a place of terrors, but to me they are not terrible at all. With every hour that passes here I feel more keenly that I have come home. Why would I leave? How could I leave? How could I ever to go back to dreary old England, to face my debts and duties, knowing that the wind is blowing through these woods, and the deer are running . . .'

'Is he under some enchantment?' Will asked Aish.

'Only if love is an enchantment,' said Aish. 'For it is just as possible to fall in love with a place at first sight as it is with a person.'

'Indeed it is,' said Constantine, grateful that she

understood him. 'I feel as if this is where I was always meant to be, and what we call the real world was just a tawdry stage-set.'

'But that feeling may pass, Constantine,' said Will.

'Or it may deepen,' said Aish. 'It seems to me that somewhere down among the roots of Mr Constantine's family tree there may have been a great-great-grandmother or ancient auntie who was born of the woods and wilds like me. Perhaps her love of such places has echoed down to him. Perhaps this is where he belongs, Will Dark . . .' She looked seriously at Constantine. 'You do understand that if you stay here there may be no way back into the ordinary world for you?'

'I know it,' said Constantine.

'No letters from home, no hot baths or feather beds, no doctor to call on if you fall ill, none of the conveniences folk in England are accustomed to?'

'In England I felt half asleep, dear Mrs Dark: here at least I shall be wide awake.'

Aish watched him carefully, and faint golden lights shifted in her eyes like sunbeams touching the bed of a stream, as often happened when she was thinking. 'You do not think that you will come to lord it over the woodlings, I trust? For they know this place far better than you.'

'I hope only to learn from them,' said Constantine.

Aish smiled, and went to the woodlings who were

following. 'This man wishes to remain with you,' she said. 'He is a good young man, though he does not know much. I hope you may look after him.'

The woodlings looked uncertainly at Constantine. 'They think I am a poor exchange for you, Mrs Dark,' he said ruefully.

But they were only bashful, and once they had overcome their shyness they gathered around him, eager to welcome him into their world and explain its ways to him.

Will hugged him, and Aish kissed his cheek, and there they left him, to embark upon stories of his own.

'Poor Constantine,' said Will, as they followed the trail of white stones back to their own world.

'*Lucky* Constantine, you mean. He has found the world that he belongs in.'

'Just like I did, when I washed up on Wildsea?'

'Just like that. Some people never do find the world they long for. Others are cast out of it, like Stone, and they yearn always to return, until the yearning makes them sad and bitter.'

'You sound almost as if you are sorry for Stone . . .'

'I am very sorry for him, and I am very certain that he must not get his way. Oh, Will Dark, I thought I would never see you again, and that our babies would grow up as woodlings, and that I would never see my own beloved hills again. And then I too might have grown sad and bitter, and behaved as badly as Stone does . . .'

Will was about to answer that he could not imagine her ever behaving badly when he noticed that the trees they were passing were not the giants of the Underwoods but only ordinary-sized grey willows and dwarf oaks. They were back on the island at the edge of the world, and someone was calling, 'Dark! Will Dark! Constantine!'

Will led Aish out of the shelter of the rocks. He felt rather as he imagined Orpheus must have when he led Eurydice out of the Underworld, and he was very careful not to glance back at her until they were safely out in the open air. There they found Mr Samuels and one of the midshipmen, who had been sent out as a search party when he and Constantine were discovered to be missing. They went back together to the landing place, where Will presented Aish to his shipmates, and explained Constantine's decision.

'Another world, eh?' asked Captain Bulstrode. 'Perhaps we should all follow Mr C's lead and make ourselves at home there. For I have been pacing the beaches since first light, observing the currents from every vantage point this island offers, and I am sorry to say I see no way we may ever sail away from here, not without being washed over that almighty cataract.'

But Aish said, 'What cataract, Captain Bulstrode? I do not see any difficulty.'

And somehow she was right. Will and the others looked about them and realized that it was not spray blowing across the beach at all, but only a little Scotch mist. That rushing in the air was not the voices of all the waters of the earth tumbling over its brim into eternity, just the west wind stirring the trees on the hill. And as for the sea, which had seemed torn by such deadly currents a moment ago, why, it now moved only in a gentle swell. They stood upon the shore of an isle that Will had observed several times from Sundown Watch, and sure enough, as he gazed out from the beach, he saw the hills of Wildsea in the distance, and sunlight glinting in the windows of the Watcher's Tower.

'Have we been here all along?' asked Mr Samuels. He looked at his hands, which were blistered from the desperate rowing of the day before. 'Did we only imagine the cataract, and the current that almost took us over it?'

'You did not imagine it,' said Aish. 'And yet you *have* been here all along. For you are in the Hidden Lands, where times and places get all mixed up, and one thing can become another, and there is seldom much point asking how or why. And it is no place for people like yourselves, or even for a person like me . . .' She paused, looking thoughtful, and pressed a hand to her belly. 'And it is *certainly* no place for children,' she went on. 'And since mine seem to be tired of being cooped up inside of me, and mean to come out soon and have a look about, I hope you will be able to sail or row us to Wildsea as fast as ever you are able.'

The men stared at her, not understanding at first, and then understanding all too well and looking quite appalled. Bulstrode started shouting orders, Mr Samuels began offering medical advice, Will and Hard-tack Joe helped Aish down to the cutter (although she insisted she did not need helping) and the midshipmen hurried about gathering up grass and moss to make a bed for her on the cutter's bottom-boards. And when it was all accomplished, and the cutter was making its way out into the swell, Will looked back at the island and whispered a private thank you to the Gorm.

But the island was already no more than fog upon the water, and the Gorm made no reply. *She is not here,* thought Will. *Perhaps she has conquered her fears, and gone to save Utterly from whatever strange seas Utterly is adrift in.*

And he hoped with all his heart she would succeed.

# 31

# NIGHT FISHING

Professor Stone was afraid that Utterly might try to leap into the sea and swim away, so he kept a tight hold of her wrist even when she was seated in the dinghy. It was a strange dinghy. Utterly thought at first it had been made from yellow logs, but the logs were a shiny fabric of some sort, plumped up with air. It looked most unseaworthy, but it floated well enough. Professor Stone pulled a cord, which set an engine buzzing like an angry bee, and the dinghy butted its way through the small waves and went very quickly out to the *Sea Witch*, where Jim and Nigel were standing by to receive Utterly as Stone lifted her bodily up to them.

'Straight into the rig with her,' ordered Stone, following Utterly aboard. 'We can't risk any more delays.' His face had a greenish look, but he seemed to have decided that a little seasickness was a price worth paying for the capture of the Gorm. The black cage stood on the deck behind the *Sea Witch*'s wheelhouse. Jim and Nigel led Utterly to it, and Stone opened it and pushed Utterly inside. Harriet came down from the deckhouse and attached various wires to her, and a kind of harness, which was tethered to the cage by a thick, springy tether.

'I'm sorry, Utterly,' Harriet whispered as she worked. 'He's threatening all sorts of trouble if we let you escape again. It's best if you just go along with him.'

'Something to say, Miss Castle?' asked Stone, watching her carefully.

Harriet made a face, and finished her work in silence. Then Professor Stone came and closed the cage. He tapped the bars with his knuckle. 'I had these forged from a meteorite that fell in the Atacama Desert,' he told Utterly. 'It's the driest place on the entire planet. These bars have never known the touch of the sea. And those panels you see around you . . .' He pointed to nine oblong plates which were bolted around the sides of the cage, pointing inwards. Utterly's reflection showed dimly in each, nine ghosts trapped in nine dark mirrors. 'The sea witches of old built circles of stone to try and hold the Gorm,' said Stone. 'Their reasoning was sound, but they lacked the right materials. Here is my stone circle: nine sheets of volcanic glass, coated with powdered moon rock I obtained from my contacts at NASA. The moon has power over the sea, as you know, and the glass was formed by the fiery breath of beings far older than the Gorm. Once she is between them . . .'

He clapped his hands, and turned to where his crew stood glumly watching. 'Well, people, what are we waiting for? The hook is baited. Let's go fishing.'

Something powerful churned in the little ship's insides and she dug herself down into the sea and surged away from Blanchmane's Cove, following the path the low sun laid across the waves until Wildsea was just a low line on the eastern horizon. There the engines were shut off, and in the sudden quiet that followed, Utterly heard gulls calling and the waves slapping mindlessly against the hull. Professor Stone's people stood about expectantly while he strolled along the ship's side, looking suspiciously at the sea.

'This is about where the *Acantha* was when they sent down the diving bell,' he said. 'I daresay if we took a sample of the bottom we'd find primroses.'

'Primroses?' asked Nigel.

'Don't mind me,' said Professor Stone. 'A memory from another time. Let's get the rig in the water, and keep an eye on those instruments. Keep a lookout, but remember, we can't trust our eyes alone.'

A new engine started up, shattering the silence again. *How do the people of this century put up with all the din?* Utterly wondered. The cage lurched. She stood up, holding tightly to the bars as the crane lifted her clear of the deck and swung her out over the ship's side. The sea rose and fell beneath her, pale blue in the long, evening light, and most inviting.

*Perhaps I may slip free and swim away*, Utterly thought. *Perhaps the Gorm shall come, and find a way to let me out . . .*

Clinging to strong bars and fragile hopes, she was lowered down until the waves started to wash into the cage, soaking her trousers again and making her gasp at the cold as the water rose suddenly past her waist. Jim, operating the winch, paused, reluctant to submerge Utterly entirely, but Professor Stone shouted: 'Lower away!', and with a rush Utterly found herself beneath the sea.

She took a breath, as she done so often and so easily when she was underwater with the Gorm. But now that she was no longer with the Gorm, it seemed she had forgotten how. Salt seawater swirled down her throat and made her choke. She tried another panicky breath, and in came more. Very quickly she found that she was drowning, and she began to flail and struggle desperately, and beat with her hands against the bars and moon-dust mirrors of the cage, in the hope the watchers on the ship above would notice her distress and haul her up.

And the cage did start to rise. Later, she would learn

how Jim had seen what was happening and tried to save her. But Professor Stone had ordered him to leave the cage where it was and knocked him down when he refused. So, after one brief, hopeful, upward lurch the cage went down again, deeper than before. Professor Stone knew what the sea witch Thurza Froy had guessed all those years before: if there was one thing certain to call the Gorm out of her seclusion, it was danger to her daughter.

And the Gorm came. Utterly's eyes were fading by that time; she was too weak to struggle any more, and the sea seemed to darken around her. But there, in its unguessable depths, a light appeared, and grew until she was sure she could not be imagining it. And then the water in the cage was full of the scent of the Gorm, and the Gorm herself was there, swimming around and around outside the bars, staring in.

The cage had slid open invitingly. Utterly tried to find the strength to kick her way out of it, but she could not escape her tether. The Gorm hesitated, and then swam inside with her, but even her hands could not break the cord that held Utterly.

'Oh, child,' she said, taking Utterly in her arms.

'I am sorry I came here, mama,' said Utterly, recovering both her voice and her ability to breathe seawater. 'But you must swim quickly away, for he is only using me to trick you.'

'I know,' said the Gorm.

And even as she spoke, the cage closed upon them both, and she was trapped.

# 32

# THE RESCUERS

Ted Kennett was not a bad man, but he had heard the way Professor Stone carried on when Jill and Nigel and the others let the kids get away that afternoon, telling them they'd be out of a job if they tried such tricks again, and that he'd make sure they never got another. Kennett couldn't afford to lose his job, so he was making sure to do whatever the professor told him and not ask any questions. 'Take the boy back to Belfriars Bay', he'd said, so that's what Kennett did. Egg put up a fight, but Kennett was so much bigger and stronger that it was a very one-sided affair, and it ended with Egg being dumped unceremoniously on the back seat of the red car while Kennett got in the front and started the engine.

'It's for your own good, Prof Stone says,' he reassured Egg, glancing at him in the rear-view mirror as he backed the car out onto the coast road. 'You'll be safer at the Centre.'

Egg slid himself around on the shiny seat and tried the door handles, but the doors were locked, and the car was beginning to move at speed along the road. Egg had thought bikes went fast, but it was nothing to this. He left off his struggles with the door and clung on tight as the world went hurtling past outside. It was terrifying at first; then thrilling, and if he hadn't been worrying about Utterly he would have whooped with excitement. The speed pressed him into the soft cushions of the seat, and when Kennett suddenly brought the car to a screeching stop it flung him forwards, slamming him against the back of the chair in front.

'Ow!' said Egg. 'What did you do that for?'

'Out the way!' yelled Kennett, but he was not yelling at Egg. Scrambling up from the floor, Egg peered out through the big window at the front of the car and saw that the road ahead was blocked. Three bikes had stopped there, their wheels and handlebars gleaming in the sunset, their riders glaring at Mr Kennett.

'Flippin' kids!' grumbled Kennett, getting out of the car. 'Hop it!'

'Let him go!' shouted Luke.

'We saw you grab him!' Splodge yelled.

'You're a kidnapper!' screamed Sharon. 'We'll get the police on you!'

The mention of the police seemed to calm Mr Kennett a little. 'Come on, kids,' he said, in a more reasonable voice. 'This is Prof Stone's business. This lad belongs at the Centre, down Belfriars Bay. He'll be looked after there . . .'

Egg, meanwhile, was busy worming his way between the two front seats of the car. He slithered past the steering wheel and out through the open door, dropping onto the road behind Kennett. Kennett turned and saw him. 'Run, Egg! Run!' yelled Luke, Sharon and Splodge. Egg gathered himself up and ran, off the road and into the rough ground on the clifftop. Kennett came after him. For the first ten yards or so Egg could hear the big man panting close behind him, but then the sounds faded, and when he stopped and looked back Kennett was returning, winded, to his car, while the Gorm Sands Gang sat on their bikes and jeered at him.

Egg went on a short way and flung himself down in a dell at the cliff's edge to catch his breath and come up with a plan. Out on the sea, a boat was heading west along the path the low sun laid. Egg wondered how long he would have to live in this world before he got used to the sight of boats moving without sails or oars.

'Twit-twooo,' said someone in the gorse thickets behind him, trying to sound like an owl. Someone else repeated the call, a little further off. Egg grinned.. He cupped his hands around his mouth and did his own, rather more convincing, owl call. Soon afterwards, the bracken at the dell's edge rustled and Luke and Sharon appeared.

'I thought you'd given up on waiting for me,' Egg said. 'I was right glad to see you.'

'Splodge is watching the road in case that man comes back,' said Sharon. 'He drove off down to Belfriars. Maybe he's given up.'

'Or gone to get help,' said Luke.

'They've took Utterly,' said Egg.

'We know,' said Luke. 'We saw. We waited for you by the track, but you were gone ages and we had to get home for our tea. We came out again straight after though. We'd just got to the top of the cliff by the old house when we saw that red car pull in. We saw that geezer take your friend away.'

It looked like he was taking her down to the beach,' said Sharon. 'I bet he put her on that boat. Where's he taking her?'

Egg shook his head, then hid his face in his hands, as if the answer might be written on his own grimy fingers. It wasn't. He thought hard for a moment and said, 'We've got to tell someone.'

'We can't tell our mum and dad,' said Luke. 'They'd kill us if they knew we'd been up here. We said we were only going down the playground. If they knew we'd been fighting off actual kidnappers and such . . .'

'The police?' suggested Sharon.

Egg shook his head. That just sounded like a way to make things even more complicated, with lots of questions and bother. Meanwhile, Utterly was out there on that boat, a black mote now in the eye of the sinking sun.

'Dan and Mim,' he said. 'They'd help. Least, I'm pretty sure they would. But they're all the way up on the Dizzard . . . Do you reckon you could get me there on your bikes?'

Luke shook his head and checked the watch he wore strapped to his wrist. 'We're meant to be home by dark, and it's nearly that already.' He glanced at his sister, and made a big decision. 'You can borrow my bike, Egg.'

'But I don't know how to ride it.'

'It's easy. We'll teach you. Come on.'

'If it isn't young Egg,' said Dan Smy, opening his front door an hour after sundown. 'I wondered if you'd be back.'

Moths fussed around the lamp in the roof of the Smys' porch. Egg stood miserably in the pool of light beneath it, weary after his long ride from Sundown Watch. Luke's bike, slightly battered, leaned against the side of the porch. The Gorm Sands Gang had given him a five-minute lesson in riding a bike before they said goodbye at Marazea. He had picked up the finer points by trial and error on the way.

'I'm sorry I ripped the trousers,' he said. 'Some fool has made a wiry fence with great sharp prickles all over it and I tore 'em climbing over. And then I had that there bike to ride, and it weren't as easy as Luke and Sharon and Splodge made out, so I kept falling off – that's what the holes in the knees are.'

'I reckon Mim can patch those up,' said Dan. 'The main thing is, you're safe and sound. When we found you'd run off like that this morning we was worried, Mim and me. Mim had me drive right round to Merriport looking for you. Tess missed you too.'

Tess, hearing her cue, writhed her way past Dan and out into the porch. Egg crouched down to tickle her.

'Course, I know why you went off,' said Dan easily. 'You're in some sort of trouble, aren't you?'

Egg looked up at him. 'That's what I come back for. I thought I could sort it out myself but I ain't enough, not against Professor Stone and his crew. And you're the only folk I know on Wildsea nowadays except Luke and his lot, and they had to go home.'

'Professor Stone? You mean that scientist fellow, down at Belfriars?'

'He's got Utterly.'

'Got utterly what?'

'Utterly Dark. My friend. He's kidnapped her, and she escaped, but he got her back and now . . .'

Egg stopped, uncertain how to explain Stone's magic

247

or his scheme to catch the Gorm to someone who probably didn't believe in either. He felt he had already gone too far. Dan Smy must think he was raving.

But Dan just nodded. 'You'd best come in then. Mim and me, we generally have a cuppa and a biscuit this time of night. You come and join us, and you can tell us the whole story.'

'Well,' said Dan, twenty minutes and half a packet of chocolate digestives later, when Egg had told them everything. 'What do you think, Mim?'

Mrs Smy shook her head. 'I don't rightly know what to think,' she said. 'I've heard about the Gorm, of course I have, but I always thought she was just an old wives' tale. And Wildsea always has been a bit different from the more usual sorts of places. But all this travelling through time . . . are you sure about that part, young Egg?'

'It would explain the old-fashioned way Egg speaks,' said Dan. 'And those clothes he was in when he arrived. And why he's so surprised by photos, and the radio, and chocolate biscuits, and how come he doesn't know what barbed wire is. If he ain't come here from the old days then he's a proper good liar, and Egg doesn't strike me as a liar somehow. So the question is, what do we do about it?'

'Well, you can whip those trousers off, Egg, and let me stitch up them holes before they get any bigger,' said

Mim. 'And then we should do something about this Utterly. If they've really got a girl held prisoner at that research centre, we need to get her out.'

Dan looked at Egg. 'Mim has a knack of getting straight to the heart of things,' he said fondly. 'And the heart of this business is your friend Utterly. We need to make sure she's safe before we do anything else.'

'They were taking her out on their ship,' said Egg, eyeing the biscuit tin and wondering if this would be a good time to ask for another. 'They was going to use her as bait to catch the Gorm.'

'Well, we can't do much while they're at sea,' said Dan. 'But I'm guessing whether they catch this Gorm or no, they'll be heading back to Belfriars Bay, so that's where we'll go too. I'd like a word with this Stone.'

'It's a job for the police, ain't it, Dan?' asked Mim. 'I mean . . . kidnappings and all . . .'

'It would be a job for higher-up police than the Merriport bobbies,' said Dan. 'They'd have to report up to Lamontane or Scotland Yard or somewhere, and I don't think Scotland Yard would believe Egg's story as easy as we do. Here on Wildsea we're sort of at the edge of things, so believing stuff comes easier to us. I'm not saying we couldn't convince 'em, but it would take time. No, we need to find Utterly first. Then we'll call in the police, if we still think we need 'em.'

He stood up and went out into the hallway. Egg

realized he was putting on his coat. 'I'm coming too!' he said.

'No, you stay here, Egg,' Mim told him.

'We'll all go,' said Dan.

# 33

# DRY CONTAINMENT

The *Sea Witch* sped back to Belfriars Bay with her catch. The cage sat on deck, and Utterly sat inside it, while her mother raged, and shrieked, and vowed terrible revenge, and strained with all her might against the bars. If she had been able to turn herself into a wave or a weed-thing she should have been able to snap such spindly little bars like spills of wood, but there was no weed here to weave a giantess from, and within Professor Stone's circle of moon-dust mirrors she seemed dreadfully weakened, just as he had said she would be. She was no stronger than a mortal woman now, and all her struggles achieved nothing, except to make her weaker and still more furious.

And then they were at the quay, and the cage was

unhitched from the *Sea Witch* and manoeuvred onto a sort of motor wagon, which towed it to the building at the base of the cliffs. Utterly had not been in there before, and when the big doors were slid open to let the wagon drive inside, she found she had not been missing much. Lamps hanging from the metal roof filled the bare interior with harsh white light. The floor was smooth, and in its centre was a circular hole, like a dry well, ten feet deep and ten wide. Into this the cage was lowered, but it was not unlocked, even though Utterly did not think she could possibly have climbed out of the well. Machines ranged along the walls rumbled steadily, filling the place with a headachey drone. Professor Stone ordered his people out and strolled around the well's rim, looking down.

'So this is the Gorm,' he said. He had kept out of the way during the voyage home, afraid of her sea magic while he was at sea. Now a horrible confidence filled him. 'You are in my dry containment facility, my lady,' he said. 'Even if you were to find your way somehow out of the cage, this chamber is far above the tideline. De-humidifiers keep the air in here as dry as the Sahara. None of your deep-sea trickery can help you here. You have lost the game, O Gorm: I, Stone, have outwitted you.'

The Gorm stared up at him with ice-white eyes. She opened her mouth and roared like storm-waves breaking on a shingle strand. Stone only laughed.

'There is only one way out of here for you and your child. It is very simple. You must give me what I want. The power to move as you move, through all the different ages of the world.' He squatted down on the well's edge and looked down at his prisoners quite earnestly. 'Open a way into deep time for me, and I shall let you go, O Gorm. For I wish to walk on rock unsullied by the slimes of life, and hear the songs of the Oldest Ones again, and behold them for myself in all their fiery glory.'

The Gorm went on hissing, went on raging. Stone might as well have said his piece to a winter sea, thought Utterly. But slowly her mother collected herself enough to say, 'Never! Never! Only I may swim the seas of time.'

Professor Stone shrugged. 'As you wish,' he said, rising to his feet. 'I shall leave you here in this dry well a while to think it over and see if you change your mind.'

He walked away. The white lights went off one by one, and a door opened and closed. The machines droned on in darkness. The air was so dry it made Utterly's eyes feel scratchy. Beside her, the Gorm made soft sobbing sounds. Utterly reached out and found her hand and held it.

'Egg is here,' she said. 'He'll save us.'

'The boy is powerless against Stone,' whispered the Gorm. 'Even I am powerless here.'

'That is why you told me not to come,' said Utterly. 'I did not know. I thought you ruled the sea in all times.'

'I wanted you to believe it,' said the Gorm. 'It was my pride, I suppose. But, Utterly, the age you were born into is the last age when magic dared to show itself, and the tide was turning even then. Humans had already begun to grow too clever, and now they have grown cleverer still, and there is no place left for the old things in their world. That is why I drew a veil over the Hidden Lands, and venture no more into the seas of men. But Stone has used the humans' cleverness to make his own small powers far greater, and he has lured me out. I have never felt so far from the sea. I cannot live, so far from the sea.'

'It is my fault,' said Utterly. 'It is my fault.'

She felt terribly guilty, and terribly sorry for the Gorm. And how strange that felt, to pity the Gorm. For all Utterly's life the very name had been a source of terror, a thing to whisper, *the Gorm, the Gorm*. All the power of the sea had been in that name, the deep inhuman power that drowned people and ships and cities and re-made the land. And now here the great Gorm cowered, caged, the glow of small lights on machines somewhere above lighting up the curve of her pale face like the faintest misty crescent of a new moon. In this new century her power was as nothing next to the strength of men.

'You must do as he asks,' said Utterly. 'You must help Stone swim back to the beginning of things.'

'Never,' said the Gorm. 'Even if I did, he would not spare us. The war between the land and the sea has raged

254

through all the ages of the world. Stone scents victory at last. He will not let us go.'

Her voice was failing. Utterly could sense her growing weaker. 'You must rest, Mother,' she said. The Gorm subsided to the dry floor, and Utterly held her and stroked her drying hair as if she were the parent and the Gorm her sickly child. 'It will be all right,' she whispered, and she still thought it might, because she was an optimistic sort of girl, and she hoped Egg might yet think of something. If only she could carry the Gorm back to the sea's edge, she thought, she could swim away, and leave this unpleasant century behind.

But time went by, unmeasured and unmeasurable in the dark, and the Gorm's breathing grew fainter and fainter.

At last, the lights came on again, filling the well with their arctic glare. Utterly was shocked at how small and helpless the Gorm looked. Her skin was blotchy, her dry lips chapped. Her hair, no longer stirred by unseen currents, draped limply over her face.

Professor Stone's shadow reached down into the well. 'So,' he said cheerfully. 'You have had some time to think. What have you decided?'

Utterly had thought her mother was past hearing; unconscious; already at the threshold of death. But at the sound of Stone's voice her eyes moved behind her closed eyelids and her lips parted a little, and she whispered, 'Never.'

Utterly felt Professor Stone's rage coming off him like the heat off an oven. 'Then you shall lie there, and dry there, and die there,' he said. 'And when you are gone, I shall be the one to step into your place.'

Utterly squeezed her mother's hand. She had come to realize, as she sat there in the dark, that it would be her job to confront Stone while the Gorm was in this weakened state. She had been afraid that she would not be brave enough. But now the moment had arrived, and it was not a question of being brave or not; there was simply no alternative.

She rose to her feet, looking up into the white glare of the lamps. 'No, Professor Stone,' she said. 'You are right that when someone like my mother dies something else assumes their power and steps into the void they leave. But that someone will not be you. It will be me. You have left me sitting here an hour or more while my poor mother grows weaker, and as she weakens, I feel myself grow stronger.'

And in truth, she did feel rather strange. She had only meant to unsettle Professor Stone by saying what she did, but now she wondered if she had stumbled on a truth. There was a sort of dizziness that had been rising her, a sort of deep trembling excitement, which she could not entirely put down to the terrors of her situation. And although Professor Stone had closed the door when he came in, she found that she could hear the sea very clearly. Beyond the research centre's chain-link fences small waves were breaking on the shore, and as each one broke she felt the tug of the sea drawing it back.

'It is for this that I was born,' she said. 'Why did the Gorm have me when she did? Perhaps it is because she knew great change was coming, and wanted a daughter to inherit her powers. A human daughter for a human age.'

Professor Stone snorted with laughter. 'You? But you are nothing! No one! We proved yesterday that you can no more open a way for me than you can fly to the moon.'

'I am stronger today,' said Utterly.

'You will die with your mother. Then the power that is flowing from her into you will all be mine.'

'Will it?' said Utterly. 'The Gorm swims through time, and you cannot swim at all, old stone. You do not even like going out to sea on your iron boat. But I could guide you, because I am of the sea *and* the land. If you promise to spare my mother, I shall take you to where you want to go. I mean, I suppose, to *when* you want to go.'

Professor Stone watched her carefully while she spoke, and did not laugh at her this time, and Utterly knew that she had convinced him. He clapped his hands together. 'Very well,' he said. 'It is a bargain. Open a way for me, and I shall let her go.'

Utterly did not believe he meant to keep his word, but what else could she do? She had no hope of escape while she was in his cage. If she were outside of it, however, something might occur to her. So she whispered good-bye to the Gorm, and told her to be strong until she returned. Meanwhile, Professor Stone came down a ladder of metal rungs set into the wall of the well and unlocked the cage, keeping a watchful eye on the Gorm the whole time. Utterly climbed up the ladder, and Professor Stone locked the cage behind her and followed her up.

'Might we not give her just a cupful of seawater?' asked Utterly, looking down at the lifeless figure of the Gorm. 'Just a thimbleful, till we return.'

'A nice try, Miss Dark,' said Stone. 'But even a drop might be enough to start her working her magics against me. Show me the way into deep time. Then, perhaps, we shall attend to her.'

# 34

# THE BEACH

Outside, the night air was cool and filled with the smell of the sea. A big yellow moon was rising above the headland. It was a good night for magic, Utterly thought.

Professor Stone started walking towards the building with the sea-pool where Utterly had tried and failed to see the Hidden Lands the day before. But there was something too square and enclosed about that pool, thought Utterly. So she made him take her to the beach instead, right at the southern end of Belfriars Bay, where long ledges of naked rock sloped down into the waves.

'You plan to have me slip in and drown, I suppose?' said Stone, as Utterly climbed onto the nearest of the ledges.

She shook her head. 'Take off your shoes, sir. Then you won't slip so easily.'

Stone stood watching her, certain she had some plan and trying to understand what it was. But Utterly had no plan at all. Perhaps if she really could take him back to the world he so longed to see, she thought, it might melt his heart, and persuade him to free the poor Gorm after all. It seemed unlikely, but it was the last hope she had left.

He climbed up onto the ledge behind her, and Utterly started to lead the way down towards where the waves were washing over the rock, very pale and clear in the moonlight. One came foaming over her bare feet, and at once she felt what she had not been able to feel the day before. The sea was full of tastes and flavours, just as it had been when she was swimming with the Gorm. It was like a tapestry of many coloured threads, and every thread was a current that led to another cove, or another deep, or another island, or another time.

The moon tore free of the scratchy scrub on the cliff top. The waves sighed. Behind the square, golden windows of the building where Stone's scientists lived and ate, music was pulsing faintly, adding its own rhythm to the complex rhythms of the sea. Out on the dark horizon, beneath the stars, Utterly saw the faint shapes of islands rising where no islands should be.

'The Hidden Lands,' murmured Stone, sounding ready to cry.

'Come,' said Utterly, taking his hand.

She went forward one step and then another until the waves were lapping around her knees. Stone stayed on the dry rock beyond their reach, his arm outstretched, holding tightly to her hand. The waves tugged at Utterly's ankles, and sea magic tugged at her mind, inviting her to follow this current or that to seas where whales were playing or clouds of bright fish swirled in giddy formations like flocks of birds.

She ignored them. Closing her eyes, she sought through all the whispering strands of the sea until she found one that carried the scent of sulphur and the earth's deep fires. It had come a long way, that scent, through ages unimaginable, and it was so faint she almost lost it, but her senses seemed keener than before, and she kept hold of it, and since she was of the sea and of the land she did not even have to swim; she just stood there knee-deep in the waves holding Stone's hand, and the tides of time carried them both away.

The cold stars wheeled overhead. The old moon waxed and waned. Like slow breaths the sea sighed in and out, in and out, and beneath it all lay the slow heartbeat of the earth itself as it whirled on its endless course around the sun. And there stood Utterly upon another beach, or on the same beach perhaps but in another time, and the waves that washed her feet were warm as bathwater, and Stone let go of her hand, and cried out in wonder.

For Utterly had brought him to the world he longed for. No blade of grass stirred as the hot wind blew; no tree raised its leaves beneath the smoky, sullen sky. No life at all seemed to exist here yet, unless the gaudy patches of slime which coated the rocks along the sea's edge were alive. The sea itself seemed weary, flopping in little exhausted wavelets against the shore. Further out, bleak stacks of shattered stone broke the swell. The air tasted of burnt metal.

'It is as I remember!' said Stone. 'It is just as I remember it! A world of stone and fire! I have been waiting so long . . . Thank you, Miss Dark!'

But Utterly felt something was wrong. This world did not feel like any she had visited with the Gorm. Why was the sea so slack and greasy? Why was the smoke-streaked sky so strange?

She turned. Inland, the horizon was rippling. The sky above it filled slowly with an awful light. A great dome of dull red fire was rising from the shattered skyline. It widened, and heaved itself upwards, and became a sun; huge, swollen, ancient; a dying ember in the hearth of space. It filled the eastern sky entirely, and as it rose the hot wind gusted, blowing dust and sulphurous steams into Utterly's face, making her eyes sting, catching at her throat.

'Oh, Professor Stone!' she said. 'This is not the world that you remember! This is a world that is yet to come!'

She turned round and around, looking everywhere for some sign of human life. Even a ruin would have been encouraging; even a few bleached bones would have felt companionable. But there was nothing. Aeons had passed, empires had risen and fallen, everything she knew or could imagine had lived out its allotted time and passed away, and now even the sea was dying.

'I have made a mistake,' she told Stone. 'I have not brought you to the beginning of things, but to their end!'

Stone raised a trembling hand to bid her be silent. He did not seem angry with her. Indeed, all the anger and sternness seemed to have drained away from him. His face, lit by the glare of that dreadful sunrise, looked kinder and more handsome than before. He seemed enchanted by this place. 'Listen!' he said. 'Oh, *listen!*'

And Utterly heard it. The sound had been too deep for her small ears to catch at first; just a low vibration thrumming in her bones. Now it rose a little, and a little more, then it deepened again. She realized it was a song; an immensely slow, immensely long song, sung by things of unimaginable size swimming just beneath the world's scorched skin.

'They are here!' laughed Stone, and his delighted laughter echoed strangely among the scorched black rocks and the valleys of dust. 'The Oldest Ones!'

The ground heaved. The hills behind the beach twisted and shuddered and finally tore apart. Utterly thought it was as if the earth was a Seville orange, and the hot red hands of the sun were squeezing it until its skin split and the bright juices spurted out. Fountains of lava leaped into the sky. Rivers of molten rock gushed their way down the mountainsides and spilled across the coastal plain. Wherever they touched the sea, it erupted into steam.

'Professor Stone! Professor Stone! We must depart!' Utterly shouted. She was afraid the sea would boil away entirely and leave them with no means of escape.

But Stone had utterly forgotten Utterly. He did not care that he had come to the end rather than the beginning. The old things of the world were singing, and their songs were the songs he remembered from his earliest days, and had missed so bitterly in all the lonesome years he had lived through since. He raised his hands in exultation and ran towards the cataracts of fire. For a moment, squinting through the falling ash, Utterly kept him in sight as he leaped between the streams of lava. Perhaps it was only the fiery light playing tricks upon her eyes, but she thought he changed as he ran, losing his mannish shape and becoming something larger, craggier, and harder to describe, until he was lost entirely in the brightness. And something too huge for Utterly to comprehend burst free of the world's crust and unfurled itself into the sky in pillars of smoke and wings of golden fire.

The world rang now with the slow, stony song of the Oldest Ones. They had sung the old earth into being, and now they were singing it towards its end. Utterly turned and fled, down the slope of that last beach and into the warm waves. Plunging through the film of greasy ash that clogged the surface, she swam down, down, until the light of the dying sun was only a deep red glow far above her. And there at last, in the black deeps where the world's last tiny creatures wriggled and squiggled through their brief lives, she caught a faded scent of her mother, and of Wildsea.

The sea cooled around her. A wave gathered her up and carried her ashore, and she staggered out of the surf only a yard or two from the shelf of rock where she had been standing with Professor Stone.

It was still night. Indeed, it was still the same night, judging by the big moon gawping down at her. Across the beach the beams of electric torches wavered. Feet scrunched on the shingle, and voices shouted, 'Utterly!'

Utterly stumbled towards them, seawater squirting from her wet sandals. Harriet caught her and said, 'Utterly! Where is Professor Stone? Jim said he saw you both going down to the shore . . .'

Torch beams blinded Utterly. The others surrounded her: Nigel, Jill, Jim.

'The kid's wet through . . .'

'I think she's in shock . . .'

'Stone must have fallen in . . .'

Jim ran towards the sea, shouting for Professor Stone. His voice rang from the cliffs behind the bay. Up at the top of the steep road, the lamps of a motor carriage appeared, and started down.

'I must help my mother,' Utterly said, pulling free of Harriet, and trying to shake away the memories of that other beach, and the dying world around it. 'You have to let me in to see the Gorm . . .'

## 35

# THE SEA RISES

Harriet, Nigel and Jill went with Utterly to the building at the cliff's foot where the Gorm was held. Nigel had spare keys on a chain attached to his belt. When he opened the door dry air rolled out, flavoured with dust. Jill turned the lights on. While they were still flickering Utterly ran to the well's edge, and looked down.

The Gorm sprawled on the floor of her cage. She did not appear to have moved since Utterly left her.

Jill ran to fetch medicine, but what good could medicine do the Gorm? Utterly climbed down into the well, and Nigel took the keys from his belt and threw them down to her. With an effort, she unlocked the cage, and went in, and knelt down beside her mother.

'Oh, Gorm!' she said.

The Gorm looked not much bigger than Utterly now. She was not beautiful any more. She had lost her lustre, like one of those pebbles that shines with a hundred delicious colours when you find it in a tide-pool, but turns dull and grey when you bring it home and set it on the mantelpiece. If the pulse still beat in her throat, it beat so faintly now that Utterly could not tell.

'Oh, Gorm,' said Utterly again. 'I have swum in the last sea, at the end of all things. I left Professor Stone there, and now I am back.'

'Utterly,' said Harriet, watching from above. Nigel hushed her.

The Gorm said nothing at all.

Utterly was trembling. The memory of that final beach still haunted her. She could not forget the taste of ash, or the deep song of the things that writhed under the earth. She felt that she would never be able to forget it. To have been through all that and still have failed was more than she could bear.

Tears filled her eyes, and trickled down her face, and tickled saltily at the corners of her mouth. Each drop was like its own little sea. First one and then another fell, and wet her mother's lips.

The Gorm's eyes twitched fitfully behind their lilac lids. Her mouth opened just a little, and the tip of her blue tongue emerged and moved left and then right, tasting the salt of Utterly's tears.

Wild hope jolted Utterly into action. She was suddenly aware of the discomfort of her damp clothes, still soggy from their soaking in the sea. She squeezed the fabric of her T-shirt until water welled from it. She shook her wet hair and drops of seawater fell like small rain upon the Gorm's dry face.

'Oh, Gorm, Gorm!' she said.

'Is she all right?' asked Nigel, up above. 'Shall I call an ambulance?'

'Shhh!' said Jill.

The Gorm opened her eyes. They had turned to the colour of dry sand.

'Gorm?' whispered Utterly.

The Gorm looked at her, and her eyes moistened, and turned sea-blue, and then sea-green, and then midwinter-storm-sea-grey. The power that Utterly had felt filling her as her mother faded all drained away now, flowing out of her like a tide, flowing back into the Gorm.

'Utterly,' said the Gorm, and then, more loudly, 'Utterly,' and then, as she remembered where she was and how she had come there, she shouted, 'UTTERLY!'

The sea answered her. The sound of the waves on the beach mingled with the rising howl of a storm from the western deeps. The whole building creaked as the wind leaned on it. The white lights flickered nervously. Jill said, 'It's turning rough out there . . .'

'Mama,' said Utterly. Her mother's anger felt as fierce

as the undertow that sucks water and sand and pebbles down the slope of the beach before a great wave breaks. 'Stone is gone!' she promised. 'He is gone quite away, and the other people here have all been kind me, you must not hurt them, you need not be angry at them . . .'

But the anger of the Gorm could not be calmed so easily. She sprang up. She ran out of the cage and up the ladder and cried out again to the sea, and the sea came at her call. As Utterly followed her up to where the others waited, the big doors at the far end of the building burst open as if a battering ram had struck them, and white water came tumbling in. The lights died. Someone screamed. The wave closed over Utterly and swept her off her feet. She flailed and struggled, upside down, and the Gorm's hand caught hers and the Gorm's cold fingers interlaced with her own.

'Let us leave this place, Utterly,' said the Gorm.

And the wave drew Utterly and her mother and the struggling scientists out through the shattered doors.

Dan had told Egg to wait in the van, but being Egg, he let himself out of it and stood in the cool sea air to listen while Dan and Mim went to the gate and had words with Mr Kennett.

'Shame on you, Ted Kennett, taking up with kidnappers and the like, and you a good Wildsea lad who ought to have no truck with such things!'

'But . . .'

'I thought it was fish or currents or something they were looking into here, anyway. Why's your professor fellow locking kiddies up? What's the need for this big old fence? He's carrying on like the baddie out of one of them James Bond films . . .'

'I . . .'

Egg was starting to feel faintly sorry for Kennett, who just sat there in his box, lit up by a little lamp in the ceiling, opening and closing his mouth and never getting a word in. He looked like a fish in a bowl. At last he gave up. The gate clanked open. Dan and Mim started walking back to their van, ready to drive through it.

'Hop back in, young Egg,' said Mim.

But by then the wind was getting up, and Egg's attention had been drawn to a dark wall which was rising behind the buildings on the shore, and the roaring that it made, and the fleets of the sea birds who came blowing landward through the air above it.

He had just worked out that it was a wave, when it began to break. He turned to get into the van, but the sea got there first, rushing up the course of Belfriars Brook, overwhelming the little bridge, and spilling out over the banks, rising quickly past the wheels of the parked van. The van, which had seemed so huge and heavy, started to bob and turn like a boat on the tide as the water lifted it. Dan yanked Egg backwards as the sea came swilling up around his knees. He ran with Dan and Mim for higher ground, in through the gate with the water following.

'Over here!' Mr Kennett shouted, running out of his hutch and heading across the car park to the building with the lighted windows. But now another wave was rolling in, even bigger than the first.

'This way,' said Dan. 'We'll get up on the cliff . . .'

They ran, and the wave broke, white water flecked with broken planking from the quay, folding the fences flat, lifting cars like storm-tossed coracles, shouldering whole buildings aside, while the gulls rode the storm-wind above it and screeched like vengeful ghosts.

Utterly broke the surface, up through the sliding foam and into moonlight. Belfriars Bay was all sea now, with crates and bins and upturned boats and cars and people bobbing on the flood. The box files that held the records of the centre's work had been washed out of the room where they were shelved, and rode the swell like a fleet of tiny barges until one by one they were overwhelmed. Something huge swept past Utterly, and as the moonlight struck its side she saw it was the *Sea Witch*: the wave had ripped her from her moorings, smashed her against the cliffs, and was carrying the wreck of her back into the sea.

Out on the horizon, the Hidden Lands raised their rugged summits to the moon.

'Utterly,' roared the Gorm. Although Utterly could no longer see her, her voice seemed to be everywhere; in the crash of the surf against the cliffs, in the gurgle of white water gushing back down the rocks, in the cries of the whirling gulls. 'Utterly!' The wave held Utterly firm and safe, and began to carry her towards the Western Deeps.

And another, smaller voice, from somewhere not far away, shouted above the noise of the catastrophe, 'Utterly!'

'Egg!' said Utterly. 'I cannot go without Egg! I cannot leave him here!'

The Gorm was not listening. The Gorm was drunk with the joy of her own wild rage. She was weaving a new form for herself, out of shattered fragments of the *Sea Witch* and the quay and the weed which grew in the deeps beyond the bay's mouth. She was rising from the tumult of the waters, not quite as large as she had been when she knocked down the Watcher's Tower, but big enough to make the screaming humans caught up in her flood scream more loudly still. And among their screams that small, familiar voice was still shouting, over and over, 'Utterly!'

Utterly turned and struck out for the shore. For a while she made no progress at all against the strength of the great wave dragging her seawards, but then another wave came in and caught her up, and she rushed with it towards the cliffs. She could not tell if the Gorm had sent this new wave to help her, or if it was only a wave and simply doing what waves did. A big motor carriage was wedged on its side in a cleft between two rocks, and Utterly washed up against its wheels. She snatched hold of an improbable little looking-glass which jutted for some reason from its side. As the wave retreated, and before another could take its place, she climbed up onto the rocks, and hands reached down out of the dark above to help her. There, perched like a puffin on a grassy ledge half-way up the cliff, was Egg.

## 36

# THE STORM BREAKS

'Utterly!' Egg said, helping her up onto the ledge with him. 'You're wetter than I am,' he added, stepping back and regarding her. 'Look at us - like two drowned rats.'

'Like four drowned rats, you mean,' said a man who Utterly had not noticed till he spoke, rising from the shadows behind Egg. 'You must be Utterly. I'm Daniel Smy, and this here is Mim.'

'Egg brought us to find you,' said Mim. 'We was just giving Ted Kennet at the gate an earful when all this happened . . .'

'Quite a storm,' said Daniel. 'And sudden too. I never seen a tide so high . . .'

They stood and watched. Belfriars Bay, with its beach,

its quay, its car park and its clustered buildings was gone. In its place was a bowl where white water boiled, and a huge shaggy shape surfaced sometimes to crush pieces of floating wreckage. Only one of the buildings still stood. It was the one with the canteen and the offices, where Utterly had answered so many questions, and been subjected to so many tests. On its roof the staff of the research centre cowered, bedraggled and afraid, while the sea tugged and worried at their little island.

'We must help them!' Utterly said.

'But they're Stone's lot,' Egg objected.

'They helped us! And we can't just let them drown!'

Egg eyed the twenty feet of wild water that separated their bit of cliff from the rooftop where the scientists huddled. A big wave hit the building, and part of it was torn away. Black against the wall of foam the wave threw up, Jill, Harriet and the others flapped their wet arms. 'Help! Help!'

'You might be able to swim out there, Utterly,' Egg said, 'but I don't reckon they could make it back to shore, not unless they're half-fish.'

'No one could swim in those waves!' said Dan, shocked at the idea.

'Utterly can! She did already – that's how she found us. Utterly's ma is the Gorm herself, there's no sea she can't swim in.'

Dan and Mim looked at Utterly with odd expressions

of respect. The thing in the bay surfaced again and bellowed, and Mim said, 'If that's your mum, dear, maybe you could have a word?'

'Mother! Stop!' shouted Utterly, into the wind and spray. But the Gorm was too furious to hear her, or too busy with her revenge to pay any heed.

'She is a moody old thing,' confided Egg. 'Not even Utterly can make her peaceable when she's in one of her tizzies.'

'There is a rope in the back of my van,' said Dan. 'Sixty foot of it. But how do we get it out of there?'

'What is a van?' asked Utterly.

The van, it turned out, was the machine that she had been washed up against, the one the sea had wedged among the rocks below. Carefully, carefully, drenched again and again by the furious waves, Egg wriggled his way down to it, with Dan holding on to the back of his trousers, and Mim holding onto the back of Dan's trousers, and Utterly looking on and fearing that if the Gorm sent a bigger wave their way they would all be drowned together.

The van had come to rest on its side, with its back end tilted up towards the sky. It was not locked. Egg waited while a wave broke over it, then heaved the door open and slithered down inside. The moonlight came in with him, showing him Dan's toolboxes, old dust-sheets, and the rope, all tumbled together in two foot of seawater at the far end. He dived inside and started to untangle them while Dan called, 'Hurry up, Egg! Get a move on!'

The wave that had just broken was withdrawing; any moment now a fresh one would roll in, and it would fill the van with Egg inside it if he wasn't careful. He looped an end of the wet rope over his shoulder, tied a clumsy knot, and started to scramble back out.

'Quick, Egg! Quick!'

He could hear the wave coming. Dan was leaning through the open door, reaching down to him. Moonlit seagulls flashed across the sky behind Dan's head. The roar of the wave filled the world. Egg caught Dan's hand, and threw himself up out of the van, onto the old rocks. The weight of the wave fell on them all, and they clung together under it, Dan braced against the rocks, Mim holding tight to Dan's belt, Egg holding tight to Dan. Utterly, watching from further up the cliff, saw them all vanish beneath a smother of white foam. It lay there like a spent avalanche, as if it were reluctant to return to the sea. When it finally withdrew, the van went with it, but Egg, and Dan, and Mim were left behind. They shook themselves like half-drowned dogs, and came up to where Utterly waited.

And now it was her turn. There was no way they could throw the rope to those poor people on the roof, not against the battering wind the Gorm had summoned up. So Dan tied one end of it around Utterly's waist, and took a firm hold of the other, and Utterly went down the cliff a way and let the next wave take her. She did not swim as gracefully as she had when she was swimming at the Gorm's side, but she still found her way easily enough under the waves and up again beside the building, which was smaller by half than it had started out. A tangle of splintered beams and wet tar-paper hung from one side of it, and she scrambled out on them and called to the soggy scientists who cowered on the far corner of the roof. She saw their faces turn towards her. Jim edged across the roof and shouted something that she could not hear. Utterly untied the rope and passed it to him.

'The Hidden Lands!' he shouted. 'Stone was right! We have seen the Hidden Lands!'

The building lurched under a tremendous blow. Utterly wondered if the Gorm knew she was up here on its roof, or if, in her anger, she cared. Jill and the others were creeping closer now, making ready to follow the rope to safety. Jim and Mr Kennet held the end of it, bracing themselves like a tug-of-war team to keep it taut. Over on the cliffs, Dan and Mim and Egg did the same. In the gaps between the waves Utterly could hear them calling out encouragement. The rope made a black line against the foam, just far enough above the waves that a swimmer could keep hold of it and use it to guide them to shore. She watched until Jill and Harriet had strug- gled their way across, and Nigel was setting out. Then she went to the roof's edge and let herself slip off into the sea.

It was so much quieter underneath the waves. The wind was silenced, and the deep rushings and roarings of the waves were somehow soothing. Utterly soared over the ruins of the research centre through fans of moonbeams.

'Mother,' she said. She circled the Gorm's vast, weedy flank. 'Mother . . .'

It took time for her small voice to be heard over the tempest of the Gorm's rage. But slowly the immense tantrum subsided; slowly the vast weed-thing her mother had become grew shapeless, and began to drift, and came apart, shedding shards of broken buildings, and startled eels that had been caught up in its coils. The waves still rolled shoreward over a sea floor that had been beach and quay and car park until an hour ago, but they rolled with a more regular rhythm now.

The Gorm in her human guise appeared out of the slicks of weed. She hung in the water before Utterly, lifting her face so the moonbeams caught it and showed her to advantage.

'You are right, Utterly,' she said. 'We must not stay. They have eyes even in the heavens in this peculiar age. Already they will be looking down, and wondering, and who knows, perhaps there are men as clever as Stone, who will dream of new ways to ensnare me. Let us swim away together and find friendlier seas.'

She held out her hand, but Utterly hung back. 'Not without Egg,' she said.

'He will be safe. I was careful not to drown him.'

'But you brought him here! You have to help him home!'

'I made him no such promise,' said the Gorm. 'Now come.'

'I shall find my own way,' Utterly said.

'The paths of the sea will be closed when I am gone,' said the Gorm. 'I will not show myself again in this age.'

'I will not go without Egg,' said Utterly.

'Come,' said the Gorm, as if Utterly were being foolish, and she had grown tired of humouring her. 'Come with me, or must I leave you here to find your own way home?'

She caught Utterly's hand, and turned, and Utterly sensed the current that would carry them westward to the Hidden Lands and backward into happier ages. But before it could seize her she wriggled free of the Gorm's grasp and kicked her way towards the surface.

The Gorm called out, and Utterly expected to be stopped, to feel a cool hand wrap around her ankle and pull her back. But it did not, and when she glanced behind her the Gorm just hung there in the moonbeams, smiling a smile which Utterly could not read.

'Very well then,' she said softly. 'At Sundown Watch.'

Utterly's head broke up through a broad sheet of

moonlit foam, and she was back in the wind and noise and confusion of the world above. She felt the Gorm depart, returning alone to her own strange realm. The waves were less fierce, but they were still big, breaking over the last remnants of the research centre. The scientists, along with Egg, and Dan, and Mim, huddled like sea birds along the ledges of the cliff. The actual sea birds seemed to have vanished with the Gorm.

Utterly rode up and down on the swell, wondering what her mother's last words to her had meant. 'At Sundown Watch' were the words that had been carved above the door of her home. But why should they mean anything to the Gorm?

From his perch on the cliffs Egg saw her floating there, her small head showing dark like a seal's against the whiteness of the foam. He shouted, and Utterly struck out for the cliffs, while Dan and Mr Kennett came scrambling down to catch her before the sea could drag her away again. Utterly climbed, shivering, up the rocks, and turned to look back. The moon was high, laying its silvery snail-track west across the waves. Out there on the world's edge she saw the Hidden Lands again, but already they were fading, and within a few more seconds they had disappeared.

'Egg,' she said, 'the Gorm is gone, and without her help I do not know how to restore us to our proper time.'

Egg thought for a moment. 'Well, your mother must

think you can,' he said, 'or she would not have left you behind.'

The sea withdrew, the water level dropping almost imperceptibly at first, then faster and faster, until it was almost back at the bay's old shoreline. It left behind a strange landscape of tumbled stones, driftwood, demolished buildings and upturned vehicles, all so covered with weed that it was now quite hard to say which had been which. The wind was gentling too. As its howling faded another howling arose; a dreadful caterwauling sound which came from several vehicles descending the steep road into the bay with flashing blue lanterns on their roofs.

'That'll be the police and the coastguard from over Merriport,' said Mim. 'And that means we should be going, my dears, if you are not too tired and cold to walk. Because they're going to have a load of questions, and when it comes to Egg and Utterly here I'm not altogether sure how we would answer them.'

Dan knew those cliffs well, for he had climbed all over them as a lad, he said. A path led up by zig-zags to the top. They were half-way up it before Jill, Harriet and the others even realized they had gone.

'And what will we do now?' asked Mim, when they reached the coast road. 'We can't walk all the way to Dizzard Tor, in the dark.'

'I've done it often enough before,' said Egg.

'Look!' said Utterly, pointing north. 'There is a light at Sundown Watch!'

And so there was. It seemed the boards that hid the windows of the Watcher's Tower had been removed. A single yellow lamp shone out there, warm and welcoming, like a lantern set upon a sill to guide a traveller home. Utterly wondered if that was what her mother had meant to tell her; that there was someone at the Watch again. 'We should go there,' she said.

'Good idea,' said Mim. 'We'll ask if we can use their phone.'

They walked along the coast road, Mim leaning on Dan's arm. It was late now, and no cars passed them. At first they shivered inside their wet clothes, but the walking soon warmed them. The moon went west into a bank of clouds and the night grew very dark, but still that hopeful light shone out from the Watcher's Tower. As they drew nearer the house, they could see that other lights were shining, too, from the unshuttered downstairs windows. The fallen wall sprawled in ruins across the front garden. Utterly and Egg skirted carefully around it in case any magic lingered in the stones, but it showed no sign of growing argumentative again. On the drive was parked a bright yellow motor carriage, of a variety which Dan said was called a Beetle. They climbed the steps to the front door. Moths and a dozy hornet were pinging against the glass of an outside light. Dan rang the bell, and waited.

Still shaken after her adventures, Utterly half expected some last trick or apparition. She would not have been altogether surprised if Stone himself had answered the door. But when it opened she saw a small, neatly dressed lady, not old, but white-haired, with a kind face that seemed faintly familiar, although Utterly was certain they had never met before. Perhaps it was because the lady's features had the same slightly Chinese look as Utterly's own, and it was her own reflection that Utterly was reminded of. At any rate, she seemed friendly, for at the sight of them standing there on her doorstep she smiled delightedly and said, 'Utterly! Egg! And Mr and Mrs Smy! I have been expecting you. My name is Miss Brightling. I am the Watcher on Wildsea.'

## 37

# MISS BRIGHTLING

'Please excuse all the dust and mustiness,' said Miss
Brightling, as they followed her inside. 'I grew up
here at Sundown Watch, and when Sir Edward Dark died
the old place was left to me, but I have been travelling,
and it is a long time since I have had a chance to visit
Wildsea . . .'

She showed them into a large drawing room which
Utterly thought had been the breakfast room and part of
the kitchen once – it was all most disconcerting. There
were lamps on tall wooden stands, and big, comfortable-
looking chairs, a lot of books, and a view through the
windows to the moonlit sea. A picture on the mantelpiece showed Miss Brightling wearing a uniform like
a soldier's, and there were other pictures all around of

people Utterly did not recognize. But there, on the wall above the fireplace, hung a portrait of Uncle Will, and another of Aish, and there between them, like a strange mirror, was a portrait of herself. It was the same picture Stone had shown her on the day she came to Belfriars Bay, but this version was larger, and in colour, and she realized that the one Stone had was just a copy.

Miss Brightling told everyone to sit down, and hurried into the kitchen (which seemed now to be across the hall, in the rooms where Mr and Mrs Skraeveling had lived).

'If she's Watcher on Wildsea,' said Egg, in an outraged whisper, 'shouldn't she have been doing a bit more watching? She should have spotted what Stone was up to, and seen you come ashore, and lent a hand. But she weren't even here! The whole place was shut up till this very evening!'

Miss Brightling returned with a tray of tea things, and smiled at Egg to let him know she had heard everything. 'You are quite right, Egg,' she said. 'But I have looked into all the possibilities – I have been preparing for this night a long time – and I realized that anything I did might only upset things. After all, you have managed well enough without my help! So I stayed well out of the way, until you needed me.'

'We don't need you,' said Egg, although he sounded unsure. There was a plate of chocolate biscuits on the tray, which made him more inclined to like Miss Brightling.

'Brightling?' said Mim. 'I remember there was a Miss Brightling living up here at the Watch when I was a girl, way back before the war. The Marazea kids all said she was a witch. But that was forty year ago, so that couldn't have been you, could it?'

'Of course,' agreed Miss Brightling brightly, pouring tea into five cups and passing Egg the biscuits.

'You are her relation, I suppose?' said Mim.

'Don't eat them all, Egg,' said Miss Brightling, at exactly the same as Utterly said, 'Egg, don't eat them all!' They laughed, and Egg blushed and passed the plate of biscuits on, explaining that he had only taken three, and he thought he was entitled, after all he'd been through that evening.

'Anyway, we do need Miss Brightling,' said Utterly. 'Because the Gorm has abandoned me, and I do not know how to get home.'

'The Gorm has not abandoned you,' said Miss Brightling. 'She has just come to understand the thing that all mothers and fathers have to understand eventually. She has seen that you are your own person, and that you are quite capable of making your own way home.'

Utterly frowned. Her mother might believe that, and so might Miss Brightling, but she was not sure *she* did.

'And what will we find if we do go back?' asked Egg, remembering the things Stone had taunted him with.

'What's happened to Aish, and Will Dark? Are they safe there in 1812, or . . .'

'They were quite safe,' said Miss Brightling cheerfully. 'HMS *Acantha* and her mutinous crew were never seen again, but Uncle Will made it back to Wildsea, and rescued Aish from the Underwoods, where Stone had trapped her. The other boat the mutineers set adrift made landfall in Ireland a few days after. The loss of the *Acantha* reflected very badly on Stone, or Lord Langdale as he called himself in those days. His friends in government deserted him, and he vanished. I believe he spent many years in Australia and South America, studying volcanoes and boring deep holes in the hope of finding his beloved Oldest Ones that way. It was only when that failed that he turned his thoughts again to Wildsea, and the Hidden Lands.'

'Poor Professor Stone,' said Utterly. 'He only wanted to go back to the place he loved best. And now I am in the same predicament, because I want to see my own time again, but the sea magic I used to help Professor Stone into that dreadful era he seemed so taken with has faded out of me now, and I have no idea how to swim back through the years.'

'And yet we know you will,' said Miss Brightling.

'How?' asked Egg. 'How can we know any such thing?'

'Why, because this portrait of Utterly was done in 1814,' said Miss Brightling, pointing to the picture on the chimney breast. 'And then there is Utterly's entry in the Log . . .'

She crossed the room and opened a glass-fronted book-case. Inside, Utterly saw the volumes of the Watcher's Log lined up. She had not recognized them, because the red of their leather bindings had faded to a rusty brown. Miss Brightling took one out and came to sit beside her, opening it to a certain page. 'Look here, Utterly,' she said. 'Is this not your own handwriting?'

Utterly studied the entry. It certainly looked like her own hand.

*24th May 1812. I returned to Sundown Watch this morning, and I must write down what I recall before it is lost to me. I have visited Wildsea in the year 1971, and there met with such adventures, and seen such wonders, as should fill up this book in its entirety was I to list them all. It was thanks only to Egg, and Mr and Mrs Smy, and to the Gorm, and to my own self, that I survived, and found my way home. But all the memories are a muddle now. I can offer only this as proof:*

Below the entry, flat and faded as last summer's blossoms pressed in a cuttings book, was the wrapper from a Penguin biscuit.

'So you see, Utterly,' said Miss Brightling gently, 'you will get home to your own time. And I think you already know how to get there.'

Utterly looked blank. She *felt* blank. She could not imagine how she could go from sitting on this sofa in the

1970s to writing an entry in the Watcher's Log in 1812. She tried to concentrate, but she could find no currents in the air like those which had guided her beneath the sea.

Once again she recalled the Gorm's parting words. *At Sundown Watch.* What had she meant? Had she been telling Utterly to come here? But for what reason?

'Dan asked me yesterday if I arrived in a time machine,' Egg said. 'And Splodge talked about some doctor who's got one. If we could get a-hold of a time machine we could get back all right . . .'

'It was a joke, Egg,' said Dan. 'Time machines are just in films and books.'

'But Utterly has a time machine,' said Miss Brightling, with a mischievous smile. 'She is sitting in it.'

'What, the sofa?' asked Mim.

Utterly had no idea what Miss Brightling was trying to tell her, and then, quite suddenly, she understood. 'She means Sundown Watch!' she said. 'The house itself – the dear old house! I have lived here always. It has changed, but it is still my home. It was here in 1812 and it is here now, just like us, Egg. And why shouldn't we step from the *now* part of it to the *then* part, as easily as stepping through a door into another room?'

'Cos we ain't ghosts?' said Egg. 'Cos if things like that could happen, they would happen all the time . . . wouldn't they?'

291

But Utterly was excited. She knew now why her mother had sent her here. Her way home was here, at Sundown Watch. Time was an ocean, where everything that had ever happened was happening right now, all at once, and always. To swim in it was merely a question of finding the tides and currents that would carry her to where she wished to go. And the truest, most powerful currents were memories.

She sprang up from the sofa and said, 'Come on Egg! I know our direction home!'

Egg, however, stayed where he was, with a most uncomfortable look upon his face. Had he eaten too many biscuits, Utterly wondered. Was that even possible?

'Utterly,' he said. 'I don't want to go.'

## 38

# MORE ADVENTURES
# THAN YOU COULD
# SHAKE A STICK AT

'Egg, whatever do you mean?' demanded Utterly. 'Of course you want to go home! How could you not?'

'I like it here, Utterly Dark,' said Egg. 'I like the noisiness, and how fast and busy everything is, and the colours of it all, and the stuff, and the people. It's exciting, this place. It feels like – well, maybe not like home exactly, but like it *could* be home.'

'But Egg, you silly goose,' said Utterly, 'you have a home already! You live at Sundown Watch, in 1812!'

'I know,' said Egg. 'But what's to become of me there? You have the Gorm and the whole sea to play in, and

Aish and Will Dark will have their twins to raise, but me? There's more for me here now than there would be then, I reckon.'

'Oh, Egg, what an awful thing to say!' said Utterly. 'You could do anything! Uncle Will has often said how clever you are, and spoken of paying for your education. Or you could go to sea with Captain Varley . . .'

'I'd go further on one of these modern ships they have now,' said Egg. 'And I'd get a better education too; cos there's years and years of history that hadn't even happened in our times, that stands to reason. And Dan and Mim said yesterday how maybe I could stop with them, and maybe I could.' He looked at Dan and Mim. 'I could make myself useful about the place, and help Dan with the gardening and the lawn mowers and such.'

'But that was before we knew . . . where you came from, Egg,' said Dan. 'I don't see how – I mean, there would be questions asked about who you are and where you come from, and we'd have no answers, would we? No one would believe us . . .'

Egg looked down at his feet, and Utterly saw a tear run down his face and drip off his chin. She was ready to weep herself. What Egg had said could not be unsaid. If he did not come home with her she would miss him always. But if he *did* come, she would always know that he wanted to be here instead. She was not sure which would be worse.

Miss Brightling cleared her throat. 'I have not *entirely*

been wasting my time while I waited for you,' she said. She picked up a brown envelope which lay on a low table by the sofa and passed it to Mim. 'I met some very clever people while I was working with Naval Intelligence during the last war. They've helped me to prepare these documents which prove Egg is your cousin's child, from Somerset. There is a birth certificate, school records, the whole works. If you would like Egg to stay with you – and I know you would – then these should answer any questions the authorities might ask.'

'Well now,' said Dan, taking the envelope from Mim and peeking at the papers it contained. 'Well now, me and Mim has been thinking lately how the house is too big and too quiet without kids in it . . .'

'Oh, Egg is never quiet,' said Utterly, and again Miss Brightling said exactly the same thing at exactly the same moment, and they both laughed and then Utterly was crying; crying and crying at the thought of losing Egg.

Miss Brightling came and hugged her. 'It is all right, my dear,' she said, kissing the top of Utterly's head. 'You will see Egg again. The Gorm may have closed the ways into her Hidden Lands, but they will still be open for a few of us. You will be able to visit this Wildsea whenever you wish. And perhaps, when Egg grows up, he will find a way to visit your Wildsea too.'

'If you change your mind, Egg,' sniffled Utterly, 'I shall come and get you.'

Egg sniffed too, trying not to show he had been crying. 'Don't reckon I will,' he said. 'But you come anyway and see me. And tell Aish I'm missing her, cos I know I will be.'

*Wooo-wooo-wooo* said a startling banshee voice, through the window Miss Brightling had opened to let in some air. Blue lights flashed by on the road.

'More police on their way to Belfriars Bay,' said Miss Brightling. 'I expect they will be here asking questions soon. Professor Stone's scientists will not remember very much about tonight, since magic does not make for clear memories, but they will remember there was a girl named Utterly in their care, and they will be worried about her, and the police will come looking for her. So you should go now, Utterly.'

Utterly looked at Egg. 'Egg,' she said, 'I cannot imagine life at Sundown Watch in any age without you. Everything will be different, and I liked it the way it was.'

'Everything *will* be different,' said Miss Brightling gently. 'You have swum with the Gorm, and you shall swim with her again. You will return to the Hidden Lands, and you will have adventures in the Underwoods with Mr Constantine and his new friends. And even when you are at Sundown Watch, there will be changes, because you will have a new niece and nephew, and you must help Will and Aish to care for them. You are not a child any more, Utterly Dark.'

This seemed to Utterly the saddest thing that anyone

had ever said to her. 'How do you know?' she asked. 'How do you know all these things that will happen to me?'

Miss Brightling smiled, and did not reply, but Utterly thought she knew the answer. The banshee voices of the police-carriages still wailed, far off, descending the track to Belfriars Bay. Another engine went by, sounding this time as though it were in the sky, and a noise like the beating of great wings accompanied it, making the glass in the bookcase rattle.

Utterly read again the entry that she would write in the Watcher's Log a hundred and fifty-nine years ago. She glanced at the next page, where Uncle Will had written an account of his own adventures. Then she went to Egg, and hugged him tight, while Egg, who had never been good at giving or receiving hugs, patted her stiffly on the back as though she had the hiccoughs. When she stepped away from him she said, 'I hope you shall be very happy here, Egg.'

'You give my love to Aish, and Will Dark, and Mr and Mrs Skraeveling,' said Egg, rather formally. 'And tell them it's nothing personal, me staying here, it's just I found the place I need to be. And you make sure to look in on me from time to time,' he added. 'And if you ever need getting out of trouble, you know where I'll be.'

'I will, Egg,' she said. 'I will.'

She looked around the room, and saw nothing there at all that she remembered from the Sundown Watch of her own time. So she went out into the hallway, but that too had changed. The floors were new, the doors were new; the pictures on the walls were all of folk she did not know. She started to go towards her own little room, and then stopped, because she could not bear to see it changed. Then she went to the foot of the stairs and looked up. On the landing newel post, just where it had always been, the little wooden tortoise was waiting for her.

Egg and the grown-ups stood in the hallway and watched as Utterly ran up the stairs to the landing. She reached out and stroked the tortoise, just as she used to when she was small. It was dry and cracked, poor thing, and sadly in need of polish, but its shape was so familiar that Utterly felt lost memories unfurling inside her like flowers. She remembered being so little that she had to stand on tiptoe to reach up and stroke it. She remembered being so little that Mrs Skraeveling, or Mr Skraeveling, or even very long ago her father, had held her up, and her little baby fingers had touched the smooth roundness of the tortoise's shell, and the dimple in the top of its head, where tortoises liked best to be scratched.

And the magic in her, which she had thought had faded entirely when the Gorm left, turned out not to be gone at all, but only sleeping, and it woke now and fed upon her memories. Utterly stood clasping the tortoise with both hands, and closed her eyes so she could see more clearly. How deep and soft and red the stair carpet had been when she was small, and how bright the brass rods holding it in place. She recalled the beeswax smell at spring-cleaning time, and the pale grey light on winter mornings, and the honey-yellow light on summer evenings, and the comfortable sounds of grown-up voices in the rooms below, and the tick-tock, tick-tock of the hall clock. The memories were so intense now, so sweet and painful, that she felt she could step into them; *they are real*, she thought, *they are not gone, those lost times, nothing that feels so real can just be lost, all the moments that have ever been must be here, now, in this moment.*

And a great fluttering of light occurred outside her closed eyelids. It was the light of moony nights, and long, wet winter afternoons, and lazy summer ones, and the weird white light that lets you know as soon as you wake that it has snowed. All those lights went flickering over her, and she opened her eyes and found that she was standing on the landing in the gentle grey light of dawn, and the stair carpet was almost as red as she had remembered it, and the stair rods were almost as shiny.

She looked down the stairs, expecting to see Egg, Miss Brightling and the Smys still watching her. But the hallway was the old stone-flagged hallway, and quite empty. Then a door opened – the old oak door that led into the kitchen – and Mrs Skraeveling came bustling out, sensed Utterly watching her, glanced up towards the landing, and gasped.

'Oh! Kitten! You've come home to us! But wherever have you been? And whatever are you wearing?'

Egg had seen no fluttering of light; no visible thing at all that he could label magic. One minute Utterly was there, standing on the landing with her hands upon the newel post; the next she was simply a memory, and the landing was empty.

'Did she get home safe?' asked Mim.

'Of course she did,' said Miss Brightling. 'And she lived a very long and happy life, and divided her time between this world and the Hidden Lands, and has had more adventures than you could shake a stick at.'

'If you don't mind me asking, Miss Brightling,' said Dan, 'how come you know so much about all of this?'

Egg answered for her. 'It's because Miss Brightling is Utterly,' he said. He turned to her. 'You are, aren't you? That's why she said in the Log that she got home "with the help of my own self". You're Utterly Dark, and you've lived all these years because of the magic that's in you, and you remember all this happening to you, so that's how you knew to be here tonight to set yourself on the road home.'

Miss Brightling smiled her mischievous smile again, and Egg surprised them both by running to her and hugging her as tightly as he wished he had hugged the other Utterly before she left.

## 39

# JOURNEY'S END

Lord Langdale was standing on the cliff behind Sundown Watch, scanning the western sea with his telescope. Utterly watched him from her bedroom window while she was changing out of her strange twentieth-century clothes and putting on a decent dress. How odd it felt to see him there, and to remember things he had said and done which would not happen for another century and more . . .

She went out through the back door, into the blustering wind and the sunshine. There were no engine sounds on Wildsea now, only the sigh of blowing grass, the crying of sheep on the common, the steady whisper of the sea in the cove. Utterly went down the slope of the lawn and through the gate to where Lord Langdale stood on the cliff's edge. He heard the gate snick shut behind her. Without taking his eye from the telescope, he said, 'There is a sail out there. It is not the *Acantha*, but a much smaller vessel . . .'

'That is HMS *Acantha*'s cutter, sir,' said Utterly, recalling what Uncle Will was going to write in the Watcher's Log that evening. 'The sailors mutinied when they realized they were in the Gorm's realm, and Captain Bulstrode was set adrift with a few men loyal to him. He is bringing my uncle Will home with him, and also Aish, whom he has rescued from the place you shut her up in.'

Lord Langdale lowered his telescope then, and turned to stare at her. It was the first time he had ever seen Utterly. It was the last time she would ever see him.

'Who are you, child? How can you know of these things?'

'You should leave while you may,' said Utterly. 'Uncle Will shall certainly have you arrested for attempted murder should you be here when he comes ashore.'

'What damned impertinence!' said Lord Langdale. 'Leave? Of course I shall not leave! I must hear what Bulstrode and Constantine have learned in the Western Deeps . . .'

'Mr Constantine will not return,' said Utterly, 'and Captain Bulstrode is already forgetting everything he saw out there. Science cannot pierce the Gorm's mysteries yet, nor lure her ashore to explain them. You must go away, and wait until the time is right.'

She wondered if she should tell him when that would be. She wondered if she should tell him to be gentler with the Gorm when he finally caught her. She wondered if she could not just help him to the place he wished to be, and save him all those years of fretting and scheming. She wondered if she should push him off the cliff – he was standing quite near the edge, so it might be possible, if she gave him a good hard shove when he was not expecting it. But she recalled something Miss Brightling had said (or would say, one hundred and fifty-nine years from now). *Anything I did might only upset things.* If Lord Langdale never became Professor Stone, and did not capture her in 1971, then how would Egg reach Wildsea in that year, and what other things might never happen that were meant to?

Besides, Lord Langdale looked so shaken by what she had said that she felt quite sorry for him, and certainly not inclined to shove him off a cliff.

'You will get what you desire,' she promised him. 'You will walk one day in your world of stone again, and hear once more the songs of the Oldest Ones. But you must wait, and you should not wait in England, for there is going to be a great to-do about that ship you lost. It might lead people to notice that you are rather older than you claim to be.'

'Utterly!' shouted Mr Skraeveling, opening the back door and hurrying down the lawn. 'Lord Langdale, sir! There is a sail!'

Lord Langdale turned his back on the sea and stalked towards the house. He was going to pack his bags, Utterly presumed, for she recalled from Uncle Will's journal entry that at suppertime he would be found to be missing. No one would recall seeing him leave, but by then so much would have happened that they would have already half-forgotten Lord Langdale.

The cutter, under a sail made from stitched-together shirts lashed to two oars, made landfall in Marazea Bay, and the whole village turned out to meet it. Bulstrode, Hard-tack Joe and the two midshipmen leaped out. Utterly, splashing past them into the shallows, saw that the boat was filled with grass and wilting leaves, and that Uncle Will was sitting in it with another gentleman. Between them lay Aish, propped on a pillow of sacking and bundled tarpaulin jackets. She looked so pale and lifeless that for an awful instant Utterly thought she might be dead, and wondered if her future self had lied to spare Utterly's feelings. But as she reached the cutter's side she saw that Aish was only sleeping, and that two babies, rather damp-looking and very pink, were sleeping with her, nestled against her breast. Utterly was astounded. Amid all the excitements of 1971, Egg had neglected to tell her that Aish was with child.

'Utterly!' said Will, seeing her there. 'This is a joyous homecoming indeed!'

'For me too!' said Utterly, starting to weep for happiness.

Aish opened her eyes at the sound of their voices. 'Utterly Dark,' she said. 'So you've come home to us! Look, here are the twins, your niece and nephew. Good Mr Samuels delivered them when we were still a league off Mawgan Head.'

'As healthy a pair of children as I have ever seen,' said the gentleman called Mr Samuels, who Utterly now saw had smears of Aish's blood all over his shirt and breeches. 'And their mother is doing remarkably well, too.'

'I had hoped they would be born in my own woods,' Aish said a little sadly. 'Then I could know they were truly of the land. But they are impatient little things and would not wait.'

'They are of the land and the sea,' said Utterly, reaching out and touching the hand of the nearest twin, a hand so tiny and perfect that it seemed impossible to believe that it was real.

'And what of Egg?' said Uncle Will, when he had come out of the boat and embraced her. 'Did Egg come home with you?'

Utterly shook her head. 'He did not. Oh, Uncle Will,' she sobbed, 'we visited Wildsea as it will be in years to come, and it was full of strange sights and sounds and people, which I did not like at all, for I hated to see it so changed. But Egg thought the changes were all most wondrous exciting, and so he has elected to stay on there with a kindly couple by the name of Smy.'

'What awful news!' cried Will, hugging her close. 'And just when I thought our adventures had finally reached a joyful resolution . . .'

'If the Egg is safe and happy where he is, then it *is* joyful,' said Aish. 'We shall miss him, of course – look, I am weeping for him now, great silly thing that I am. But we always knew he would grow up and leave us one day, didn't we? And if he is happy there in futurity, then we should be happy for him. People must find the worlds they belong in, as you have Will Dark, and as your Mr Constantine has done. And we can but hope they thrive there.'

The midshipmen were telling the Dearlove children about the adventures they had endured at the world's edge, but the Dearloves did not seem to believe them, and the midshipmen were growing doubtful of the tale themselves. Utterly stood by the cutter and kept Aish company while Will and Mr Samuels and Reverend Dearlove started arranging a litter to carry her and her babies home to Sundown Watch. 'I could walk perfectly well,' Aish confided, 'but at times like this men do like to feel they are *doing* something, the good creatures. But you look sad, Utterly Dark, and why is that? Is it still the Egg running off that is upsetting you?'

'It is only that everything will be different now, Aish,' said Utterly. 'When I was swimming with the Gorm it comforted me so to think of you all here on Wildsea. But the Wildsea I left is changed already, and it will keep on changing. Oh, Aish, in the years to come there will be a lot of new houses all along behind the beach there, and Sundown Watch will be all turned-about, and there will be noisy engines everywhere, and people will dress and talk in the most peculiar ways, and the music will sound like someone dropping a lot of saucepans down the stairs, and there will be a thing called the telly, and everyone will talk about "the last war" as if they are all expecting the next one, and no one will have so much as *heard* of the Gorm. Instead of people fearing the sea, the sea shall fear people, who will catch all the fish in it, and kill all the whales, and dirty it with oil and rubbish, and I cannot bear to think of it all changing, for I love it all just as it is.'

'It is a sadness,' admitted Aish, nuzzling her babies' sleeping heads. 'But all things change. To love things that are passing away is part of being human, I think.'

'Will you pass away too, Aish?'

'I daresay I shall. But that will not be for many, many years yet, and I do mean to make them years of honey. Now, here come Will and Mr Samuels and the Reverend, and look, they are so proud about that old cart they have commandeered, it would not do at all to keep them waiting . . .'

Back in her room, while the household rearranged itself around the new arrivals, Utterly picked up the strange clothes she had brought back with her from her adventures, and wondered how anyone could ever wear such things. Her memories were already growing vague, and she rather hoped they would soon fade altogether. But in a pocket of the blue trousers something crinkled. She reached in and pulled out the wrapper from a Penguin biscuit, which she must have stuffed in there unthinkingly while she was at the research centre. She laid it flat upon the windowsill and carefully smoothed it with her fingernail. She knew that she had seen a wrapper just like it somewhere, and suddenly she remembered where. Snatching it up, she ran upstairs and climbed the Watcher's Tower to write a new entry in the Log.

*24th May 1812. I returned home this morning. I must write down what I recall before it is lost to me . . .*

Down in the house, she could hear the babies crying. *Uncle Will must be so busy and so tired,* she thought. *I should sit the Watch for him myself tonight.*

The sun was thinking about going down, and its light lay golden on the cliffs and the sea. She watched and watched, and did not see the Hidden Lands, but she knew they would be waiting there for her whenever she needed to return. And as the last light faded, she looked north to the Dizzard and thought, *up there on*

*Mawgan Head there will be a little fort built one day, for some war that has not been thought of yet. And in a far-off year a boy will sit there with his dog and think of me.*

She lifted her hand and waved to Egg.

And on an evening in the autumn of 1971, Egg, with Tess the spaniel flopped happily by his side, sat on the roof of the old pillbox, which was now the Gorm Sands Gang's new den. The others were cooking sausages over Dan Smy's camping stove, and the smell drifted up invitingly to him. But before he went down to join them, Egg looked south to where the sunset glowed upon the roofs of Sundown Watch, and guessed what Utterly would have done all those years ago, and waved back.

# ACKNOWLEDGEMENTS

With thanks to everyone at David Fickling Books –
my brilliant editors, Liz Cross and Meggie Dennis; to
Bronwen Bennie, Phil Earle, Fraser Hutchinson, Alison
Gadsby and Julia Bruce; and to Paddy Donnelly, whose
cover illustrations, maps and chapter headings have
become so much a part of Utterly's world. To Philippa
Milnes-Smith and her team at the Soho Agency. To
Sarah McIntyre and Stuart Pyle, my housemates while I
was working on this one. And to Sarah Reeve, as always,
because without her I'd get nothing done at all.